P9-DVH-681

The
BOOKSHOP *of the*
BROKEN HEARTED

McKenzie Co. Public Library
112 2nd Ave. NE
Watford City, ND 58854
701-444-3785
librarian@co.mckenzie.nd.us

The
BOOKSHOP *of the*
BROKEN HEARTED

❧

ROBERT HILLMAN

G. P. PUTNAM'S SONS

New York

#ac499

PUTNAM

G. P. Putnam's Sons
Publishers Since 1838
penguinrandomhouse.com

Copyright © 2018 by Robert Hillman
Published in the United States in 2019 by G. P. Putnam's Sons
First published by the Text Publishing Company Australia 2018
Mary Barnard's translation of lines from "Sappho" is included
by kind permission of University of California Press.

Penguin supports copyright. Copyright fuels creativity, encourages diverse voices, promotes free speech, and creates a vibrant culture. Thank you for buying an authorized edition of this book and for complying with copyright laws by not reproducing, scanning, or distributing any part of it in any form without permission. You are supporting writers and allowing Penguin to continue to publish books for every reader.

Library of Congress Cataloging-in-Publication Data

Names: Hillman, Robert, 1948- author.
Title: The bookshop of the broken hearted / Robert Hillman.
Description: New York : G. P. Putnam's Sons, [2019]
Identifiers: LCCN 2018044402 | ISBN 9780525535928 (hardcover) |
ISBN 9780525535935 (epub)
Subjects: | GSAFD: Love stories.
Classification: LCC PR9619.3.H564 B66 2019 | DDC 823/.914—dc23
LC record available at https://lccn.loc.gov/2018044402

International edition ISBN: 9780593083079

Printed in the United States of America
1   3   5   7   9   10   8   6   4   2

Book design by Elke Sigal

This is a work of fiction. Names, characters, places, and incidents either are the product of the author's imagination or are used fictitiously, and any resemblance to actual persons, living or dead, businesses, companies, events, or locales is entirely coincidental.

For Ida

The
BOOKSHOP *of the*
BROKEN HEARTED

CHAPTER 1

She didn't stay long as far as marriages go, just a year and ten months. Her note was brief, too:

> *I'm leaving. Don't know what to say.*
>   *Love*
>   *Trudy*

And Tom Hope was left injured in a way that seemed certain to kill him.

He stood at the wooden table in the kitchen reading again and again what she'd written. He thought: *It was the rain.* He pictured her standing on the verandah in her blue dress and her cardigan while the rain came down day after day from a gray sky. He read the note one more time. It was written on the pink notepaper she'd used on special occasions and dated September 10, 1962. She'd also left behind a piece of toast from which she'd taken a single bite. The indent preserved the arc of her teeth.

He kept to the farm for weeks after she'd gone. He knew what would happen if he drove into Hometown: *How's the missus, Tom?* from every direction—and he had no answer. He worked in a daze, holding himself together as best he could. Cleared the channels in the orchard, a good five days, then repaired the wire fences of the hill pastures ready for the woollies in spring. He had never wept in his life but these days his cheeks were tear-streaked all the time. When he noticed, he would shrug: What did it matter?

She barely had any family: her father missing up in New South Wales; her mother and sister, Tilly, living with some Bible bashers who'd taken them down to Phillip Island. Where could she have gone?

. . .

HE COULDN'T STAY on the farm forever. He needed tobacco, sugar, tea. He needed Aspros. He woke with a headache every morning. In town, first one friend then another expressed surprise at his long absence. When he was asked how his wife was faring, he said, "Oh, she went on her way." He didn't elaborate. He thought, *I'm meant to be alone.* He had more reason than Trudy running away to make him believe this. He'd always been awkward with people. He had to remind himself to smile. But in his heart he yearned for people all around him. Only let them not ask him to talk and smile too much. Let them just say: "Tom, good to see you," and, "Tom, look in one time and say hello to the kids." Animals forgave his unease. The mare he'd bought for Trudy to enjoy obeyed him, never her. His dog, Beau, an old heeler, loved him in the way of dogs. But then, Beau loved everyone.

. . .

LISTENING TO THE radio one evening, he understood suddenly a comment she'd made not so long before she left. She had talked a lot when she was playing the game with the three decks of cards, such things as: "Clever girl!" and "Whoops-a-daisy!" But the comment Tom had just recalled was different. At the time, he'd thought it part of her strange three-deck game. It wasn't. It was something intended for him. "Another night in paradise," she'd said, moving one small pile of cards to the edge of the low table.

Tom stood up from his armchair and stared straight ahead. Why had it taken him so long to understand? *Another night in paradise.* He stamped through the house, arms folded tight over his chest. All the things he might have done to make his wife happy crowded his mind. A record player. Songs that she could choose for herself. A television set on hire to purchase. A proper bathtub, not that half-rusted tin thing. He ran to the kitchen and found a piece of paper and a black pencil. In a frenzy, he wrote a list of the things he would do to make a difference if Trudy should one day come back. Whenever a new idea came to mind, he rushed back to the kitchen and added it to the list:

6—Picnics!!

7—Pets cat budgie!!

8—Light fire kitchen first thing!!

Outside, Beau ran yelping along the verandah from the back door to the side door, excited by the movement inside the house.

· · ·

MORE ITEMS OCCURRED to him over the following days. *Tell her about good things she does.* Such as what? *Like when she doesn't burn the sausages.*

And when he'd had that pain in the guts, she'd asked him three times if he was feeling better. *Like when she says how are you feeling.* But one afternoon in the kitchen for a cuppa he glanced down at his list on the table and noticed how hard he'd pressed the pencil into the paper. This was mad, wasn't it, making notes? *Tell Beau not to jump up on her.* An image formed of Beau listening to him, head cocked. Tom smiled and made a mental note on a different list: *Don't be an idiot.* Trudy had told him once, smiling, that he was "unbalanced" given the way that he'd stick with some problem about the farm for hours, for days, studying the habits of the codling moth until he'd all but indexed the physical and mental processes of the insect. She'd mimicked him perfectly, the way he wandered up and down, arms crossed, head on his chest, mumbling his thoughts. He'd enjoyed the mickey-taking.

.   .   .

TOM'S SISTERS DROVE up from Melbourne in Patty's big Ford to see to him. He'd been their big brother in their growing-up years but at some point, one sister then the other had adopted a protective way of handling him. It was as if their developing experience with men had made them aware that their brother lacked a type of male insistence, often very stupid insistence but maybe necessary. He was solid with men, respected by them; but a woman of a certain sort, they clearly believed, could get away with murder. And Trudy was evidently that sort.

Listen to Tom in his letters taking all the blame on himself! The sisters had come to the farm with a message: Get over her, Tommy love, and move on.

Tom had only the one strategy for dealing with his sisters when they fussed: He became carefree. Making tea in the kitchen, Patty called over her shoulder: "More fool her if she doesn't want our handsome Tom!"

Tom said, "Probably for the best!" and smiled as if he were well on top of the situation.

Claudie said, "Her and her crosswords!" She meant the crosswords in the *Sun* newspaper that Trudy had pored over, chewing her pencil.

Patty called cleverly, "I'd give her a cross word or two if she turned up now, I can tell you!" and the three of them laughed.

When the sisters left for home in the middle of the afternoon, Tom heaved a sigh of relief. But the relief was succeeded by a plunge of sadness. He had said one or two things critical of Trudy for his sisters' sake and now he felt like a traitor. "Damn you for that!" he said aloud to himself. He added to his second-chance list of ideas a new item, number 34: *Don't blame her for things!!*

. . .

A BIG SOUTHEASTERLY took a sheet of iron off the dairy roof the day Trudy returned. Tom was up a ladder in the late afternoon hammering the sheet back in place when he saw her. The Melbourne bus must have dropped her off on the town road. Everything in the world came to a stop except for Trudy struggling up the drive with her suitcase. It had been raining for a month, just as it had been when she ran off, and it was raining now. The first words that came to Tom when blood returned to his brain were: "Thank God!" He hurtled down the ladder two rungs at a time and strode to meet his wife with all the unused joy of twelve months swelling his heart.

When they met halfway up the drive he wrapped his arms around her, he couldn't help it. "I'll take this," he said, picking up her suitcase. Trudy was sobbing. Even in the rain, face all wet, her tears still showed in their passage down her cheeks. "Don't cry, love," said Tom, but Trudy's shoulders continued to heave with the rigor of her weeping.

Once in the kitchen, Tom helped his wife off with her red overcoat and sat her by the warm stove. He brought her a towel for her hair but, although she accepted it with a whispered, "Thank you," she didn't use it. She sat with the towel on her lap sobbing and shaking. Tom stood behind her with his hands on her shoulders. He said, "There, love. Don't cry now." Every now and again in her weeping, Trudy struggled out the word, "Sorry!" and once managed a little more: "Tommy, I'm sorry!" Tom was looking down on the tangled, wet mess of her fair hair. As Trudy sobbed, Tom drew the strands of her hair back from her face with his fingertips.

.   .   .

TOM DIDN'T PRESUME that Trudy would wish to share their marriage bed that night and was prepared to sleep on the sofa. But no, she insisted that he climb in beside her. She had recovered from her sobbing and something like her old, soft smile had returned. There was nothing wrong with her appetite, either: She ate a huge plate of bubble and squeak and, on top of that, a whole tin of peaches with fresh cream. And she spent almost an hour in the bathtub before bed once Tom fired up the water heater.

Trudy wore to bed a pink satin nightdress that Tom had never seen before. It had been her custom before she ran off to wear pajamas at night. Tom was careful not to touch her and only lay still beside her in the dark, smiling at his good fortune. Nor did he ask for explanations. It was Trudy who spoke first, and it was Trudy who drew herself close to him. The soapy smell of his wife could almost have burst Tom's heart.

"Tom," she said, "I went a little bit mad."

"Yes," said Tom.

"Do you know what I want? I want to forget all that. I want to forget it forever."

"Yes," said Tom. "Forget it forever."

"I missed you so much, oh so much, darling! Did you miss me like that?"

"Very much," said Tom.

She kissed him. Nothing on earth was as soft as her lips, nothing. She stroked his face. If he'd had the words, he would have blessed her for coming back to him.

She kissed him harder and said, "Will you make love to me?"

"Do you want that?" said Tom. It was something he'd refused to hope for.

Trudy sat up in bed and lifted her nightdress over her head, lay down again and pressed herself to him.

"Darling man."

. . .

TOM AGONIZED OVER the list of ideas. He wanted to show it to Trudy but feared it would seem foolish to her. She was the one with the education, two more years of high school than Tom's father had thought enough for him. A sophisticated person might consider his list a bit childish—he could see that. In the end, though, he decided that he must show her. Her mood on the first two days of her return was the best he could remember, but on days three and four she'd seemed glum. Tom hoped with all his heart that the list would cheer her up again.

"What's this?" she said. She was still in bed but roused herself to accept a breakfast cup of tea and Tom's six sheets of notepaper. Her bedside light was on. She'd been reading her book and had dozed off. The book lay open and face-up on Tom's vacant side of the bed. The cover picture showed a young woman with long golden hair shielding her breasts with loose crimson fabric. Two men leaned over her, one at each shoulder. A crusader knight and, as Tom surmised, a sultan.

"Some ideas I had," said Tom. He sat on the side of the bed.

Trudy read slowly, sipping her tea at intervals. She didn't say anything. Tom managed not to ask her what she thought of the list while she was still reading. When she was away he'd forgotten how pretty she was, how the brown of her eyes caught the light and gleamed. He wanted now to stroke her hair and to breathe in the sleepy smell of her skin. He thought, *I should've shaved!*

Trudy put the list down on the little table beside the bed. "Oh, Tom," she said. She lay back on her pillow and covered her face with her arm.

Tom in his dread didn't move. Then found the courage to stroke his wife's hair. "What is it, Trudy?" he said. "What's wrong?"

Eyes covered, she said something that Tom didn't quite catch.

"What was that?"

Trudy uncovered her face. Her eyes were wet and glowing. She reached up and took hold of Tom's shirt just below the neck and kneaded the fabric between two fingers.

"I'm pregnant."

"Pregnant?" said Tom.

"Tom, I wouldn't blame you if you threw me out. I truly wouldn't."

As Tom leaned back, the air came out of his lungs with a sound like a sigh. It was as if his body couldn't be sure that it was supposed to keep going. Finally he said, "There was someone else?"

Trudy didn't say anything. She was watching her husband's face.

Tom said, "Excuse me." He walked out to the verandah and let the screen door slam behind him.

"Dear God!" he said under his breath. So much was ruined. When his father died it was like this. So much ruined. A healthy man, who strode about like a king, killed in a week by a sickness that didn't even have a proper name. And then his mother died a year later when her heart packed up, and not the least warning. Tom looked up at the hills and said again, "Dear God!"

But even in his shock and disappointment he knew there would be no throwing out. He heard her voice behind him.

She was standing inside the screen door, barely visible in the shadows.

Tom didn't speak. Her form became more distinct as his eyes adjusted. He could see the sheen of tears on her face.

"We'll work it out," she said. "Please let's work it out, Tom? We can, can't we?"

· · ·

It was noticed in Hometown, Trudy's baby—well, naturally. She must be, what—four or five months now? And she'd been back with Tom no more than three months—about that? Or maybe Tom had been seeing her before she came back, wherever she was. Do you think? Anyone with hide enough to ask Tom Hope if his wife's baby was his, good luck to him, or her. And if it wasn't, did Tom even know? Bev Cartwright from up on the floodplain, who had been close to Tom's uncle Frank, told anyone who raised the matter: "Do you think he's an idiot? Tommy's an intelligent man."

. . .

Eight months into her pregnancy Trudy's mood changed. She stayed in bed until after eleven each morning and wept often. She said that food tasted like poison to her. She said that the world was full of crooks and liars. Tom put it down to fear. She was frightened of her baby. And yet not every frightened mother-to-be was as bad-tempered and ill-mannered as Trudy. He shared the house with her, that was all. He would show the same kindness to a stranger.

All this fear of Trudy's was there in the hospital with her when she gave birth. She screamed blue murder and so annoyed the midwife that she was eventually told to show a bit of gumption. The delivery was straightforward enough despite Trudy's carry-on (the midwife's word). Afterward she had to be ordered to suckle the child, a little boy given the name Peter.

The midwife said to Tom, "I don't envy you over these next few months, my dear!"

. . .

The boy must have felt his mother's lack of affection because even at four and five months he looked to Tom for comfort. And Tom took pains throughout his working day to get back to the house regularly. He'd put down the wire-strainer or his shovel or the slasher and stride down to the house to give the boy a few fond words and a hug and to make sure he'd been fed and changed. Trudy watched without interest, scratching at the rash that came and went on her arms and shins.

My life's gone to the dogs, Tom thought, *but the little chap's coming along.*

At other times, by himself, he thought of what a hit-or-miss business it was being married. Just good luck if it worked out, bad luck if it didn't. He shared hardly a thing with Trudy, no interests that bound him to her, and yet he had once been head over heels in love with her. Now she only perplexed and worried him. If the little boy couldn't make her happy, what could?

Yet he wished Trudy could be a happier person. He wished she would go and find her other man if that would do the trick. Only if she took the little boy with her would it upset him badly.

.   .   .

How MANY MEALS were shared before Trudy went away again? Hundreds upon hundreds at the cedar kitchen table, very little said, middle loin lamb chops with cauli and peas and mashed potatoes, grilled trout, rabbit stew with carrots and parsnips, mutton roast on Sundays. Tom fed Peter in the high chair, the little chap with his coal-black hair and plump red cheeks reaching for Tom and not for his mother. Tom called the boy "Petey" and "Peter." His mother rarely had a name for the child at all. Although every so often Trudy would suffer a fit of remorse and make more of a fuss over the boy, combing his hair flat to his head and dressing him in a strange little tweed suit her mother and sister had sent from Phillip Island. These fits could last up to half a day but always ended with the child distressed and calling in a high, imploring voice for Tom. And that was the child's name for the man who was not his father: Tom.

CHAPTER 2

This time Trudy told her husband face-to-face. She said Jesus Christ had called her to join her mother and sister down on Phillip Island. Jesus Christ had not called Peter, though, not for the moment.

It was in the bedroom that Trudy told Tom of the calling. She had stolen out of bed very early to dress and pack a suitcase. When Tom awoke for the cows at four, Trudy was sitting in the kitchen ready to catch the five o'clock bus to the city. She was wearing her maroon hat of soft felt and her green suit and best shoes. Even in the kitchen light she looked pretty, with her makeup on and her chin raised and her hands folded on her lap. She looked relaxed.

She said, "Tom, I can't stay with you anymore. I can't stay with Peter anymore. I can't stay in this house anymore, no not even for one hour more."

Then she told Tom about Jesus Christ. She said, "I'll come back for Peter one day when I understand things properly. Oh, Tom, I'm so sorry. Do you see why I must go? Do you?"

Tom had expected that he would feel relief when his wife finally decided to leave him a second time. Instead, a burden of sadness settled on his heart. He looked at Trudy, sitting composed on the bentwood kitchen chair, her hands in her lap and her fair hair grown so long now that it curled over her shoulders. He noticed that she had plucked her eyebrows into perfect arcs.

He said, "Yes, I understand." He couldn't say, *You're going because you're bored and you have no roots and there is nothing in your heart*, so he let her believe what she wished.

The lowing of the cows had just begun, and the clattering of the gate as they banged against it in their insistence.

Trudy said, "I'll go now."

"Will you say good-bye to Peter?" Tom asked her.

"No, I shan't," she said. "It will just upset him."

Shan't was a word she used now and again.

. . .

Tom DIDN'T STOP to reflect on the great difficulty of caring, by himself, for a boy of almost three while keeping up with the farm. Before Trudy had left he'd tried taking Peter with him whenever it was possible; now he would have to take him everywhere, possible or not. If he'd thought about it for even five minutes he would have seen it was no-go, so it was best not to think about it. At least the shearers had come and gone. He always helped with the shearing, and there's no time for supervising a small boy with sheep to handle.

Up the ladder in the orchard, he called down to the boy, "Whaddya think?"

Playing in the grass with his yellow truck, the boy said, "Too right!"

Among the sheep in the hill paddocks, Tom encouraged the boy to trot along beside him. He said, "Big, fat sheep up here!"

And the boy said, "Big buggers!"

When they found a brown snake toasting in the sun beside the oxbow lake, Tom crouched down to tell the boy how to behave with snakes: "You see one, you stop still. Just stop still. And you shout out, 'Tom! Big wriggler!' Okay? And I'll take care of him."

It was hardest in the rain. Tom carried the one-man tent he used on fishing trips and set it up for Peter wherever he was working. He said to the boy: "Tom's down there freeing the channels, okay? Listen, now. If you need me, you bang on this tin bucket with this stick, you got that? If you feel lonely, you bang on the billy with the stick. And I'll come."

He couldn't find a way to keep the boy close for the milking between four-thirty and six in the morning but he was able to recruit Beau for the job. Obediently, but with deep misgivings, Beau sat by the boy's cot and allowed Peter to reach out and stroke his ears and his nose when he woke at half-past five. By six the boy would have worn out his interest in Beau but that couldn't be helped. Down in the dairy Tom heard the boy howling out: "Tom! Come here, Tom!" And then: "Please, Tom!"

He read the boy stories twice a day, books from the library in Hometown. At night when Peter was asleep, Tom struggled to keep his own eyes open past nine. But he made sure the fire was set in the stove and that the accounts were up-to-date. Even exhaustion couldn't mar the enjoyment he was getting out of life. In bed he lay smiling, recalling pleasing moments from the day.

He knew Trudy would come and take the boy away one day. The thought always came to him just at the height of his happiness. He chased it away by shaking his head and waving a hand in front of his face.

. . .

PATTY AND CLAUDIE raced up from the city when they were eventually told that Trudy was away on her travels again. They found Tom in the shed repairing the manifold on the tractor, Peter nearby tinkering away with an old gearbox from the utility truck. Patty said, "Oh, Tommy, this will never do!" Tom said it would do very well; and no, Peter would not be going back to the city to be brought up with Claudie's kids.

Claudie said, "Tom, listen to me. He needs a mother's touch. It's all very well playing with car parts but there's more to raising a child than that."

But Tom was firm and his sisters returned to the city without Peter. In the car, Patty said to Claudie: "That woman, I'd have her skun! I'd do it myself!"

"Poor Tom," said Claudie. "If ever a man deserved a proper family."

. . .

IT WAS TWO more years before Trudy was heard from again. A letter arrived in the post with this to say about her new circumstances and her plans for her son:

> *Dear Tom,*
>
> *I apologize to you for letting so much time past before contacting you about Peter. I hope you understand that I have been through a very difficult time since coming to Phillip Island. Tom, I was in a very very unhappy state when I came here but Jesus Christ has found a path for me I am so glad to tell you.*

Tom, I owe my life to Jesus Christ and I will Follow Him forever in my life from now on. Tom, I must have Peter here with me to raise in the Love of Jesus Christ. This is what my Prayers have revealed to me. You saw me at my worst, Tom, but you would be very amazed to see me now. I am ready to be a Mother to my son in a most Beloved way. I am coming with Mum and my sister Tilly to pick him up on Wednesday 27th this month. I will be most appreciative if you will have Peter ready for me. Tom, I thank you for your kindness, you are a good man, I know that.

  With Christ in my Heart,
   Trudy

The hammer blow that is expected, braced for, does no less harm than the one that comes from nowhere. Tom sat at the kitchen table stunned, aching all over. He'd put Peter to bed before allowing himself to study the damage. He thought, *She has no right.* Then he said aloud: "I'll take off. We'll go to Queensland." He imagined himself making his way in the outback with Peter in tow. He could do it. He was a mechanic and welder and panel beater by trade and he could always find work. If nobody wanted a mechanic, he could find work on a farm, on a station. He could shear, so there was that. There was nothing he couldn't turn his hand to.

Before he did anything so un-Tom-like as throwing himself into a melodrama, he made an appointment with Dave Maine in Shepparton, the solicitor who'd handled his uncle's will, a good chap who knew his way about. He had to take Peter with him and the little bloke sat in a chair in Dave Maine's waiting room with a picture book and a packet of jelly beans. Dave, with his tie always worn loose, and a dark-gray suit with a slept-in look, told Tom that he didn't have a leg to stand on.

"You're not the father, old chap. She's the mother. The court will give him to her."

"After she's been away for years?"

"Doesn't matter. If you could prove some great moral turpitude, maybe. But she's shacked up with Jesus, so you tell me. The court wouldn't even give you visiting rights. You could work out something informal, that's a chance. Where's she taking him?"

"Phillip Island," said Tom.

"Phillip Island? Fuck me. Miles away! You're rooted, Tom. Sorry."

Other strategies occurred to him. He could see Trudy and her mother and sister off the property at the point of a gun. He could be away in town on the day they arrived. He looked at the boy full of pain as the days went by. It was only a week before Peter was due to start school and Tom had purchased his uniform, his books, told him what school was all about, shown him the building in High Street. Tom had said, "I'll drive you to school in the mornings and pick you up in the afternoon. You'll like it. Lots of kids to play with. Lots of stuff to learn."

"What about the milking?" Peter had said, for he'd been helping with the milking in recent months. "Tom can't do all the milking by hisself."

It was his habit to speak of Tom in the third person at certain times.

"I'll have to cope, won't I? School's important."

He started a letter to Trudy saying that Peter was ill and that she'd have to wait for a couple of months. But he didn't send it. He thought for the hundredth time of Dave Maine's words: *She's the mother. The court will give him to her.* And he saw that the game was up. Even if he took off for Queensland, they'd find him eventually.

.   .   .

THREE DAYS BEFORE Trudy was due to pick Peter up, Tom took him
down to the river to fish. This was the boy's favorite thing, fishing for
the small rainbow trout at the confluence of the creek and the river
where the water rattled over the small round stones. He'd developed a
handy way with the rod, Peter. As small as he was, he could still get
some decent loft on his cast and he knew how to flick the bale back
over the line at just the right moment and draw the line in at a speed
that kept his lure off the riverbed. When a trout took his lure, he knew
to play it at the right tension and to keep the tip of his rod up. He
couldn't net a trout while still holding the rod, not yet, but he was
pretty good all the same.

This day, Tom let him catch three little trout before giving him the
news about his mother. One of the trout was a brown, a bit bigger than
the rainbows. Catching a brown was a prize. The rainbows were maybe
more beautiful with their mottled coloring, but the brown trout were
stronger and fought harder and their hatred for the person on the other
end of the line was obvious.

The boy made a small pool in the shallows of the river using rocks
as a wall and in the pool the dead trout kept fresh. It was necessary to
check every fifteen minutes or so to make sure that crawfish hadn't
invaded the pool to pick at the trout. It was not unknown for a big
crawfish, or yabby, to drag a small trout back into the current of the
river and make off with it. Making the wall of stones that hemmed off
the current of the river was something that gave the boy as much
pleasure as catching the trout.

Tom said, "The thing is, old fellow, your mum's coming up in a few
days' time. You know who I mean, don't you?"

"Trudy."

"Trudy, yeah. And she wants to take you back with her, wants you to go and live with her."

The boy looked puzzled. But he didn't say anything. Instead he dashed to his pool to check for yabbies. Tom walked down to him and put his hand on the crown of his head.

"Bit of a bugger, isn't it?" he said.

The boy said something but it was too soft to carry.

"What's that?" said Tom.

"I can't," said the boy.

"You can't?"

"I can't," the boy said again. He'd begun to cry.

Tom crouched down, his hand now on the boy's shoulder. In the rock pool two small yabbies were making toward the eyes of the brown trout. Tom picked them up and tossed them into the current.

"Peter, it's not what I want," he said. "She's your mum, you see. It's not what I want."

Tiny squeaking sounds were coming from the boy. He was attempting to stifle his tears, but he couldn't.

"I can't," he managed to say again. Then he reached into the pool, seized the brown trout, and threw it out into the river.

· · ·

TOM HAD PETER ready at eight in the morning, everything packed in a small suitcase and two cardboard boxes. The three lengths of the boy's split-cane fishing rod were tied together with twine. His Ambidex reel with its ball-bearing spool was wrapped inside one of Tom's socks and packed in the suitcase.

It was going to be a warm day, the sky an intense blue from

horizon to horizon. At this time of a day that was bound to get hot, Beau would normally be pestering Tom for an early dip in the dam. But he looked at Tom and the boy standing at the front of the house and went to hide under an old Humber Tom had up on blocks under the cypresses.

A little after ten in the morning a red Volkswagen turned into the drive from the highway. Tom had left the main gate open. The Volkswagen pulled up at the second gate and Trudy stepped out from the passenger seat. The other two figures in the car remained where they were as Trudy opened the gate and walked to the front verandah, where Tom and her son were waiting. Her hair was cut short and she was thinner than at any time Tom had known her. She was wearing a green belted dress that had something of the look of a uniform. She walked with her arms crossed below her breasts. A silver crucifix hung at her throat.

"Hello, Peter. Hello, Tom."

She stepped up onto the verandah then knelt down and put her arms around her son. She said, "I've missed you so much." When she stood and put her arms around Tom his nostrils filled with the aroma of lavender soap. She said to Tom, "I have something for you." She reached into a small pocket in her dress and brought out a tiny parcel of purple tissue paper. She unfolded the parcel to reveal a small, gold crucifix on a fine chain. "I hope you will think about wearing this, Tom. To show that you forgive me." Tom made no move to accept the crucifix but he allowed Trudy to slip it and the purple tissue paper into the side pocket of his suit coat. He had dressed himself in his good clothes for the handover.

Tom said quietly, dipping his head close to Trudy, "It's cruel to do this, Trudy. You left Peter behind. He only had me. I love him like he was my own flesh and blood. And, Trudy, he doesn't want to go. You only have to look at him."

"Oh, Tom," said Trudy, "you just don't understand. Tom, Peter will live in a house full of love. Tilly's children will wrap him up in love. This is just a farm, Tom. A lonely, lonely farm. On the island Peter will have children his own age and a proper school, a blessed school. We can't be selfish with children, Tom."

"I'd like to come down and see him," said Tom. "Once a month, something like that."

Trudy shook her head so readily that she must have been expecting the request. "Oh no, Tom. I don't think that would be a good idea. No."

Trudy's sister and mother had stepped out of the red Volkswagen and were now standing on each side of the car. They wore identical spectacles with oversized lenses and identical broad smiles, as if this were the happiest day of the year.

Tom carried the two cardboard cartons, the fishing rod, and the suitcase down to the car in one load. He lifted the boy up and gave him a fierce hug. "Well, old fellow. You write to me, won't you? You find the time to post me a letter, won't you?"

The boy nodded in a defeated way and allowed Tom to pull the front passenger seat forward and pop him onto the backseat. Trudy climbed into the backseat beside her son. Trudy's mother took the front passenger seat and Tilly the driver's seat. The boot at the front of the car was raised. Tom packed in the suitcase, the boxes, and the fishing rod.

Then the car wouldn't start. The engine turned over and came briefly to life but one of the plugs wasn't sparking. Tom knew what the trouble was. He said: "Better let me take a look." He was ignored. Trudy's mother said: "It always does this." Tilly turned the ignition key again and again. Peter looked out of the window at his father with something like hope in his eyes.

Tom said again: "Better let me take a look." He lifted the engine bonnet at the back then went down to the shed for his socket wrenches. When he returned to the car some sort of silent tussle was going on in the backseat—Peter trying to get out and Trudy restraining him, all of this wordlessly.

Tom said, "He can help me."

Trudy released her grip on her son and stared fiercely away from where Tom was standing. The boy scrambled into the front of the car and over his grandmother. Tom opened the passenger-side door for him. Tilly and Trudy's mother maintained their broad smiles.

Tom opened his socket set and told Peter the size socket he required. The boy took the socket from its place in the set, fitted it to the wrench, and handed it to Tom.

"Got a dirty old plug here," said Tom. He removed the plug he suspected of causing the trouble and cleaned it up with a thin strip of emery cloth. He let Peter replace the plug and tighten it and fit the distributor lead.

"Give it a go," Tom said to Tilly.

The engine kicked over and roared to life.

Trudy's mother climbed out of the passenger seat so that Peter could climb into the backseat again. But the boy flopped down on the grass like a dog that doesn't want to do what it knows it will finally be forced to do, and Tom had to lift him up and return him to his mother. He kept up the same playing-dead trick on the backseat, lying hunched-up and facing away from Trudy.

Instead of turning the car around Tilly backed it slowly all the way down the drive. At the highway, she got the car facing in the right direction by fits and starts and then it was gone, swallowed up by the dip on the city-bound side of the highway just past Tom's gate, then screened from his view by the poplars along his front fence.

Tom sat on the front verandah and rolled a capstan. He kept glancing up, hoping foolishly for the red car to reappear. His insides ached so badly that he couldn't even bother with the relief of a smoke and he crushed the cigarette after two puffs. He picked up his socket set, locked the lid, and walked down to the shed. Beau, still worried, followed at a respectful distance.

CHAPTER 3

The sun dried the moisture out of the hill paddocks well before autumn that year but the grazing still pleased the woollies. Tom ran a channel down to the waterhole from a spring that bubbled up above the granite boulders. The flow of the spring came up to the world, looked around, then dived back into the earth. Ferns that couldn't be found anywhere else on the property thrived along its bed. The sheep could make their own way up to the spring, but Tom didn't encourage them. They had a way of propping there until it was dark, then the ewes would become spooked and bleat themselves silly.

Peter had been gone for two months. Tom was sure this was one of those things in life that can never get better. He wasn't a great farmer, but he had had the makings of a good father. That's what he said to himself when he was about the place and the sense of failure that troubled him became too much to bear: not much of a farmer, poor husband, but he'd made a good job of being a father. He could say that in his defense. Then one morning tramping uphill to the orchard with Beau he stopped and smiled: a moment of insight into the strain of self-pity in his fantasies of failure.

"Bloke's done his best, eh, Beau? Do you think? Not exactly fly-blown, am I? So shut up. Not you, me."

Those in Hometown who knew all the details of Tom's story—a half dozen people, Nigel Cartwright and his wife, Bev; Trevor Clissold; the Noonans—all on the land, one-time friends of Uncle Frank; Juicy Collins, the butcher—showed their sympathy by never saying a damned word about Trudy or Peter. Juicy, who'd known Frank Hope best, the uncle who'd left Tom the farm, came closest. He made a habit of singing songs with a breezy theme whenever Tom called in for snags and mince as he did each Tuesday. He called Tom "the cavalier of the hills" and sang in his creamy tenor the opening verse of "Don't Fence Me In." And then: "Don't fence young Tom in, you hear me? Don't fence our Tommy in."

"Take it easy, Juice," said Tom.

"He's the Sheikh of Araby, our Tommy," said Juicy. "Up and down the bloomin' hills on his camel, have a care for your missus. Nice to be a free man, isn't it, Tom."

"If you say so, Juice."

Juicy kept up the banter while he wrapped the week's meat for Tom in the broadsheet pages of the *Herald*. 3XY Radio played in the background—up-to-date rock 'n' roll favored by Juicy, the only man of his age, forty-three, in Hometown who had a good word to say about the Rolling Stones. On the white-tiled wall at the rear of the shop hung a portrait of the Hometown Robins of 1963 in red guernseys, premiers of that year, Aussie rules. The boys with their arms folded, half of them sitting, half standing behind; shy faces, others cocky, the three bad boys of the team wearing foolish grins.

Juicy's satire veiled a type of contempt, and Tom felt it. The real Casanova of Hometown was Juicy, who gave himself to adultery so unapologetically that past lovers would take a moment at the counter to ask about the progress of more current affairs. And it was Juicy who got about the hills—not on a camel but in his bronze and black Monaro—advertising his perpetual adolescence.

Tom had not the least interest in finding a woman to replace Trudy. His wife was divorcing him. Documents from a legal firm in the city had arrived in the mail. The grounds for the divorce were given as: *sustained emotional cruelty and abuse.* Articles in evidence included a letter written by Trudy's mother, in which she stated that her daughter had come to the Jesus Camp on the night of March 1, 1967, soaked to the skin and sobbing *as if her soul had been torn out of her body.* Tom, reading the letter, remembered Trudy arriving back at the farm three years ago, also soaked to the skin and sobbing. Was it something she'd mastered, arriving in rainfall? Maybe she had another chap lined up.

. . .

LATE IN THE summer when all the pears and apples and nectarines had been picked and dispatched on Terry Nolan's truck to the agents in Healesville, Tom wandered up to the orchard with three saws and a brace ladder to start work on the pruning. His uncle had always pruned at the end of summer rather than in winter and it was best to follow custom. He'd had Peter with him while he was pruning last season. He'd call down to the boy, "What about this bugger, Petey? Will we lop him off?" What often surprised him was how little it mattered that he wasn't Peter's true dad. He thought, *Would I love him more?* He couldn't see how that would be possible.

He moved the ladder from tree to tree, taking off the growth of the past season with the curved-blade saws, with the secateurs. It was work. You couldn't avoid it. And the day was as hot as a bastard. Tom said, "See, if you know what you're doing, Tommy Hope, you start earlier." His bare arms, stretched above him, ran with sweat. Marsh flies lumbered around his face, falling on his flesh when they saw the chance. The flies were attracted by the sheep dung under the trees, then by the blood of the scratches on Tom's forearms. He said to himself aloud, as if he were the second party in a conversation, "Life's not over yet, Tommy. Jesus Christ."

.   .   .

IT WAS TOM'S custom in the evenings to cook up whatever rubbish he intended to eat, then settle by the wireless with a bottle of Ballarat stout. He'd get some joy out of the songs on the wireless, grow mellow as the alcohol kicked in. But this evening, he took the stout up to the boulders, scaled the biggest one, and sat there studying the sunset. A huge sheet of crimson and turquoise stretched above the hills in the west. Beau lay beside him, after ten minutes of desperate attempts to get a foothold on the stone and turtle his way up. Tom swigged from the bottle and patted Beau with his free hand. He was here to vary his experience. He'd sat years past with his uncle Frank on this rock at this time of the day, this time of year, the sun setting. He'd been visiting, just by himself. Fourteen? Fourteen. His uncle had wanted him to enjoy the beauty in the sky and he had, because his uncle had wished it. But that lasted about two minutes. After that, he was merely being dutiful. He'd glanced at Frank's profile for some sign that this would all be over soon and they could go back to the house. But it had taken a long time for his uncle to exhaust his interest in the sunset.

So now Tom, trying to see what his uncle had seen, had to concede that the sunset was beautiful, but what most impressed itself on him was the loneliness of his house down there on the flat. The place was weatherboard painted a butter color, faded now, a verandah on three sides, iron roof a rusty red. The old floodplain reached for a mile on each side of the river, which you could pick out by the line of ghost gums along its banks. On the other side of the river, a couple of miles back, the pasture hills of Henty's property stood in silhouette, all of the trees taken out long ago. The hills were rounded and they graduated in size, like the knuckles on your fist.

Henty ran three thousand woollies up his hills and over the plain, barely had to bother with them from one year's end to the next, sent two thousand Corriedale lambs to the abattoir each summer. Tom kept fifteen hundred Polwarths and sent five hundred to the abattoir each year. He was building up the flock after Uncle Frank, in his last two years of failing health, had sold off all but two hundred and fifty. His uncle had brought in three shearers each year for a clip that was hardly worth bothering with. The shearers considered themselves bush royalty and asked an arm and a leg. By the time the bales went up to the railhead and on to the agent, you'd be lucky if you could fill your pipe three or four times with the profit. Tom kept a better watch on his sheep than Henty did on his. Henty kept the water up to them and blew the guts out of any dogs that came up from Hometown and went gaga in his paddocks, but he never had the vet along for a look-see; he shot any woolly that looked crook. And don't talk to Henty about disease that could spread through the flock. It had never happened and never would. Clipping the hooves of the beasts? Never. No dipping, no worming. And he was no friend to the spring orphans. Tom fussed over his sheep like a paddock nurse and was disdained for it by his brother graziers. It wasn't a quiet disdain; it was hearty and to Tom's face. "Fuck me, Tommy! You'll be buying 'em gum boots next."

The house. It was empty now. But even if Tom were inside at this moment—this is the thought that came to him—the house would look the same. He was its sole occupant. The house pitied him. It had lived through the era of Uncle Frank the bachelor, through the disaster of Trudy, the short heyday of Peter, and now once again it was the shelter of unmarried Tom.

.   .   .

HE DROVE THE ute into Hometown without any motive. No, there was a motive. He couldn't bear to be only himself any longer; only Tom Hope. It had grown on him up on the boulder with Beau. It wasn't right. He was thirty-three, there were years left to him. He'd made a poor show as a husband to Trudy, but he wasn't as hopeless as all that, surely. Another woman might be glad of him. Well, it wasn't impossible, was it? He had a proper bathroom now, and, Jesus, really, when would you get another autumn and winter like the one that had driven Trudy mad, day after day of rain? It was true, he wasn't likely to be genius as a husband. But it was something he could work on.

He drifted in the ute down to the pub, the River Queen, didn't really want a drink, asked himself what in God's name he thought he was doing but couldn't go home. His house exerted a repulsion that he wasn't ready to fight. The River Queen had a television; he could sit over a pint and watch—what? Too late for *Bellbird*, a show he'd enjoyed there a couple of times. Too late for *Pick a Box*.

He thought of Peter, of the way the boy could turn a curious gaze on anything, everything, ask questions that you could savor before answering. What was a swan-necked valve good for? Why did the points have to be set on the ute with those thin fingers of metal? Did chooks lay eggs on purpose? With Peter, something became freed in his heart. Could that happen with someone else?

He walked along the empty shopping strip and found that staring into the darkened windows was no better than being at home. On a Saturday night, which this night wasn't, the Gala Cinema would be lit up, people milling at the entrance. Not tonight. He heard boys calling to each other in the darkness, wandering the town in search of distraction, mischief, anything vivid.

Tom paused at Moira's tiny shop, the window full of tokens from distant cultures; polished stones, charms, inspiring tracts in decorated frames. A poster from the previous year's referendum was still taped to the window. VOTE YES FOR ABORIGINAL RIGHTS. The shop was only open when Moira felt up to it. It was said by many (including Moira) that she grew high-grade marijuana at the back of the Cathedral Ranges, her real source of income. Tom liked her, the only hippie he'd ever met. Her kisses of greeting were always full on the mouth. When Peter was still on the scene, Moira had buried him in the avalanche of her bosom every time she saw him. And she'd given Peter a pamphlet about the war in Vietnam. "He's not too young to know about murder." Tom didn't dwell on the war in Vietnam. His instincts told him that it was stupid, or worse, rubbish, but he didn't attend Moira's protests, her melodramatic offsiders in LBJ masks with something not quite the color of blood oozing from their mouths. And then, Morty Lewis's son, Heath, had died in Vietnam, not in combat but from septicemia after he stabbed himself in his bare foot playing mumblety-peg with a Yank infantryman. The irony of Heath's death—our allies, an idiotic game—only served to magnify Morty's grief. Tom's courtesy would never allow him to wound Morty further by standing in the shopping center with Moira's handful of offsiders chanting slogans. It was too, too much like showing off.

The last shop in the row was vacant again. A woman from the city had run a picture-framing business there until recently, but no business established on the premises had ever really made a go of it. The shop was the sad sack you find in every small town, empty for six months of the year, for the other six months leased to tenants with misplaced optimism. Some years before the picture-framing, antiques had filled the shop space, the whole country struggling out of a credit squeeze, no one spending a penny on luxuries.

Inside the shop, Tom could make out cardboard cartons stacked in piles of four. And against the walls, in the gloom, timber bookshelves— an assortment, some fairly fancy with glass doors. This was to be a bookshop? Tom murmured: "What the hell?" Maybe he couldn't prove it, but you could probably claim that not a half dozen people in Hometown had ever opened the cover of a book and got away with it. Tom himself had read only one book for grown-ups in his life, something left behind by Trudy, the story of a blond woman in the time of the Crusades who made passionate love to Christians and Saracens alike. The idea had been that he'd find some clue to Trudy's thinking, but no. He'd enjoyed the tale, though. It wasn't out of the question that he'd read another book one day.

No signboard hanging from the verandah outside the shop, and nothing on the window. Or no, there was something: a piece of notepaper torn from a spiral binder and sticky-taped to the inside of the glass. Tom squinted at it, couldn't read it, made a flame with his lighter. The lettering was in another language, not English, the strangest writing you'd ever see. He studied it with his nose close to the glass, the flame of his lighter threatening to singe his eyebrows. Egyptian, maybe? But no little pictures, just strange shapes.

Tom said, "No idea," and put away his lighter.

Home? Tom supposed so. But dear God, something had to happen. Something. He wasn't living like this for the rest of his life. He climbed into the ute and sighed like a bellows.

. . .

TOM DROVE HOME nursing his melancholy. Tomorrow, fairly early, the pears, the nectarines. And Beau at the base of the ladder, scratching himself.

. . .

THE LANGUAGE THAT Tom had studied on the window of the shop, the language that had so perplexed him, was Hebrew. Translated into English, it would read:

To the God of the Hopeless,
Bless this shop.

CHAPTER 4

Tom kept an eye out to see if the bookshop made any progress.
Nothing much after a fortnight. It wasn't Tom's habit to ask for information about anything that wasn't his business, but he broke the rule
after the third week.

"Juice, the new shop down the way."

Juicy Collins was weighing Tom's lamb chops.

"Hannah's shop," said Juicy. Then: "You want to watch me when
I'm weighing, Tom. Could have me thumb on the scales. Not above
that sort of thing."

Dulcie Nash, whose husband kept the servo on the S-bend by the
sawmill gave a snort that wasn't quite a laugh. "Don't you worry,
Tommy. I'm watching the rogue."

"Won't get away with much while you're on guard, Dulcie. Hannah's shop, Tom. Lady from the continent, as they say."

"Jewish," said Dulcie, as if the single word provided a catalog of
important information.

"That's right," said Juicy. "A Jewish lady. From the continent. What,
you've got some objections, Dulce?"

"Me? No. Have I? I don't know."

"How long's she been in Hometown?" asked Tom. He thought he'd glimpsed the woman who must be Hannah days earlier, sharing a joke with Vince Price in the licensed grocer's. He was left with a sketchy image of a well-dressed woman, attractive, a mass of dark curls mixed with gray.

"How long?" said Juicy. "A year, Dulce?"

"Might be. They usually stick to themselves. She'd be the only Jew in Hometown."

"Horry Green," said Juicy.

"No!" said Dulcie. Her basket held before her, she took a couple of quick steps closer to Juicy's marble counter where the broadsheets of newspaper sat in a pile. "Horry's a Jew?"

"More Jewish than Moses," said Juicy. He'd wrapped Tom's chops and had them ready to pass over the counter but wasn't yet prepared to do so.

"Horry? No! Dear God, I would never have picked Horry. Horry's Australian!"

"More Jewish than Moses," Juicy repeated.

Tom asked when the shop was expected to open.

"Opens on—what?—Friday week?"

"You spoke to her?" said Tom.

Juicy handed over the parcel of chops then returned to a familiar theme: "Tommy, cut up one of your woollies, enough meat to last you three months. Glad of your custom, but save your dough, Tom-Tom. I've told you before, dummy."

"Do that, Tommy," said Dulcie. "Save your money well."

Tom had no taste for butchering. He never mentioned it.

"You've spoken to her, Juice?"

"I have."

Juicy lifted the cloth cap he always wore in the shop then replaced it again. He was time-wasting, teasing.

"Got an interest, Tom? The Sheikh of Araby? I'll tell you one thing." Juicy leaned closer to Tom. "A figure like Cleopatra."

Juicy made a shape in the air.

"Oh, boy! Don't think I haven't made a few indecent suggestions. No-go. She's got me pegged for the scoundrel I am. But a young fella like you. Hoo!"

Dulcie, listening closely, reached over the counter and delivered a light slap to Juicy's cheek. "Don't you get Tommy mixed up with a creature like that! Don't listen to him, Tom. You've had enough trouble in that way." She pursed her lips. "Old enough to be your auntie."

"Forty-five?" said Juicy. "I'll take all the aunties on offer at that age."

"You already have. Give me half a dozen savs and leave Tommy alone."

.   .   .

THREE DAYS LATER, Tom came within a whisker of driving back into town to see what the bookshop lady was up to. But at the last moment, he switched off the ute's ignition and sat there baffled by whatever it was he thought he was doing. He climbed out of the ute with a sigh, gathered a ladder and tools, and set to work soldering a gap in the guttering above the living room windows. Whenever it rained the water dripped down onto the window ledge and had begun to lift the paint. Tom sanded the window ledge and applied a coat of red lead to the exposed timber. With the soldering, it was the work of a good two hours. An old, demented ram he treated as a friend butted him repeatedly as he sanded and primed—not hard, just affectionately. And

Beau in turn chewed on the old ram's leg. Tom asked himself aloud: "What do you expect her to say to you, you nong? 'Hello, it's a nice day'? For God's sake." He was a practical person who never thought of fate and things that were meant to be. He could take apart an engine, stand surrounded by its thousand parts, find what was causing the problem, put the engine back together. He might daydream, but he knew that the dreams were foolish. He daydreamed of a time when Peter might contact him—a letter. There would be no letters. Peter would grow closer to his mother and forget him. He would become a Christian and it would be Jesus he loved. Tom these days—since Trudy—remained faithful to what seemed likely. He didn't chase rainbows.

Except that he did. He'd think of Peter during the day and fashion prayers for the boy's happiness. He would say: "Nothing wrong with Jesus. Let him have Jesus." And then he'd think: *I'll drive down to Phillip Island one of these days and park outside this Jesus place. I'll see if I can get a glance at him when he comes out.* Tom was hoping for no more than thirty seconds. He'd stay far enough away to avoid strife. Maybe catch Peter playing footy with the other kids. Thirty seconds. Then he'd drive back to the farm. Six hours driving, there and back. Well worth it.

. . .

IT WAS MIDDAY by the time he'd finished the soldering, the sanding, the painting. Once he'd packed the tools away, he said to himself, *Why not now?* He could leave Beau to bark at the woollies for a minute or two in the evening, remind them that the place was still attended. He'd get Juliet Henty from across the highway to do the milking this once. The mare, Josephine, and the Clissolds' blind pony he'd taken on, Stubby, could care for themselves in the oak tree paddock, so long as they saw his headlights when he got back. Stubby was all Jo wanted in life, after all.

. . .

HE PACKED A lamb sandwich and a bottle of tea, kept on the clothes he was dressed in and headed off down the Melbourne Road to the highway. He took the old Studebaker his uncle Frank had left him to give it a good run with the new rings and valve seals. His thoughts as he drove were of Peter, of moments when he thought: *This is the best thing*. Peter with his stick poised above the upturned billy, on the lookout for snakes. "How long for a snake, Tom?" He wanted to beat the billy, to sound the alarm.

But Tom thought of the bookshop lady, too. He knew nothing about Jews, except that they'd been knocked from pillar to post in the war. He knew Horry, of course, who ran a book on the city races, everything squared away with the police; Kev Egan at the station, in particular, who enjoyed a punt himself. Horry was what people call dapper. Smart suits, narrow-brimmed hats. On big race days at Flemington and Caulfield and the Valley, Horry went about the Hometown shopping center in a green velvet waistcoat with gold buttons, a young clerk in tow who kept whispered wagers in a notebook held five inches from his nose. People paid coins into the Hometown Urban Fire Brigade box on Second Saturday song nights at the River Queen to hear Horry duel with Juicy in front of the open fire in the saloon bar. Horry's baritone, Juicy's tenor. "The White Horse Inn," "On the Road to Mandalay," "White Christmas" from Horry. And from Juicy, "Your Cheatin' Heart," "Cool Water," and "Let's Call the Whole Thing Off." It was usually Horry who won the duel by acclamation, because of the vibrato he got into notes at E above middle C. He'd say, "God smiles on the baritones," and immediately donate the twelve shillings prize to the Brigade box. The Jewish lady, maybe she had a little bit of Horry's flair. When Tom saw her with Vince Price that time in the licensed grocer's, she'd turned for a second or two. Seen him looking, given him a smile and tilted her head to one side. Two seconds.

·　·　·

HE CAME TO the city, to its thousands and thousands, to the demented traffic, then down the Nepean Highway; never out of third for long stretches. Both sides of the highway were lined with shops and each shop had its sign and the shops and the signs and the striving lowered his spirits. The years on the farm had changed him. Up a ladder a month back, pruning the apple trees, the nectarines, the pears, he could feel his heart seeking, even when he was unhappy, even when thinking of Peter brought tears to his eyes. What could you seek here?

·　·　·

HE CROSSED THE bridge at San Remo at two-forty-five in the afternoon, the sky a high, hard blue, the sun still hot even though the season had advanced to mid-autumn. Skinny boys burned black leaped from the bridge railings into the tidal waters below. A slip of paper with the address of the church on the main road out of Cowes sat on the seat beside him. He found the five main buildings of Jesus Mercy on a bare patch of earth fifty yards back from the road. A signboard behind a low chain-link fence advertised the place as: CHURCH OF JESUS MERCY AND CHURCH OF JESUS MERCY PRIMARY SCHOOL. A larger sign set farther back read simply: JESUS CAMP. Pastor Gordon

Bligh was named as the principal of the school. The buildings were identical—gray fibro, pitched iron roofs painted a rusty red. Above the gable of the building that served as the church rose a timber cross that had faded in the weather to a driftwood gray. The cross was too big, too hefty for the modest scale of the church building.

Set farther back than the five main buildings were a number of plain weatherboard cottages, all alike, shaded by sugar gums and with garden plots of geraniums and petunias crowded around the two steps leading up to the verandahs. The front door of each cottage bore a plaque with the name of an individual book of the Bible printed on it in flowing script. Tom could read the nearer names from where he sat in his car: Deuteronomy, Romans, Hebrews, Obadiah, Nahum.

Tom had calculated the time of his arrival to coincide with the end of the school day—assuming that Jesus Mercy kept the same hours as Hometown Primary. It was only that thirty seconds he needed. He realized that he might catch sight of Trudy, too, but he wasn't concerned. The great power of wounding that had once been Trudy's had lapsed. He watched from the Studebaker, window down. At three-thirty, with no warning bell, children began to straggle from the front door, many of them, more and more, perhaps a hundred, a mixture of ages, and there he was, Peter in a navy blue school jumper and gray shorts. Tom thrust his head out the window to call to the boy, then remembered. But there was joy in seeing him shuffling along with his head down and turned a little to one side, a gladstone bag held by its handle in one hand. Tom said: "Don't they ever give him a haircut?" Even from this far away, Peter's hair looked like the raised crest of a black cockatoo. Tom bit his lip, yearning to step out of the car, take a few steps, crouch down, and let the boy race into his arms.

Peter knew the Studebaker. He'd helped Tom with the engine a dozen times, building up phrases of car chatter. "Is the carby crook,

Tom? The timing's off, do you reckon? Black smoke out the exhaust, Tom! No good!" He looked up and saw the car, cream and red, the distinctive grill. His face flared with glee. He dropped his gladstone bag, burst through the gate, and ran with pounding strides in the clodhopper boots he was wearing to the passenger side of the car. He wrenched open the door, climbed in, slammed the door shut, flung himself into Tom's arms. He said: "Take off, Tom! Take off!" Tom kissed him, tried to push down his hair, but even as he was doing this he was telling the boy that he couldn't take off, couldn't drive away. Peter clutched at him, grabbing handfuls of shirt. A face appeared at the passenger window—a big face, big smile. The man, whoever he was, short-sleeved white shirt and suspenders, motioned with his hand for Tom to wind down the passenger-side window. Tom lurched across the seat, Peter still grasping him, and turned the handle. The man pushed his head and shoulders inside.

"You'll be letting that boy go," said the man. His face was a burning red; perspiration trickled down his forehead from a great mane of white hair. He was old, certainly, but with a vigor that belonged to a much younger man. "You hear me, then? You'll be letting that boy go." His smile kept its place.

"We're not going anywhere," said Tom. "I'm Tom Hope. I know this boy."

Peter, his voice reduced to a squeak, exhorted Tom again to take off.

The old man withdrew his head and now opened the passenger door of the Studebaker. He reached in, took hold of Peter with both hands, and lifted him out of the car. Tom slid across the front seat and out onto the roadside. The man stood with Peter under one arm, the boy's limbs hanging limply. He was a tall man, broad chested, powerful forearms. His face, creased with age, was a handsome face, except that the smile of brilliant white teeth, maybe dentures, was more menacing than genial.

"This boy lived with me for a couple of years after his mother left him," said Tom. "I'm not a stranger."

He was trying to keep any note of apology out of his voice.

The man nodded. "You get along now," he said. "You get along, Tom Hope."

His smile didn't falter.

Peter had reached out and taken a grip on Tom's belt. Tom worked the boy's fingers free. He lifted Peter's chin to look him in the eye. "This gentleman's right, Peter. I'm not your dad. I shouldn't've come. I just wanted to see you for a few seconds. But it was wrong."

"You get along now, Mr. Hope," said the man. "I'm the pastor here. I'll be speaking to the police."

A small number of kids and three adults were watching, absorbed, from the school gate, Trudy and her sister and mother not among them. The pastor nodded in the direction of the Studebaker. Tom reached out to tousle the hair on Peter's head, but with the boy under the arm of the pastor, thought better of it. "Better go, old pal."

As he pulled out and drove off he saw Peter, on his feet now, being led away. The pastor stooped and picked up Peter's gladstone bag. The children and the three adults were patting Peter, comforting him, so it seemed.

· · ·

HE REACHED HOME at seven in the evening, the three hours of the drive from the island to the farm given over to angry remorse. A foolish thing to have done. Peter would be in strife. Better if he'd parked farther away. Better if he hadn't taken the Studebaker. The police might call. What could he say? "I wanted to see Peter, no he's not my son, no I'm no relation."

Oh, but so good to have seen the boy. "Take off, Tom! Take off!" Yes, Peter, but to where? We don't fit in. And you can see the law's point of view. What? "I love him, she doesn't, give him to me." For God's sake, Tom.

·   ·   ·

THE HORSES, JOSEPHINE and blind Stubby, were waiting by the fence. Tom gave them a toot of the horn. They tossed their heads in delight then followed the car up along the fence to the top gate. Tom went into the shed and came back with two apples for each of the beasts—blemished apples that he kept aside from the harvest. Beau waited on the front verandah in an agony of obedience, knowing that he had to stay until called.

"Beau! Rouse yourself, pal! Come on!"

The dog flew off the step and reached Tom without his paws touching the ground, or so it seemed. He leaped to Tom's shoulder and buried his nose in his ear, licking away wetly, teeth clicking. The woollies had kept to the hill pastures below the boulders, which was all right. Tom fed the horses a scoop of grain each, doled out a tin of Tucker Box to Beau from the cupboard on the back verandah. And found, half under the back door, half out, a sheet of paper folded exactly into four. He opened it up and read what was written in the remaining evening light.

Dear Mr. Hope,

It's Hannah Babel. You won't know me, but I am living in the town now—for a year, thirteen months, in fact. I am opening

*a bookshop in the shopping center and I need someone—you—to
do some work. I have a sign to hang and I am informed that it
must be welded. Mr. Collins in the butcher shop says that you can
do such things, and so, here I am. I tried to ring you this
afternoon—no success, so I came here, to you. Will you ring me on
the number at the top of this page? Or call at the shop tomorrow
in the afternoon, before 5. Maybe a "cuppa"? I am putting this
under the back door because people tell me that the back door is the
"business end" of the house on a farm. But just to be sure I am
going to copy this note and leave it under the front door, too.*
And a signature.

At the head of the page, printed in blue:

*Hannah Babel Diploma of Music Budapest Institute of Music
Lessons by appointment: Piano and Flute
5 Harp Road Hometown
Telephone Hometown 0817*

Sure enough, another note under the front door, identical except
for this: *Your dog is very friendly!*

Tom sat with the notes at the kitchen table. He read each twice,
opened a can of beer, lit a smoke, and read them again. Outdoors, the
big white owl that perched itself at night on the rear timber rafter of
the old barn gave its deep three-note call every ninety seconds. Tom
lifted his head and listened. His uncle had told him that it was a sign
of good luck on its way if an owl took to perching nearby. He'd mentioned this to Trudy one time, and she'd said his uncle had it wrong.
It was a sign of bad luck. Common knowledge, she'd said.

CHAPTER 5

Jacket and tie? Tom tried on his corduroy coat over a white shirt and blue tie. He looked at himself in the mirror inside the wardrobe door. The expression on his face startled him; as if he were off to a funeral. He tried a smile, another, a series of smiles of varying breadth, then waved his hands about in annoyance. What the hell? He was calling on Mrs. Babel to talk about a welding job. Why in God's name would he wear his cord jacket and a shirt and tie and his brown slacks? He threw off his jacket, ripped off the tie, the shirt, and left the slacks on the bed and dressed himself again in his work trousers and a green twill shirt. He gave himself a smack on the side of the head. Would he ever—ever!—have any sense? Would he?

· · ·

HE TOOK THE back road into town because it was a longer journey, by about a minute. He needed thinking time. Or not so much thinking as reproving. He asked himself why he was carrying on the way he was. This Mrs. Babel—Hannah—had a job of work for him. She wasn't interested in anything except his ability as a welder. She wasn't going to ask him out to the pictures. She was a music teacher, twelve years older than him. So why, Tom? Could he answer that simple question: Why? He knew nothing about music. Beethoven. Nelson Eddy. He knew nothing. Beethoven had been a great favorite of Uncle Frank's; he'd left behind twenty or more long-playing records. A foreign chap with a violin. And oh! It came back to him now—the violin chap was Jewish, too. Uncle Frank had mentioned it when he was explaining the name.

"Jewish cove on the violin, lots of 'em are."

"Lots of them are what?"

"Musicians. Violins, pianos."

It was an odd thing about Uncle Frank, an odd thing having all those records. He'd lean back in his armchair beside the record player, beating time in the air with his arthritic finger that he could never straighten. "Have a listen, Tommy. How does a bloke do that? Hey? How does a bloke do that with a violin?" Tom couldn't have been less interested if his uncle had been listening to a recording of squeaky doors.

.   .   .

HE FOUND HANNAH in her shop-to-be attempting to negotiate the mechanism of an ancient cash register, something from the ark. The day was warm enough for her to be wearing a yellow summer dress patterned with tiny red flowers. The dress revealed a lot of her bosom and she wore black high heels, as if keeping shop called for more style than any other woman in the shire would have thought necessary. Tom knew immediately what the bosom-revealing yellow dress would do for her reputation in Hometown, and winced. That head of hair, a great mass of curls. The gray appearing just here and there.

"Mr. Hope! Lovely to see you. Help me with this. When I press down the keys—like this—nothing happens. Nothing! You do it."

She nudged him to the cash register, put her hands on his shoulders and positioned him over the keys. "Now. Have I been swindled, Mr. Hope? Do you think? The man in the shop where I bought it, he said, 'A child can use it.' A Greek fellow, up near Victoria Market in the city. A Greek. Beware of Greeks bearing bargains." Whenever she smiled, she lifted the arcs of her eyebrows, as if to say, *We're having fun, don't you agree?*

"Pardon?" said Tom.

"Make it work, Mr. Hope. Madame Babel is on her knees, begging you. Still, it's very beautiful. Is it beautiful? I think it is."

A movement over by one of the stacks of cartons caught Tom's attention. It was a little yellow bird, shaking its wings on the topmost box. When Tom saw the bird, the bird saw Tom. In a motion too quick to be followed, it was on his shoulder.

"Woo!" said Hannah Babel, and she laughed with delight. "David, suddenly so bold! Mr. Hope, he has chosen you out of thousands. Say something to him. Be his friend."

Tom, blushing, his head turned toward the bird, struggled to imagine what he might say. Finally: "Hello, little bloke."

The bird gave a hop and came to rest on the top of Tom's head.

"Oy!"

"Relax yourself," said Mrs. Babel. "He's not an eagle, Mr. Hope. He won't harm you. Whistle for him. His name is David."

Tom attempted to whistle a few notes of "Mary Had a Little Lamb."

"Try C major, Mr. Hope," said Mrs. Babel. "Work within your limits."

The bird left Tom's head and alighted on Hannah Babel's shoulder.

It had a candid look in its perfect eyes. "David, too, comes from the Victoria Market," she said. "I was there maybe a month ago for shelves in Abbotsford Street. The Greek fellow. I walked through the market where the birds are sold—you know where I'm talking about, the pet place? An amazing thing—I came out with David on my shoulder. Could anything be more propitious, Mr. Hope? Befriended by a bird."

Tom's guess was that *propitious* meant "lucky." He said, "Good."

"He came with me in the car, on the dashboard all the way back. Can you imagine?"

"Good. In the car. Good."

Hannah offered a finger to the bird and returned it to the top of the stack of cartons.

"You can do some welding for me? Will I call you Tom?"

"Yes. Please."

"And you'll call me Hannah."

. . .

MADAME BABEL—HANNAH—showed Tom the job. An oblong iron frame suspended from the shop's verandah was left with an aperture into which a sign could be fitted. The many failed businesses run from the shop had each displayed a sign, rescued from the frame once utter defeat had been admitted, and taken away by the various proprietors. Hannah had been informed by Juicy Collins that the frame that held these signs was in a precarious state and would need to be rewelded to the iron struts that attached it to the verandah ceiling. Tom brought a stepladder from the back of the ute and climbed up to inspect the damage. He scraped away at the rusted struts with the tip of a screwdriver, scrutinized what the investigation had revealed, made a few clucking sounds of concern of the sort that tradesmen employ whatever the job, and called down to Hannah: "Juicy's right."

"You are saying? 'Juicy'?"

"Mr. Collins. Bob Collins."

"Ah!"

Hannah, facing west, was shielding her eyes from the afternoon sun. She was smiling as if this appraisal of her signboard frame gave her real pleasure. Which it could not, in any sensible way. Unless everything gave her pleasure. Because Hannah was smiling, Tom smiled. For a few seconds they were smiling at each other, for each other, with that liberty we sometimes enjoy before intimacy exists. Then Tom realized what he was doing and resumed his troubled-tradesman expression. A frown and shake of the head, a squinting, worried look in his eyes.

"Yeah, I dunno," he said.

Hannah said, "It is what? Not possible? The welding?"

Tom said, "Yeah, I dunno. Maybe."

He scratched his head above his right temple with the tip of the screwdriver.

"Maybe," he said.

He climbed down the ladder, maintaining his air of preoccupation with the issue of the rusty frame. Hannah had kept her smile. She reached out and picked a flake of rust from the shoulder of Tom's twill shirt, standing about an arm's length closer to him than either a woman or a man normally would in Hometown. In Melbourne, in Australia more broadly. And that smile. She touched the palm of her hand to Tom's chest above his heart.

"Cuppa?" she said. She spoke the word as if satirizing it. "Cuppa, Tom Hope? I have some special Hungarian tea. Magyar fruit tea. Come in."

An electric kettle sat on the floor by the power outlet, along with a bag of sugar, two cups with saucers, a pint bottle of milk, a china teapot—bright red—a tea caddy, and teaspoons. Hannah crouched by the kettle in a manner that preserved her elegance.

"So," she said, "what is your verdict, Tom Hope? Can the sign be fixed? Tell me."

Tom stood awkwardly among the cartons, shooting a glance at the yellow bird every few seconds, anxious that he didn't again become a perch. It was only that he'd suffered from a young age with a sense of appearing a fool. The bird studied him teasingly, head to one side.

"Yeah, I'll need to replace those two struts," he said. Hannah smiled up at him from beside the muttering kettle. "You can't weld rust, Mrs. Babel. But what I can do is— Pardon?"

"Hannah," said Hannah. "You must call me Hannah. Okay?"

"Right, right. Hannah. Sorry. What I'm saying is that I can replace those struts with new ones, if that suits you. Pardon?"

"It does," Hannah said again. "It suits me, Tom Hope. Very much."

Hannah spooned tea leaves into the pot. "Hungarian tea. Good for your complexion. Shining skin. Have you ever enjoyed Hungarian tea? Fruit tea?"

"No, no, I haven't. No."

"My friend sends it to me from Budapest. We don't use sugar or milk in this kind of tea. But I should ask you. Would you like milk and sugar?"

"No," said Tom, with a prescient conviction that the tea he was about to be served would be a trial. "No. I'll go without." Feeling that he would do well to keep talking for the sake of avoiding Hannah's difficult comments, he explained that this was the oldest shop in the town, ninety years since it was built, those leadlight windows down the side and in the fanlight above the door. And the frames of the plate glass sections, that was copper. If Hannah scoured off the verdigris with steel wool the copper would shine.

"A bit of steel wool, come up lovely, Mrs. Babel—"

"Hannah. Here's your tea. Let it cool for a minute."

"Hannah, sorry. Come up lovely, Hannah. Verdigris, the green stuff. Verdigris."

Hannah stood before him with her teacup and saucer. She held up the cup and turned it a little left and right. "And the cups, too, from Budapest," she said. "You see the pattern? The flowers and the birds? Do you see how lovely?"

Tom said, "Hmm."

"When can you start work?"

"When? Well. When would you like?"

"Now."

"Now?"

The tea was horrible. Tom sipped it, but barely.

"Not so good?" said Hannah. "You don't like it?"

"No! No! Lovely."

"You hate it. That's okay. I hate it myself. Just for the complexion. So you can start now?"

Tom drove back to the farm for the welding gear, returned, cut the steel strips for the new struts, welded the frame in place. By which time it was five-thirty, the light failing. Hannah asked him if he could also make some more shelves for the shop. Torn between self-preservation and his liking for the lady from the continent, he said he'd make the shelves. He'd measure up and come back the next day. If she wanted cedar, he had a heap in his workshop.

"Cedar. Good," said Hannah. "So you'll come back tomorrow? In the morning? Up until three. After that I have students."

The yellow bird had taken up its perch on Hannah's shoulder. It turned its head rapidly this way and that, its eyes on Tom. All at once it let out a few notes of song, a sound that filled the shop.

"David! Yes, I see very well, my darling. I see very well."

And to Tom: "David likes you. That is what he said."

Tom nodded. He had accepted that Hannah was a fruitcake. It didn't ruin his liking for her.

"One thing, Mrs. Babel. Hannah. Sorry. One thing, Hannah. You're not worried that you'll lose money? People in Hometown don't read books."

Hannah closed her eyes and widened her smile. She opened her eyes again. "They will read. They will come to Madame Babel. Don't worry."

Now she reached up and placed a hand on Tom's cheek. "You have a beautiful face, Tom Hope. Do you know?"

What the hell? Tom's beautiful face reddened to the hairline. He attempted to say something. His mouth opened, no sound came out. Then: "It's not."

He took Hannah's hand away, gave it back to her.

She was laughing, softly. "Tomorrow morning," she said. "Cedar."

. . .

DRIVING HOME IN the ute, Tom said aloud: "Is she mad?" She must be. *You have a beautiful face.* Dear God! And yet . . . and yet what? And yet she made him happy. The way she kept moving, clasping her hands, laughing, reaching out to touch his arm, smoothing her yellow dress over her hips. He felt like a great block of stone talking to her, but she was *interested* in him, that's what it felt like. He had never before in his life been made to feel interesting.

Something else. Tom didn't think of himself as observant, astute.

He didn't notice things. He more *failed* to notice. But when he pictured Mrs. Babel's face—sorry, Hannah's face—as he did now, her eyes, her green eyes, he grasped that she was suffering. That huge smile, all of her teeth on show—one at the side a bit discolored—but she was suffering.

He had suffered. In the same way? He didn't know.

CHAPTER 6

MAY 1944

The train had stopped twenty times or more during the three-day journey, sometimes for hours. It was different this time.

The small window high in one wall of the wagon was not showing any light. Hannah's guess was that it was well past midnight, not yet dawn. All wristwatches, pocket watches had been surrendered at the start of the journey. The only timepiece in the wagon, an alarm clock with a black enamel housing and a white face, belonged to an old woman with oversized dentures from a town outside Budapest. She took it from her leather suitcase every so often to wind it. Others called to her: "Madame, the time!" She held the clock up above her head so that everyone could see. But her winding hadn't been vigorous enough and the clock had stopped. Hannah attempted to keep track of the time in her head but there had been lapses into unconsciousness, when she knew she was asleep while remaining aware of everything. She'd even said to Leon, "Take Michael, I'm asleep." And Leon had relieved her arms of the child and left his wife standing, the shoulders of those packed against her supporting her weight.

Destinations have a way of announcing themselves. Hannah and the other adults in the wagon, all but a few with children in their care, sensed in the silence that this was as far as the train would carry them. At other stops they would hear nothing for five minutes, then there was a grating sound followed by a sharp jolt, the great iron mass of the train coming to rest with reluctance. And they might hear a voice and a response. Then the train would begin moving again, slower than walking pace, gradually gathering speed, the regular *thud* as the wheels hit the cross-ties, the journey continuing. They enjoyed a few minutes' relief to know that they had not yet arrived, succeeded by dread that arrival was still ahead. On the first day of the journey, Hannah, in a whisper, had asked of a man who kept a bakery in her neighborhood in Budapest: "What will happen?"

Jacob Cahn the baker had lifted his eyebrows, turned the corners of his mouth down. "They will kill us," he said.

For a further hour by Hannah's count, nothing. Her arms ached so badly that she thought she would simply drop Michael to the floor, without apology. And yet she knew that she could hold on for another hour if she had to; for longer, two, three hours.

Leon said quietly, "Let me take him."

Hannah shook her head.

The boy's hand reached for her face. He said, "Mama."

She said, "Shush."

In a wagon of ninety human beings, Hannah knew maybe fifteen, some from the Dohány Street synagogue, a few, like Jacob Cahn, from daily contact. All were Jews, but how much did that mean? Thrust together in this way, after watching others relieve themselves in buckets, listening to one another weep from exhaustion, still no intimacy beyond a shared sense of injustice. Hannah felt the reluctance of her heart to embrace the whole complement of the wagon as a failure. She wished she were more a Jew who rejoiced in the bond of the faith. Instead, she thought, *If we die, let me hold Michael, the rest I don't care about*. About Leon? Yes, let her care for Leon as she died, but Michael above all. Also, let her care for Jacob Cahn, who had flirted with her in the bakery in such a clever way, speaking the English he'd mastered during a twenty-year sojourn in London, in Spitalfields: "Radiant maiden, how may I serve you?"

She kissed the crown of her son's head, a mistake. The boy had drifted into a dazed state that gave him relief from hunger, but the pressure of his mother's lips, perhaps more forceful than she'd intended, woke him with a roar. She told him to be quiet—first in Hungarian, then in English. She'd been teaching him English and, for some reason, the child was more inclined to take instruction in that language. Other children in the wagon, inspired by Michael's rebellion, raised their voices in solidarity. Leon said, "Give him to me." Hannah allowed him to take the child, but then seized him back. She didn't want to be scrambling wildly for her son when the door opened.

And the door was opened, a sliding door that crashed against the frame with great force. Dogs began barking in a barnyard frenzy, as if they'd picked up the scent of foxes among the chickens. Torch beams played over the faces of those huddled in the wagon. In the glare, Hannah could make out the shapes of the dogs striving against the leashes that held them. Commands were being shouted, not a single voice but a number. German was one of Hannah's languages and she understood the orders: *Get down on the ground! Get on the fucking ground!* But even those who didn't speak any German knew exactly what was being said. Hannah had to hold Leon's jacket to stay upright, such was the crush behind her. She slid to the ground with Michael in one arm, and was immediately shoved toward a group formed by others from the wagon. Suitcases and bags were wrenched from hands and flung into a heap. Twenty other wagons were emptying at the same time, eighteen hundred men, women, and children.

It was May of the year 1944. Dawn would come early. Hannah judged it to be maybe five in the morning. She had a great need to see where she was. Now and again a torch beam swung toward the loco-motive end of the train and she glimpsed the rails stretching ahead, dead straight. Jostled in the melee, she reached again and again for Leon, never able to grasp him. The command now was for men and older male children to move into a separate group. To demonstrate, the soldiers—they were SS—seized one man after another and pushed each into the group that was forming. The dogs reared on their leashes in their ex-citement. Hannah called: "Leon! Husband!" She caught sight of his face for no more than a second at a time in the sweep of the torch beams. He looked helpless; no suggestion of defiance. Michael with maddening insistence was attempting to turn his mother's face toward him. "I don't like the dogs!" Hannah, still struggling for a sight of Leon, at last glared into Michael's face. "Shut up!" Then, of course, he howled.

Hannah called in German to the nearest SS officer, "Ist das Ausch-witz?" Even in the din of pleading voices, her voice carried. The officer looked directly at her with an amused curiosity.

"Is das Auschwitz? Ja, das ist Auschwitz. So konnen Sie Deutsch?"

"Herr, ja, ich sprechen Deutsch, ja."

"Ja?"

"Herr, ja."

"Sie sind Ungarisch, nicht wahr?"

Yes, she was Hungarian.

The officer beckoned her, instructed her to follow him. He placed her at a distance from where another SS officer, apparently the most senior, was directing the new arrivals into two lines. One of the lines received many more of the inductees than the other. The men were sent to a third line, farther away. Hannah was told to remain exactly where she was. The officer then left her. In the thin light she could now make out buildings at some distance. This was Auschwitz. It had been the task of Leon's monitoring group in Budapest to impress on the Soviet Foreign Office that Jews were being held in great numbers at Auschwitz, and at dozens of other camps. And the Russians had accepted the claim, had conveyed their sincere regret. It was unfortunate that nothing could be done.

Hannah did not know if she and her son could evade death. It was not possible to say what she would have to do to keep first Michael alive, then herself. But she would not disobey the order of the SS officer that she stay put with Michael—she knew that much, at least.

.   .   .

WHAT WAS TAKING place before her eyes she couldn't properly grasp, but it seemed that the distinction between the two lines of women was that one received those with small children in their care, and also the aged—the grandmothers. The other line, nearer to her, comprised younger women, mothers with daughters of about ten or older. The light—it could not yet be called dawn—was just clear enough to see what was unfolding, a great bewildered crush of humanity taking orders from soldiers who intervened to push people in one direction or the other, always shouting, like human bullhorns. The senior SS officer stood in the midst of the shouting and shoving in a state, so it seemed, of profound self-approval. He was tall, good-looking, intent on showing a bright set of teeth. His gesture of assignment was a brief wave of his gloved hand—you there, you there. The soldiers kept glancing at him to see which line he was indicating and everything they did, everything they said was impatient, insulting, and terse with authority:

"Bewegen Sie, Sie, Arschloch!"

"Sind Sie verdammt taub?"

Hannah had to put her hand to her mouth to stifle protests when the SS soldiers flung people about who were slow to comprehend. She thought: *Listen to me, keep your mouth shut.*

It went on for an hour or more. The senior officer never once lost his composure. It was as if he were on stage, full of relish for the role he was playing. He twice gave a short, rather feminine laugh, but even as he laughed he kept up his flawless routine: You there, you there.

Nobody in Leon's Budapest monitoring group could say for certain that the Jews who were sent to the camps were being murdered. Two Bohemian Jews, men in their twenties, had been interviewed by the group—it was their claim that they'd escaped from Auschwitz and made their way to Budapest. They said that the Jews in the camp were shot and buried; also Russian POWs, Poles, others. But their stories were full of holes—differing versions of how they'd escaped and of the number of Jews in the camp; one said tens of thousands, the other said about a thousand all up. Also, both were plainly mad. Their testimony was disregarded.

But it was accepted all the same that a program of extermination was under way. Jews had been murdered in large numbers in the towns and villages of their birth all over Europe, in front of many witnesses, some with cameras. If the Lithuanians were murdering Jews in the open, the Poles bludgeoning Jews in town squares, the Ukrainians, the Romanians, the Germans themselves in every town, it must be true that the SS were killing Jews in the camps. Leon, scrupulous about evidence, said, "Probably." But he wouldn't insist to his Russian friends that camps like Auschwitz were made for murder.

Hannah, her child at her feet barely awake, knew she should give up any doubts of her own. She believed that the women with small children were destined for some killing ground, allowed to keep their children to avoid outbreaks of hysteria. The other women with older children—maybe they were to be made to work somewhere, perhaps in the camp, perhaps elsewhere. She grasped it. But better to believe that she was wrong. And why was she here, set aside with Michael? Because she spoke German. Surely. Would it save her and her son? She would speak German without ceasing for a year if she had to. She would grovel as she recited Goethe. Leon had whispered to her on the train: "If we are to die, don't plead." She had wanted to hit his face, to bite him. Don't plead? Of course she would plead.

A soldier strode angrily toward her. When he was close enough to hit her, if he chose to, he shrieked, "Was machst du denn hier, du Fotze?" *What are you doing here, you cunt?*

Hannah said quickly that his colleague had ordered her to stand where she was: "Herr, Ihr Kollege sag te mir, hier zu stehen."

The officer in charge had seen the exchange. He called out in a musical voice that carried above the noise, "Lass sie, zu sein, Trotell!"

The soldier, chastised, turned back to the officer, executed a quick bow and hurried off. The officer called to a subordinate to take over his role, then strolled across the bare, open ground to Hannah. She thought as he approached, *Such vanity,* for that was the most obvious thing about him. He stood before her smiling, not too close, much taller than her. The small gap between his front teeth gave him just a hint of incongruous boyishness.

"Ich bin informient, gnädige Frau, dass sie Deutch sprechen."

Yes, she said, she did speak German; she went on a little to demonstrate how well. She had learned German from her flute teacher, who'd lived in Berlin for a decade and spoke an inflected Weimar version of the language, every phrase carrying a freight of mild irony.

The officer was not as impressed as she'd hoped. He nodded

without emphasis, then bent down to look more closely at Michael. He took the boy's face in his two white-gloved hands, studied the eyes, a brilliant green like Hannah's own. Then he stood and held Hannah's face in the same way as the boy's. He kept up a commentary in a sing-song Bavarian German. "Ja, das interessiert mich, ich muss sagen . . ." He asked Hannah if she was Hungarian, if she was from Budapest, whether her parents were also from Budapest. Strange, certainly, but also fascinating, he said.

Hannah wished to ask what was strange but also fascinating, but didn't dare.

Then the officer said abruptly, "Gut, hier bleiben." *Good, stay here.* And he strode back to his post: directing the Jews from the train this way, that way.

She let Michael sit at her feet. He was by now too tired to complain, too tired to think of hunger and thirst. He rested his head against Hannah's leg and said nothing at all.

Nearby, workmen had commenced erecting a new fence: galvanized metal poles driven into holes dug with a pick. The workmen weren't wearing uniforms, only overalls or baggy twill trousers. They paid no attention at all to the inductees being pushed around, the shrieks and curses. Three were smoking, the cigarettes clamped in their lips while they shoveled out the yellow clay. They might have been anywhere. Two rolls of wire mesh and two of barbed wire were waiting to be stretched between the poles.

Hannah woke. She didn't understand that she'd been unconscious where she stood, but was aware, for a second, that some different state had intervened between her last sight of the workmen and the present moment. And then Michael was not at her feet and panic like a torrent surged through her.

She ran toward the inductees, stopped, searched in the melee for the boy. One of the SS guards charged at her, smacked her on the side of her head with his open hand, grabbed the shoulder of her coat. She escaped his grasp and ran to the workmen. She asked in German if they had seen Michael, a boy, three, a gray jacket, gray pants. They looked at her with flat expressions that offered her nothing.

"Bitte, ein kleiner Junge in grauen Hosen! Bitte!"

The guard seized a handful of her hair and hauled her back toward the inductees, pulling harder when she resisted.

CHAPTER 7

The cedar in Tom Hope's workshop had once been the rafters, floor-boards, and architraves of Teddy Croft's place down on the river. A spring flood in the late fifties lifted the river above the level of Salt's Flat and took the house off its stumps. Rather than repair the house, Teddy and Leanne rebuilt in brick fifty yards farther up an incline and the old place was offered about for a song. Tom Hope in his second year at the farm bought it with the idea of dressing the timbers and selling them off. The hard work of running the farm by himself and then the catastrophe of Trudy got in the way of Tom's project but the cedar was of the highest quality, branded on the non-facing side of each plank with the heat-etched Black Goanna trademark of a specialist timber mill in the Atherton Tablelands. Building shelves in Hannah Babel's shop seemed like a good use for it.

.   .   .

HANNAH HAD ALREADY purchased ten ill-sorted sets of shelves but she accepted Tom's suggestion that they dispense with all of them except for the glass-fronted bookcases with their lozenges of crystal. Tom said, "Rows of divided cedar along three walls, all the way up to the ceiling, and a row down the center. I can fit a brass rail for a sliding ladder so you can get up to the top shelves. Maybe keep books up the top nobody wants."

Hannah said, "Nobody? Tom Hope, for every book, someone loves it."

"Is that right?"

"You think maybe someone writes a book for two years, three years, it could be ten years and nobody loves it? Okay, I'll climb up the ladder. Make the shelves."

Tom unbolted his bench saw and buzzer from the workshop floor at the farm and set them up in the back room at the shop. He fetched in all of his tools, also jars and boxes of bolts and coach screws and self-tappers and sturdy brass Phillips heads. A workbench was required, and he put something together from ash and red gum from the farm, bolted into the wooden floor of the shop. He rose at four to get the milking out of the way, checked on the woollies, then started work at the shop at eight in the morning before Hannah was even on deck. He brought Beau along to give the animal a change and the dog sat among the curls of cedar shavings with a fixed expression of gratitude, tongue lolling, tail swaying. By the time Hannah arrived, Tom's face was a terrain of wood dust traversed by shallow valleys carved by sweat. It was Hannah's habit to greet him with a kiss on his dusty cheek, so strange to Tom that he would tense at first sight of his employer. Yet the moment of contact of lips and flesh was quickly becoming something to live for. He thought, *Remember, she's mad.* But, of course, he was in love with Hannah, besotted, and would bear anything.

Later, seven days into the job, Hannah found it suited her better to kiss Tom on the lips.

. . .

SHE PREPARED HIM proper tea, Bushells, and at lunchtime bought him sandwiches made with a dense, dark bread Tom had never come across before, and hated. Hungarian salami and Jarlsberg, mustard pickle, tomato and cabbage fried in olive oil. The first of these sandwiches he thought would kill him, but he persisted. Hannah watched him eating. She said: "Tasty?" And Tom said: "Mmm!"

. . .

SHE WORE A different dress each day and different shoes, not always high heels. And she appeared to own a treasure-house of jeweled brooches and necklaces, bangles and bracelets of gold and silver and enameled brass. She came to work each day groomed like a queen. Her massy curls were sometimes taken up and worn as a great furry bun on the top of her head, held in place by colored plastic combs. Since the days were growing cooler with the approach of winter, she sometimes wore pleated woolen skirts and a finely woven jumper with an artful scarf. No woman in Hometown came close to her for care with costume and Tom was aware that as a result, she was widely despised by other women for going posh when simpler attire would do just as well. Not by everyone. Bev Clissold would call in at the shop to say hello to Tom, and if Hannah were there she would step back and admire her garments and face and figure.

"Puts me to shame," said Bev. "Here I am in my pinny."

. . .

The conversation was mostly on Hannah's side. Partly because Tom was determined not to bore her, as he'd bored Trudy. Partly because Hannah had accepted Tom's expertise in establishing the shop's architecture and there was little for her to do but talk until the time came to unpack the books and fill the shelves. She hung about watching him at work, her back against something that supported her, hands clasped in front, feet crossed. She seemed transported by admiration. "And those holes, Tom, so that you can change the height of the shelves? So clever! You are using that— What do you call it? A spirit level? Using that spirit level so that each shelf is straight? Tom, you take such care!"

Tom knew that Hannah was offering flattery in place of the contribution she was untrained to provide with a hammer, a screwdriver, bench saw, and buzzer. And he knew that the flattery was sugar. But Hannah was so candid in her way of going about it that he couldn't help but smile. He said, "Hannah, this is all easy stuff. It's not magic."

. . .

When she wasn't admiring Tom's carpentry, she chatted about anything at all. Often about politics. She followed the whole business: policies, scandals, disasters. She was the first person Tom had ever known who took any of it seriously. In the Tramways Union, political talk was just tribal abuse or encomiums for Red Clarrie O'Shea, the union secretary.

"This fellow Henry Bolte who looks like Khrushchev, who would vote for him, Tom? Who? A little thug. Can't they see? You know what I read in the newspaper? He has a farm, and the road is paved up to his gate, after that it is dirt. Just to his gate. Who do you vote for, Tom? If you vote for this Henry Bolte, I have to leave you."

Tom, not sure if Hannah was joking but glad that he could reply in the way he was about to, said: "Labor. Like Uncle Frank."

And books, she spoke about books. Solzhenitsyn. Tom suffered, with grace, an account of *In the First Circle*, just out; she'd finished it in three days. And then she started in about a new book by "Your Thomas Keneally."

"Can't say I've heard of him," said Tom.

"He trained to be a priest, you didn't know? Madness."

She studied him beveling the front of the cedar shelves with a hand plane, the timber held securely in two vises on the workbench.

"I want to choose you a book. A novel, for you to read."

"A book? Righty-o," said Tom, remaining cheerful in the way he'd perfected while eating Hannah's sandwiches.

"Well, I have chosen," said Hannah.

"Good-o."

"Would you like to know the name of the author?"

Hannah, whose plans to make Tom a reader were apparently well advanced, produced a green-covered Everyman edition of the book from behind her back. "Charles Dickens," she said. "Have you heard of Mr. Charles Dickens?"

Tom laid the plane on the bench and frowned with the effort of recalling.

"You know, I think I have, Hannah. Yep, I have. Charles Dickens. Uncle Frank was a bit of a reader. He read me something by Charles Dickens. Couple of pages. I was, what? Eleven? Twelve? Did he write a book about Christmas? Charles Dickens, about Christmas?"

"So he did," said Hannah. She was delighted. *A Christmas Carol.* "So he did, Tom."

Tom nodded, pleased that he'd heard of Charles Dickens; pleased that he'd pleased Hannah. He stood beaming.

Hannah held the spine up for him to read. "*Great . . . Great Expeditions . . . Expectations*! *Great Expectations*. Good-o. What's it about?"

"Being alive," said Hannah. "Being a human being with hopes and fears. Tom—what a treat you have waiting. I am being honest with you. What a treat you have waiting."

"Right you are. I'll get stuck into it. *Great Expectations*. Good-o."

He returned to the beveling.

Hannah interrupted him by placing her hand on his shoulder, caressing the muscles there. She put the book on the workbench, among the shavings. She held herself against him, her body entering the contour of his back, her hands crossed over his heart.

"I adore you," she said. They had been lovers for five days.

CHAPTER 8

It had begun like this, at Harp Road, Tom with his pocketknife scraping away at the flaking blue paint on the railing of the back verandah. There was no need for him to trouble himself with the paintwork of a rented house. It was just his habit. See it, fix it.

He no longer wore his wedding ring, Hannah noticed, not for a week now. His left hand, free of the ring, rested unoccupied on the railing. She reached out and closed her own hand over it. Tom, for a minute, less, gave no indication of what Hannah had done, had declared, but then ceased scraping with the pocketknife and became still.

"Come with me," said Hannah.

She undressed him in the bedroom, first kneeling to remove his boots while he kept balance, holding on to the tall chest of drawers. Then stood to unbutton his twill shirt, the top of her head at his chin height. Unbuckled his belt, freeing the tail of the shirt. Negotiated the buttons of his fly, slipped down his khaki trousers, disposed of his socks and Y-fronts leaving him in his singlet.

"This is a new singlet?"

Tom attempted a spoken reply, but some occlusion in his throat obliged him to settle for a nod.

"You wanted to impress me?" A smile in her voice. "Take it off."

His chest, its sparse fair hair, the symmetry of the nipples wrenched her to him in a greedy browsing over his face and mouth. Then the surprise, as Hannah was overtaken by Tom's initiative, an avidity in disrobing her, shaping her that belonged to a more emphatic man, one she'd never met. Hannah wanted to say: "Where does this come from?" but also, "Don't stop."

Raised above her, filling her, smiling, he whispered endearments, kissed her face. She said, "Don't make me come too soon, I don't want to come too soon," but she did. Then gave herself over to a breathless babbling in a language Tom wasn't equipped to understand—Hungarian? And tears, too, a continuous stream. She wriggled free and took a Kleenex from a box on the bedside table, dried her eyes, her nose.

"You see? You make me too excited. Did you know?"

"Han, I was taking it slowly."

"Yes, yes. It's me. But, Tom, you didn't come? I want you to come. Is something wrong?"

"When you're ready," he said.

"I'm ready. Ready ready ready."

She straddled him, bent low, and kissed him.

"This is the sweetest thing, Tom, the sweetest thing in my life, I promise you, Tom."

Hannah had left music playing on the radio, string quartets.

"You like this music?" She was tracing the features of his face with her fingers.

"A bit mournful," said Tom.

"A bit mournful. But not you. You are not mournful. Smiling Tom. Why are you smiling?"

"It's so good, Han."

She took a deep breath, cried out, collapsed on Tom's chest, and they were back with the babbling and tears. And then—more. Took more, had more, wanted more, skin slick with sweat, monsters in their need to go too far.

A man with land to tend in bed at midday was sinning. Tom was surprised at how little it bothered him. Beau would keep the sheep from the worst they might attempt; the morning milking was out of the way. It was as if he'd become aware of a feature of nature hidden from him all his life: a second sun, a mountain range that dwarfed the familiar hills. Hannah said, "Tom, you are wonderful for me, I promise." What Tom believed was that Hannah loved him, and for that reason, was likely to say anything. But he smiled. He had never once smiled in bed with Trudy. A warm, happy mystery was in attendance. This, then, was "making love."

Scrambled eggs, toast, and coffee in the kitchen at one in the afternoon, sunlight bathing the table, softening the butter in its crystal dish. Hannah had slipped her red silk dressing gown over Tom's frame, too much of him to cover, like a present wrapped in paper that won't quite join up. They spoke in sentences of one or two words.

"Good?"

"Good."

"More?"

"No thanks."

"Sure?"

"Sure."

"Stay, please?"

"Yep."

Back to the bedroom, sprawling sex that moved them up and down the bed, onto the floor, into the living room, where two crested robins that Hannah fed watched with curiosity at the window.

The cows, the Ayrshires, the everlasting cows. Tom dressed without showering, kissed Hannah, and promised he'd be back. He roared down the highway forty minutes late, having had to stop to haul the aged Sally Morse out of the ditch she'd failed to avoid for the hundredth time on the Moon Hill bend.

The cows were complaining at the dairy gate; Beau walked in circles with a reproachful frown. After the milking—and the cows could sense his resentment—Tom fed Beau, took a half dozen loin chops from the fridge, and raced back to Harp Road.

Hannah was tutoring two evening students in piano duets, the Hilary twins, Denise and Delilah: "Alouette," "William Tell." The girls were distracted by Tom in the kitchen grilling chops and boiling cauli, carrots, and potatoes. They knew Tom well, and not as a man who ought to be occupied in their piano teacher's kitchen. They were old enough to imagine sex, too, but Tom? Mrs. Babel? Mysterious, fascinating, also disgusting.

He slept at Hannah's house in Harp Road three nights in a row. Her bedroom frightened him a little. The walls were hung with what appeared to be rugs, richly colored and patterned. On the walls? Did people do that? And paintings, one of Hannah naked that shocked him. ("My husband who is dead. He painted me fifty times maybe. Two husbands, Tom, both dead.") On the third night, Hannah left the bed to strike a pose beneath the painting identical to the one portrayed. Playfulness in the bedroom startled him. He had slept with only one other woman apart from Trudy—an episode of mutual consolation with one of Juicy's castoffs, and that with a demeanor more determined than inspired, on both sides.

Two husbands, both dead. Tom, in bed at the stage when questions are asked, questions that have been saved up (his head next to

Hannah's on the same plump pillow, twice the size he was used to, allowed his face to be caressed in silence). But he asked his question eventually.

"One went to the gas chamber," Hannah said. "One was shot."

"To the gas chamber?"

"In Auschwitz, Tom. In Auschwitz."

The room was lit by a lamp in the corner with a fabric shade of creamy gauze. Tom's leg rested across Hannah's midriff. He felt the muscles of her abdomen become tense and saw the same sort of tension stiffen her face. It would be better not to ask her anything more about these two dead husbands. But a gas chamber?

"Auschwitz?" he said.

"Then you haven't heard of Auschwitz? Okay, who needs it? A horrible place, Tom."

"In the war?"

"Yes, my love. In the war."

In some distress, so it seemed, Hannah turned away from Auschwitz, shrugged Tom's leg off her stomach, and raised herself above him.

"Do you know what we have to do?" she said.

Her smile had returned.

"What we have to do?"

"Yes. Do you know?"

"No. Tell me."

She studied Tom's face, pushed his hair back off his forehead. But she didn't say what she might have said just for the moment.

"In this light," she said, "your hair is fair. Blond. Do you know?"

"It was blond when I was a kid."

"When you were a kid. All those many, many years ago."

"Well, it was a while ago now. I'm thirty-three, Hannah."

"I know, my darling. I know exactly how old you are. I know everything about you. Everything important."

She settled back on her side, her face next to Tom's.

She said, "Dear God, don't die. Three times, I couldn't bear it, Tom Hope."

"I'm not going to die, Hannah. Nobody's going to shoot me."

It appeared for a few moments that Hannah might give way to tears. Then: "Nobody's going to shoot you, Tom Hope," she said. "Come inside me again. Make me happy."

. . .

ON THE FOURTH and fifth and now this sixth night, Tom had to leave at ten. He didn't want to, but the woollies were being stalked by town dogs that had gone bad. He'd lost eight sheep over the space of a week, bellies torn open, the dogs frantic for blood. When dogs go bad, they give up the whole structure of a future; blood in the mouth is all that matters. The five-dog pack that had been killing sheep for a fortnight had been reduced to three by Augustus Henty. They'd started on his flocks first and he'd recognized two of them—a mangy Labrador with a bit of collie and a one-eared mutt with a bit of everything—without being able to get a clear shot. He went to the homes of the owners, hauled the dogs out, and displayed the crusty blood on their muzzles: guilt written all over their hairy faces. Henty was given leave to shoot them, but even if the owners had protested, he would have tethered the dogs and shot them anyway. In a town that relied on grazing, vigilante justice prevailed.

This time Bobby Hearst was with Tom, camped on a rise upwind from the northern paddock. Beau was left home. If he'd seen the pack he would have charged in and been ripped to pieces. Bobby was Hometown's Dead-eye Dick, sixteen years old and jumping out of his skin to get to Vietnam. He used a Mauser 98 stamped with its Wehrmacht serial number, its date of manufacture (1940), and the eagle and swastika emblem. Bobby had traded a modern Anschutz .22 and a wartime Webley flare pistol for the Mauser, which was modified with a long-range flip-up sight welded to the barrel halfway down. The sight required you to take aim above the target: The bullet's trajectory, if your judgment was reliable, would take it smack into the target a yard below your point of aim. Strictly speaking, he was too young to carry firearms, but the person you had to please if you were underage and wanted to tote a Mauser about was Kev Egan at the station, and Kev didn't mind.

Tom and Bobby were up the hill before midnight, but hoping the dogs would come closer to dawn. Hard to hit a target seventy-five yards away without a little light. The flock had separated into four untidy groups spread across the big northern paddock, each group loyal to a particular ewe. The sheep suspected that Tom and his offsider were up the hill, but they weren't curious. Whenever the moon escaped the clouds it revealed the woollies in each flock unaltered in their sleepy positions by so much as a turn of the head. Now and again, a soft bleat.

Tom smoked drowsily; Bobby sipped from a bottle of warming Melbourne Bitter, commenting in his chirrupy way on the local footy and the statewide competition and the overfastidious girls of the town who wouldn't put out for love or money. Tom would have preferred a silence to fill with thoughts of Hannah but if the dogs were going to be shot, it would have to be Bobby's Mauser that did the job. Tom, maybe as good a shot as Bobby in his day, had no relish for killing dogs. He was likely to pass up a target—as he had the past two nights—unless he could be sure of hitting the head. Bobby could get off three rounds in ten seconds with a bolt-action rifle, each shot insanely accurate. He went for the gut.

Long before dawn, Beau, half a mile away on Tom's verandah, let out a plangent howl. He'd picked up the scent of the pack—what remained of the pack after Henty's intervention—and this was his combined protest and lament. The sheep, all four groups, set up a panicky bleating. Tom and Bobby stretched themselves out full length and scanned along the paddock with their sights. Everything was shadow, the huddled sheep a lighter shade of dark than the scrub and the ironbarks. But it was possible to make out the dogs streaking toward a clump of isolated woollies between two closely packed groups. Tom could see no prospect of a shot.

Bobby could. The big mongrel, who must have been the boss, reared in its frenzy and Bobby hit it twice while it was still on its back legs. The second dog leaped sideways when it was struck, then collapsed. Tom shot the third dog, the fool of the three, when it propped at the sight of the big mongrel licking its own innards.

"Did you see that big bastard up on his back legs, Tommy?"

Bobby was on his feet, excited and happy. His voice was shrill. Tom stood and gave him a pat on the shoulder.

"But did you see that big ugly bastard up on his back legs, Tom? Pop, pop! Hit him twice while he was rearing! Fuck me!"

He was ecstatic. He stomped around in small circles, the Mauser clasped in one hand.

"Jesus, Tommy. Did you see that big bastard rear up? Hoo-eee!"

"I saw him, Bobby. Great shot."

"Two shots, fuckin'! Two! While he was rearing!"

"Two shots. Terrific."

McKenzie County
Public Library

The woollies had backed well away from the dead dogs, but once they caught sight of Tom their alarm faded and they drew closer. But not too close. It was as if they were tugging their skirts back from something unseemly, although interesting.

The mutt Tom had shot was good and dead, pretty much intact except for the small hole in its head. Tom's rifle was a .22; a kid's gun, really. The red kelpie, Bobby's second kill, was pulling itself and its guts along the ground as if toward some imagined sanctuary. Tom shot it through the skull. The big mongrel, hit twice, was still licking its own intestines. It stopped every couple of seconds to growl futilely at Bobby, who was leaning over it with a long-bladed Japanese bayonet.

"Kill it, Bobby," said Tom.

Bobby made a motion with his hand, as if to say, Not so fast.

"Bobby, kill it. It's in agony."

"Deserves to be," said Bobby. But he plunged the bayonet through the dog's neck.

They threw the dogs over the top fence into the scrub. Tom would dig a ditch and bury them in the daylight. He was grieved a bit walking back to the house with Bobby, thinking how little he resembled any decent sort of farmer. Uncle Frank had never given a second thought to putting a bullet into a dog's brain. A dog that had gone bad had to be shot. That was all there was to it.

Tom drove Bobby to his home on Ben Chifley Road then parked outside Hannah's darkened house. Should he go in and wake her? She might say: "So selfish when you know I'm asleep." No, she wouldn't say that. She would say: "Tom, I'm so glad." He was at that stage of loving in which insight and confidence are only there for moments at a time. He knew Hannah in the whole of her being with passionate certainty; then he doubted everything. And it was in those minutes of doubt and not in the moments of belief that he left the ute and went to her back door and knocked quietly, sure she would be too deeply asleep to answer or that she would hear the knock but decline to stir herself at such an hour.

Hannah came to the door in the satin slip she wore at night, hair disarranged, sleepy and smiling. She kissed Tom on the lips, then kissed him again with the generosity of a woman who knows her heart.

Later, hours later, she showered with him. The showerhead protruded out over the green enamel bathtub, a plastic curtain depicting tropical fish of many colors and shapes hanging down. The novelty of being in the shower with another person, a woman, Hannah, most beloved, put a smile on Tom's face and the smile spilled into laughter. What now? From a shelf built into the fringe of the bathtub a clear glass bottle with a cork stopper, the bottle half filled with an amber liquid. She had Tom lather her hair, shrieking instructions above the hiss of the water in two languages. Tom felt—what?—foreign, from Paris or somewhere, sharing a shower. Is that what happened in Paris? Showering together? Then she dried him so slowly and carefully that he burned with embarrassment, kneeling down to get between his toes, all of this with such close attention to detail that you would have thought him a statue of amazing value being prepared for display.

Breakfast. Something from Hungary. "Not kosher, but who minds?" said Hannah, and then had to explain *kosher*. "Some things we can eat, some things we can't. Jews, you understand? All the good things, we can't eat." Tom watched the preparation with a fixed smile. As the ingredients multiplied, many of them in packets and jars never before seen in Hometown, Tom's unease increased. It was a type of pancake: thick, with a filling. Tom swallowed each mouthful without chewing, but some of the flavor escaped onto his palate.

"Hungarian?" he said. Hannah, at the other side of the kitchen table sipping coffee made with a clever device, watched on with an indulgent frown and also a small, satirical smile.

"Hungarian. *Hortobágyi*. You like it?"

"Very nice," said Tom. Meaning, *Inedible*.

Hannah came to her feet, crossed to Tom's side of the table, whipped the plate away, dropped it and the large, remaining portion of *hortobágyi* into the kitchen sink. Baffled, he blinked up at Hannah as she stood with arms crossed. She was angry? It was possible in Hungary to get angry if someone didn't enjoy your *hortobágyi*?

"If you don't like something, say, 'I—don't—like—it.' Hear me, Tom! 'I—don't—like—it.'"

"It was good," said Tom.

Hannah took two steps to the table and seized Tom's chin between thumb and fingers.

"No! You don't like it. You can say if you don't like it. Don't try to be so nice every minute, Tom."

She softened. "Stay nice. It's okay."

She kissed him. "I'll make you fried eggs. Aussie fried eggs. Now, what's the recipe? Oh, yes. 'Melt butter in pan, throw in the eggs. Serve with tomato sauce.'"

As she fried the eggs, she asked Tom if he'd been reading *Great Expectations*.

"I'm up to page thirty."

"You like it? Don't be nice!"

"I like it. I like Pip and Joe. Pip is like Peter."

"Peter? Peter is who?"

"Trudy's boy. Trudy I was married to. I told you about her. Some of it."

Hannah at the stove turned to look at him. She held a spatula in one hand. Her hair had dried and formed curls. She was wearing the yellow dress that Tom admired. She studied Tom warily.

"A boy. Her boy? Not your boy? Are you not his father?"

"Another fellow."

"Another fellow. Not you?"

"Not me."

Tom looked away from Hannah's gaze. He felt as if he'd blundered.

Hannah served him his eggs. She put the Rosella sauce in front of him and the salt and pepper. The lip of the bottle wasn't darkened with dried sauce in the normal way; Hannah always wiped the outlet before she screwed the lid back on.

"So, a boy," said Hannah. She'd seated herself opposite Tom. She hadn't made any *hortobágyi* for herself; only coffee. "Where is he? With the woman?"

"With Trudy," said Tom. And then, with an obscure sense that it would betray Peter not to say more, he told Hannah the story.

She paid attention.

"Now he's with these Jesus people for good?"

"Yep, with them."

"But you love him."

"Yep."

Tom risked a question. He'd been wondering about this but hadn't seen an opening. And the possible answers worried him.

"You've had children, Hannah?"

She didn't respond. She sipped her coffee.

"You'll go home before you come to the shop?" she said.

"Have to feed Beau. Do one or two things. The cows, I'm running late with them. I'll be at the shop about ten."

Hannah took Tom's plate away. As she passed behind him, she touched his neck for a second with her free hand.

"Sleep for a few hours, Tom Hope," she said. "Okay?"

The touch of her hand told him that something had gone out of her. He knew it. He wanted to ask her if she was upset, but he didn't.

CHAPTER 9

NOVEMBER 1944

It was possible to think of nothing. For hours at a stretch, nothing. In a dormitory of a thousand women, she might lie on a wooden bunk with a stranger on each side, her mind a stone. The women beside her held her close for warmth. But not only for warmth. Each thought Hannah still in possession of her pride and her wits. They wanted to be as near to her as they could be, as if she might suddenly do something extraordinary, reach under her bunk and produce a saucepan of soup, maybe that. It would require only a few words to disabuse them, but Hannah kept quiet. The women clasped her in a way that cost her little. Best if they believed what comforted them.

· · ·

HER REPUTATION WAS based on a lucky find in the feather factory where she worked each day, a huge wooden shed in the east of the camp. The task of the forty women who were assigned there was to empty *doonas*, cushions, and pillows confiscated from Jews who arrived at Auschwitz by train. The feathers were gathered in big wooden tubs and would be used to fill quilts, cushions, and pillows for sale in shops in Germany. Some would become padding for cold-weather military coats. The room was a blizzard of feathers from the timber rafters of the ceiling down to the floor. The Polish *kapos*, wraiths who had survived in the camp for years, Jews themselves, shuffled through the drifts of feathers murmuring in uninflected voices: "Miss nothing, miss not one feather . . ." She'd found a loaf of bread hidden in a pillow—someone had expected food but not pillows to be taken away—hard bread but not a spot of mold, and a prayer book, the siddur, nowhere else in Auschwitz would a siddur exist. She'd eaten a few mouthfuls of the bread, given away a portion and saved what was left for Michael, if she should ever find him. But what she'd hidden had been discovered and devoured. It was an omen. She would never find Michael. She had been told by the *kapos* that he was dead; up the chimney. And Leon. Typhus. Then the gas chamber. He'd lasted ten days. What could you expect? A runny nose used to send him to bed for a week. Her grief for Leon came in one huge gulp. She was not ready to grieve for Michael.

· · ·

As a woman, she should not read aloud from the siddur, but everyone agreed: In Auschwitz, it's okay. She read the Hebrew prayers to a gathering of fifty or more each night, for a week. The *kapo* who was in charge of the dormitory listened in silence. On the seventh night, the woman's wits left her head and she ran into the gathering and snatched the siddur from Hannah. She stood railing against Jews as if she'd been raised in the bosom of the Third Reich. It was the only time she'd shown emotion of any sort. Her rage gave way to a storm of tears and she ran away with the siddur and did not return for three days.

. . .

IF YOU WERE sick of life, sick of Auschwitz, there was an easy way out. At the selections in the mornings—a couple thousand women in rags in groups of five, the standard cohort—you could cough, keep on coughing, and the SS soldiers would be directed by an officer to take you to the gas chamber. Thirty minutes after your coughing fit, you would be burning or, if there was a backlog, an hour. Hannah felt the urge to cough herself crazy each morning, but didn't. It was said that Michael was dead. Well, all sorts of things were said and many of them were not true. It was said that the Americans were in Berlin, but they weren't. That the camp commandant had ordered an end to the gassing in order to get the place in shape for liberation by the Allies. No, the gassings went on, the chimneys sent up their columns of black smoke. That Adolf Hitler had shot himself through the head. Well, so what? If every SS guard and every SS officer in the place shot himself through the head, okay. But Hitler? Fuck him. Do you know what would be heaven, what would be a miracle, the best thing ever in the world? A glimpse of Michael in warm clothes with rosy-red cheeks and stout little shoes. Maybe in the arms of the officer who'd spoken to her that first morning; him with the white gloves. That would be okay. White Gloves takes a shine to the boy, keeps him alive as a pet. That's fine, fine, fine. That Michael would still be alive when the Germans were defeated and that she would still be alive and that the officer would by that time have cut his own throat—fantasy. Just Michael alive. To know that, okay, gas me, go ahead.

. . .

IT WAS POSSIBLE to think of nothing for hours at a time, but not forever. She remained furious with Leon, who was dead. She whispered to him about his foolish conviction that the Germans would never invade Hungary, never come to Budapest. "They've lost the war. They don't care about Jews now." Oh, really? He was thought to be the gentlest, the most compassionate man on earth, but he was an arrogant individual underneath. "Hannah, eight hundred thousand Jews in Hungary. They can't afford to bother with the Jews now. They've lost the war." Oh really? All this came from his friends in Russia. But what was she talking about, his friends in Russia? All Russians were his friends. He wanted a Russia in Hungary. The workers of Russia, the workers of Hungary, their hands clasped for eternity. He who had never used a hammer in his life, who barely understood the function of a sickle. But so dear, in his way; in his stupid way. The Polish *kapo* said, "Up the chimney," rubbing the tips of her fingers together as she raised her hand: the upward motion of smoke.

. . .

MARTA, WHO HELD Hannah so close at night, whispered to her: "Come and hear. Come and hear the Litho." Who? A Lithuanian by the name of Elizabeth. Everybody respected the Lithuanians, who'd come to the camp in the middle of summer and now, in November, were running small classes for Hungarian women who wanted to learn Yiddish. In Auschwitz, a Yiddish school. Absurd. In the darkness, no pens or paper, to women starved and exhausted who might well be murdered in the morning. Elizabeth gave her instruction in German.

Most of the women knew half the German language by now. Also classes in philosophy. The Lithuanian Jews had apparently spent their lives with their noses in books. Good for them. Hannah went to the corner of the dormitory where Elizabeth was talking in a strangely tranquil way about Rousseau. The Lithuanians knew nothing about their faith but everything about a thousand *goyishe* philosophers. Hannah was enthralled. She'd read all that Rousseau had written, and yet what Elizabeth had to say was welcome. "You ask me, 'But what is *freedom*?' It is what we are born with. The baby comes, the midwife counts its toes, its fingers. She says: 'All there.' She should say, 'All there, everything, and a beautiful free soul.'"

Someone called out: "Not here!"

Elizabeth said, "Even here."

. . .

THE SS NEVER came to the dormitory. It stank, and God alone knew what diseases clogged the fetid air. But this morning Hannah's dormitory was visited by an SS officer who looked a little too young for the job. A few others that she caught sight of from time to time on the way to the feather factory—too young. The war was going badly for the Germans, maybe not so many grown men left. So this boy soldier would have been thrown into the job of visiting the dormitory by his superiors. He announced shrilly that all the women in the dormitory were to ready themselves for a hike to the railhead. The officer added that "workers" were permitted to take their belongings with them. A low murmur of laughter ran through the dormitory. Belongings? The officer looked about in alarm. He repeated the invitation to the workers to take their belongings. This time, no laughter; just a few snorts.

She wouldn't go. The prospect of even glimpsing Michael taken from her forever? At the selection she would cough. She produced a practice cough as soon as the officer departed. The dormitory was rowdy. Many, many rumors. The Polish *kapo* who had run away with the siddur was back. The women asked her: "Where are we going? To the gas chamber? Tell us!" The *kapo* was in an agreeable mood for some reason. She said: "To Stutthof, in the north. No selection. All of you go to Stutthof."

.   .   .

IN THE LINES that formed for the exodus to the train station, to Stutthof, Hannah coughed loudly whenever an SS guard came close. She was ignored. The order was given to march. Hannah, forced along, kept her eyes on the ground. She would have wept if that were possible, but it wasn't; nobody wept in Auschwitz after the first month. Instead she whispered to herself: "He is alive. No one can say that he is dead. He is alive." By the time she passed out of the gates of Auschwitz, she had stopped whispering. She thought nothing. But the tears had come.

CHAPTER 10

If nothing else, they had fashioned a beautiful shop. The cedar shelves shone under three coats of varnish and on the only vacant area of wall Hannah had hung a tapestry from her native Hungary depicting a king being entertained at court by jugglers, a magician, and dancing girls. The tapestry was said to be very old. Elsewhere, Tom had left alcoves in the shelves where Hannah displayed a series of colored lithographs of Holy Days, Jews at a table feasting and talking, Jews at prayer.

Hannah had arranged the titles in standard categories—fiction, biography, travel, and so on—but she'd also included, without much prospect of reward, a hundred volumes of poetry, both anthologies and individual collections. And she'd made a feature of contemporary Australian novelists.

The only advice she'd taken from Tom so far as the stock was concerned was to give a bit more thought to it before she went ahead and ordered various German, Russian, and French classics, untranslated. He said: "Darling, nobody will buy them. Nobody speaks German in Hometown. Nobody speaks Russian."

She had a temper. "Why? Anyone can learn German in two weeks.

Am I to run a bookshop for lazies?" She gave an hour or more to ugly ranting, complaining that Tom himself was one of these people who would rather listen to football than study a German primer.

Tom had indeed brought a transistor radio, a little Sony, to the shop one Saturday afternoon to catch the footy call from the stadium in the city, much to Hannah's disdain. But if her sense of betrayal found irrational expression, she always recovered. She ridiculed the call of the game all through one quarter, then repented and apologized, called herself a little bourgeois snob and listened to the next quarter with Tom, holding his hand. "Which team is your special one? Blues is it called? Blues? I want Blues to win this game, Tom. Blues will be my special ones, too."

A few tasks remained. Tom had to put up the ladder tracks but hadn't yet made the ladders themselves. He fetched in the timber he'd need, good aged oak from planks he'd been hoarding, cut the lengths on his bench saw at the shop, and was about to head back to the farm to turn the rungs on his wood lathe when Hannah appeared. She was wearing black slacks, a big black woolen jumper with a wide neck, and what looked like the sort of boots a stylish mountaineer would choose, laced up almost to the knees.

She said, "Take me with you, Tom. Show me your farm."

Tom had to smile. God forbid she should simply pull on a pair of jeans and a windcheater.

. . .

HE WALKED HER down among the woollies in the big north paddock, showing her how the sheep could pick out the grasses they preferred and the way they stayed close to their leaders, lifting their heads to keep track. "In every flock," Tom said, "there's a genius. And the sheep know who the genius is."

"Ai! Do you imagine? One is a genius!" Hannah was thrilled. Her accent grew more pronounced when she was happy.

She wanted to know how the sheep could tell each other apart.

"They look the same to us," said Tom, "but they know who's Sally and Sue among themselves."

Hannah was full of admiration for Tom's knowledge. At the shop, she'd praised his carpentry in the same way. It had seemed excessive to Tom; he would have been happier if Hannah's compliments had been commensurate with achievement. It took only bare competence to fashion dovetail joints, after all. He'd come to understand, though, that it wasn't really flattery; instead, it was a sort of delight that was roused in Hannah for anything she didn't know; anything new to her. She could never come to the end of all that pleased her.

Now the orchard; five hundred trees: pears, nectarines, apples, gray-green lichen on the side of the boughs away from the northerlies. Hannah put her hand to the crusty bark of one of the older apple trees as gently as if touching flesh.

"Tom, all this, such work you do."

She wanted him to stretch out with her on the grass under the apple trees, but open-air lovemaking was beyond anything that Tom could contemplate. They went indoors.

For Tom, daylight meant labor, and he betrayed a certain eagerness to be up and about once Hannah had signaled her satisfaction in a torrent of Hungarian. She said, "Lie still." He did, but he thought of the old ram needing tick treatment and of the cows impatient to be let into the broad paddock with the wattles. He had to be told a second time, "Lie still."

Tom had to admit that he was capable of enjoying Hannah's languid caresses and her endearments and it was only that it was wrong and bad to lounge about in the middle of the morning that prevented him from melting into a pool of butter under the warmth of her hands.

.   .   .

She said, "Tom, I was unhappy, so unhappy, Tom, I can't tell you. And now I love you. This is how I like to be."

Such candor unsettled him, but in some part of him newly made, he grasped that Hannah was someone he must listen to. Phrases came to life in him from he knew not where; words that he had never employed. He said them aloud to himself during the day: "Bless you" and "My dearest one." As much as anything, he enjoyed her teasing. She said, "You are so polite, Tom. Somebody trips over. What do you say? 'I'm sorry.' Not your fault, but you are sorry. And you blush like a boy. Will I whisper something? Listen to me. Listen to what I whisper."

Only, there was the sorrow. She looked away from him at strange times, and he was nothing to her; insignificant. He said, "Hannah, tell me." Then she recovered and was gay and loving. But not a thing was shared.

"Darling," he said now, as Hannah caressed his body, pausing at his chest. Flattening her hand against his heart. "Darling, tell me."

Her hands stopped drawing him to her.

"Tell you what?"

"Why you were unhappy."

"I lost two husbands. Do you know? Two husbands."

She threw back the covers and swung her legs out, pausing naked beside the bed. She was about to speak, but whatever she might have said she caught before it came out, smiled at Tom fleetingly, and went out to the bathroom with her clothes clutched in her hand. He heard her washing. Then nothing. She appeared again, sat on the bed and pulled on one boot, drew the laces tight.

"Drive me home," she said. Every trace of tenderness had left her.

CHAPTER 11

She came back to him the next day. Tom was at the shop tinkering with the cash register when she walked in. She kissed him with feeling, and this time something was said. "I'm not right in my head for a few minutes. Is that awful, Tom?"

"No," said Tom, it wasn't awful.

"Listen, Tom. This is Nietzsche. Have you heard maybe of Nietzsche? No, no, no. Impossible. In university if you went, you would hear."

"Hannah, I haven't been to university."

"Okay. Rubbish. It doesn't matter. Plenty went to university who became fat Nazis. But listen. This is Nietzsche. If you look over the edge, you see nothing, nothing. But if you stare at nothing, it looks back at you. Do you see?"

"Nothing looks back at you?"

"Do you see?"

"Hannah, I don't. I'm sorry."

"It's okay. It's rubbish. Will you fix my machine? My cash register?"

She was miserable. Tom put down his screwdriver and took her in his arms. He could feel the clenched distress of her body.

As he held her, her face against his chest, she said, "Tom, this is something I don't say. To Leon, never. To Stefan, never. My husbands, you understand?"

"Yes, I understand, Hannah."

She stepped back and looked up into his eyes.

"Don't leave me. Please."

She was holding his face with both hands. He hadn't shaved and she pushed against the pale stubble. The gaze of her green eyes was so intense that he would have found it painful if he'd been forced to lie to her. But no, he could tell her the truth.

"Hannah, I'll never leave you. I promise you."

"But can you say, 'never'? Do you promise me?"

"I promise. Never."

"But you don't say, 'Hannah, marry me.' If you say 'never' why can we not be married? Why, Tom?"

Before he could answer her—"But we can be married"—she flung herself away from him and buried her hands in her hair.

"Forty-five, Tom! That's what I mean. Tom with his mother! Ha ha ha! I might slap someone, maybe. Okay, we don't get married. But you stay with me. When I'm too old throw me on the rubbish heap, I don't care."

"Hannah," said Tom. "I want to marry you. That's what I want."

"Are you saying?"

"I want to marry you."

Hannah looked down and nodded her head. Her mood had changed.

"Tom," she said quietly, "no babies. You see?"

Tom nodded. He didn't have to be told that there would be no babies.

Hannah cast her gaze here and there about the shop. She walked over to the tapestry.

"Do you know where I got this, Tom? Will I tell you? Okay. In Budapest. I came back in February 1945. A few friends were still alive. They stayed in the Swiss embassy. Most of the Jews were dead, but a few left alive in the Swiss embassy. And these friends had captured a Nazi. A stupid Nazi from the SS. Somehow they caught him before all the SS ran away, back to Germany. They wanted to shoot him, Tom. Execute him. But nobody wanted to pull the trigger. He showed them treasures he had stolen from Jews. This tapestry. It is two hundred years old. He wanted to buy his life. So I took it. I said I would shoot him, the stupid Nazi. He was in a cellar. I pointed the gun at his head. He said to me in German: 'Madame, please don't delay.' But I couldn't shoot him. We gave him to the Russians to stand trial. They shot him in front of us. I took the tapestry to my apartment. I put it on the wall. I never knew what Jewish family it was stolen from."

She had pointed a gun at a German. She had wanted to shoot him. Hannah? He had no stories like this. He had once balked at shooting a tiger snake because it seemed wrong for it to be dead. He'd watched it wriggle into a hole in the earth. What could he tell her? "Listen to my story. I saw a tiger snake. I didn't kill it." His uneventful life. Trudy had shown him that replacing iron on a roof, soldering up a gap in the spouting, and dipping woollies could make a woman feel as if she were drinking poison, each day a few drops, enough to kill her. All he knew was that day followed day. If the sheep weren't dipped, they'd be full of lice and ticks and fungus. If he didn't solder the spouting, the water would drip onto the window ledge and lift the paint and rot the wood. What could he have said to his wife? "Trudy, it's a farm, it's not Luna Park." She'd once asked him to tell her something amazing. "Anything that's not usual. Nothing usual." She was already willing him to fail. The one thing he'd thought of was a kookaburra years ago that used to sit with him on the back verandah while he sipped his tea. Then one day a blue tongue had squeezed under the back door and into a pile of kindling. He'd heard a tapping, and when he'd opened the door the kooka stalked in, threw the kindling aside, picked up the lizard in its beak, and strutted out. That wasn't what she meant.

"But you will, won't you? Marry me," said Tom.

He thought they'd agreed, but something he'd noticed: Hannah could go about beating a drum, then put down the sticks and shrug as if the matter had suddenly lost all of its importance.

She said, "We must open, Tom. We must sell some books. Tom, make the cash register work."

CHAPTER 12

⌘

This time Hannah stayed the night at the farm. While Tom prepared dinner, she looked around at the pictures: the work of Uncle Frank, who had taken up oil painting in the last few years of his life with a death-or-glory abandon. All the canvases had been grandly framed in gilt with an aged look and all were the same size: eighteen inches by twenty inches. Three of the pictures were of waterfalls: long curtains of blue running down the middle of the canvas hemmed in by fat clumps of greenery. One was a portrait of a sheep's face. By the looks of it, Uncle Frank had found the nose very difficult to render; but he had tried, and the nose achieved the status of a separate portrait within the portrait. The two landscapes looking uphill toward the big boulders on the hillside above the farm gave the viewer the impression that a breath of wind would knock the stones down the slope, so slightly were they anchored to the earth. Hannah adored them all. In particular, a self-portrait in a farmer's hat with corks suspended from the brim, which, with their jiggling, were meant to frighten away the flies.

"I like them," said Hannah. "Are there others? We could hang one up at the shop, what do you think?"

Tom was keeping an eye on the leg of lamb, the roasting potatoes, the pumpkin. For greens, he was providing string beans. And as a special touch, because he knew how to do them, dumplings, his mum had taught him. In answer to Hannah's comment, he said, "I wouldn't want to take them down. Old Frank was proud of them." Then he added, "They're probably rubbish."

Tom had the door of the woodstove open and was peering in. Hannah bent beside him.

"Ready?" she said.

"Fifteen minutes."

He put the beans on the hot plate. He wore a tea towel around his waist, tucked into his belt. He seemed especially cheerful.

He went to the big, old, murmuring Kelvinator and fetched out a bottle of wine. "Red with meat?" he said. "Is that right? Moyston claret."

Hannah raised her eyebrows. In the refrigerator? She said, "Beautiful," as Tom placed the bottle on the table. A search high and low had turned up a white linen tablecloth donated to the household by Tom's sisters. Without a steam iron, he perhaps could not be expected to have smoothed the creases out and so ridges ran north to south, east to west on the cloth.

Hannah sat at the table to forestall the intervention she might not be able to resist. It gave her pleasure to follow Tom's determined movements, even the awkward ones. He attempted to withdraw the baking tray from the oven with too little of the tea towel, burned his fingers, tried again, and was forced to stride quickly to the bench and crash the tray down. Meanwhile, the gravy was curdling. But with persistence, he was finally able to fill two big unmatched plates with roast lamb and veggies. He sat down, then jumped to his feet to fetch the cloth serviettes, again the gift of his sisters, and the salt and pepper.

"I should've made mint sauce," he said. "And cheese sauce for the cauli."

"Tom. It's perfect. Enjoy it."

In fact, this was the first time that a husband or lover had prepared a meal for Hannah. It was surprising that she hadn't insisted on it over the years. She'd been raised in an Orthodox household, not overly strict but strict enough. She'd turned angrily away from the harping of her mother on stitching and baking. Her four sisters were obedient girls in their very souls. Hannah's father was her champion. "You want five of a kind? Have one blessed with a mind of her own." He'd sent her to university when it was impossible for Jews to enroll—he'd managed it. His ambitions for her had not quite extended to the neglect of the oven and the ironing board. And since she'd loved him in the way she had, she'd made mottoes of his priorities: Keep a kosher kitchen, feed the husband, study, practice the piano.

And when, in her first year at university, she became pregnant and married, it was to a man incapable of opening an oven door. Leon, an intellectual giant, apparently believed an invisible spirit kept his household running smoothly. When Hannah spent three weeks in Pavdac Hospital with pneumonia, Leon had come to look increasingly homeless and unloved, his shirts more rumpled than if he'd slept in them. She'd kept house for two husbands without any resentment; wrote her thesis on the Hungarian Baroque while nursing a baby and baking challah.

. . .

LEON WOULD SIT at the table lost in a volume of Proudhon while she followed a furious choreography of provision all around the kitchen, Michael in a sling on her hip. After Auschwitz, when Leon was dead, she married Stefan, who sat at the table lost in a volume of Berenson while she slid one plate then another under his poised fork, this time without the baby, without the child. In 1956, Soviet tanks in the streets of Budapest, she slid plates under the raised forks of ten or more fire-brands from the Council of Workers who'd piled into the apartment after throwing house bricks at Russians, and was rewarded (if that was the word) with a kiss on the cheek, a squeeze around the middle.

Nothing in her life had prepared her for Tom. She'd understood all there was to know about him at a glance that day in the shop, and was wrong. She'd come to Australia, understood everything in ten minutes, then didn't. The same experience. Not the sort of heart, Tom's heart, she'd known in the past. Not the same anything, not even his mannerisms. He pushed his fair hair off his forehead with his upper arm. When he wished to tell her something difficult, he looked to his left, then at his feet, then raised his head and met her gaze. A little catalog of these ways he had was added to each day. The details of love. And something she particularly enjoyed—his long, clean limbs. Why did his limbs matter? She stroked him all along his legs, his arms, and thought—this was ludicrous, of course: *Mine, all mine.* At forty-five, suddenly sick with the jealous need to lock a man away from other women? It had always been beneath her. Now—God knows. This country. It brought unfamiliar things to the surface in her. At first she'd thought, *Australians, children, they know nothing.* It was what she'd thought of Tom.

But there was more that needed to be said—she knew that now.

. . .

SHE ASKED HIM as they ate if he'd read more of *Great Expectations*. He had. He'd carried it about the farm in his big back pocket and had read from it leaning against the wall of the dairy, of the hay shed, as he doled out pellets to the chooks. He could get through thirty pages in an hour. Miss Haversham—she was mad, right?

"Do you think she was mad?" asked Hannah, recognizing in her own manner, regrettably, the demeanor of the tutor.

"Well, yeah. Yeah. All the stuff going moldy on the table. That's mad, do you think?"

Hannah said, "Disappointment can be a passion." Thinking, *Dear God, will you listen to yourself!*

"Pardon?"

"Her feelings of betrayal—she lives for the passion of disappointment. She is faithful to it forever. It means more to her than marriage ever could. Do you see?"

Tom thought about it. "She wanted to be jilted?"

"No, Tom. Not that. But look at the purpose it gives her. For her whole life."

"I think you've lost me."

They enjoyed the steamed pudding, Golden Syrup, new to Hannah. Finished not one but two bottles of the chilled claret, then washed and dried the dishes side by side. Hannah thought: *If he says marry me again, be less stupid, be less bloody stupid, say, "Tom, yes, with all my heart."*

They made tipsy love.

Before she could sleep, she had Tom open the curtains of the bedroom to let the moonlight in. "It's the war, Tom," she said. "We hid in dark places days and days. Now I have to see outside all the time."

He kissed her on her shoulders, her breasts.

"Tell me," he said.

She thought about it for a few minutes. Then she said, "No, I don't think so."

. . .

HE ROSE FOR the cows at four-thirty but left her asleep. So he thought. She lay in bed turning her gaze from the dresser to the cupboard and into all the shadowy places, raised her head to listen to the cows impatient for Tom. He milked by hand as she knew, just the twelve cows, the hundred-pint yield per day destined for the elderly Swiss couple on Brown Dog Creek who made Tiltsin and exported it to their native Basel. She'd asked Tom once about the smoothness of his cheeks. He told her that he milked with a cheek against the cow's flank, turn-and-turnabout. A milkmaid's complexion. She heard the sheep in the paddocks, bleating because the dawn was coming into the sky. Tom said that sheep woke hopeful each new day. Optimistic beasts, not quite as stupid as they looked. Hannah thought: *If he goes away, I'll die.* Then she caught herself. *No, I won't. Less melodrama!* But what she really believed was that she would die. She hoped so.

She threw back the covers, wrapped herself in the spare blanket Tom had left beside the bed, shuffled about the house studying items on ledges and shelves. She switched on the light in the living room, its ugly green sofa and armchairs made shapeless by collapsed springs. This is what she was looking for—a picture of the boy, Peter. It was propped on the mantelpiece, the embers of last night's fire still vivid between the andirons below. She stood holding the blanket closed with one hand while in the other she held the photograph.

"So," she said, "the child."

The picture showed a boy of five or so in a school uniform, a bag hanging by a strap from his shoulder. The boy's dark hair was neatly cut, neatly parted. His smile was as wide as he could possibly make it, so it seemed. Hannah recognized the corrugated iron wall of the workshop behind him, the bushy cotoneaster with its clustered pomes rising to the roof. Sitting at the boy's feet was the dog, Beau, head to the side in the puzzled manner of a pet who'd been told to stay, stay. The sun was in his face, in Peter's face, and he was squinting at the camera. The shadow of the person with the camera was thrown forward into the scope of the picture. It was Tom; she knew his shadow shape.

Hannah let her gaze rest on the boy in the picture for minute after minute. The golden-red light of the embers reached up to her face. She replaced the picture on the mantelpiece and walked with her head bowed into the kitchen and sat. The Saxa salt packet with a hole for pouring punched in it near the top still sat on the center of the table. She roused herself to look toward the dairy from the back porch. The lights were on. Tom would be nearing the end of the milking. She shuffled back to the bedroom and slipped under the blankets. It wasn't long before the screen door slammed. She heard Tom undress. How he knew what she wanted she couldn't say, but he did. He held her from behind, embracing her shape, kissed her on the neck, and trickled endearments into her ear.

CHAPTER 13

The date of the wedding was agreed, September 20 or thereabouts, six weeks away—after the ewes had lambed, a civil ceremony at the old redbrick Mechanics Institute. Tom said that Horry Green the bookie, also a justice of the peace, would officiate, if asked. For the time being, they told no one. Oh, and before the wedding, the grand opening of the bookshop. The name? Madame Babel's Bookshop. But really?

"The thing is, Han, nobody in Australia is called 'Madame.' People will think you're putting on airs. Too posh."

As soon as he'd uttered the word, Tom wanted to take it back.

They were in the shop, shelves of books competing in allure, arranged by title rather than writer—Hannah's democratic bias. She didn't want sections of shelves turned into colonies of titles by the same author. Writers had to muck in together. At the same time, she would ride roughshod over any rule in order to save a book from the jeopardy of an unsympathetic shelf companion. *The Making of the English Working Class* was not expected to sit beside *The Making of Americans*, a book Hannah disliked. As a buffer between the two, she had placed a skinny softcover booklet, *Making Your Own Jam*.

"'Posh'? People will think I am giving myself airs? Posh is saying that, isn't it? Giving yourself airs?"

"Some people."

"Oh, just *some* people. Madame Babel gives herself airs, some people will say. Madame Babel who ate the corpses of rats in Poland. Madame Babel who begged at the feet of the *kapos*. This Madame Babel is the one who gives herself airs. I see."

Tom hadn't been told of the rat, of the *kapos*, whoever they were. He exchanged a glance with David the canary, who had taken to Tom as a favored habitat, sitting on his shoulder and nibbling at his earlobe.

"So I can tell the sign writer when he comes, 'The Bookshop of the Hungarian Woman Who Gives Herself Airs'? Or you have something better?"

Tom extended a finger, took David on board, and transferred him to the top of the cash register.

"Hannah's Bookshop. Don't you think?"

"'Hannah's Bookshop,'" said Hannah. "Nice and plain. Nothing fancy, God forbid." And then, without evident motive: "Tom, I had a son once. His name was Michael."

She went to the door of the shop and quietly pressed it shut.

Tom said, "I'm listening, Han."

Hannah shrugged, looking away. "I wanted to tell you. When you came back to bed after milking the other day. That's when I wanted to tell you."

Something was working in her. Her glance moved back to Tom, then toward the shelves, back again. The gaze of her green eyes, the light, was something she could intensify or subdue in the space of seconds. Tom waited. He knew he had to be still. If he put his arms around her now she would push him away.

"But you didn't," he said, since it seemed that he was being asked to fill the pause. "You didn't tell me."

"No, I didn't."

"But now?"

Hannah lifted her shoulders and let them fall. She said, "Now, yes." Was that all she had to say? She picked up a book from the counter: a red cover with a yellow band. She studied it.

"Maybe a new book, Tom? This is excellent for you. *Crime and Punishment*. Dostoyevsky. Do you think?"

"You don't want to tell me more about your boy? About Michael?"

An expression of exasperation passed over Hannah's face, as if Tom were trying her patience.

"Tell you more what? He is dead."

It was risky, but now might be the right time. Tom stepped forward and put his arms around Hannah. Even if she wriggled and pushed, he intended to hold her. But she didn't. Instead she circled him with her own arms and held him close, the book still gripped in one hand. She lifted her face so that she could see him. "I am too difficult, Tom. I know it. You can leave me, I promise you."

Then she rested her chin on his shoulder.

"But, Tom, please don't. Please don't."

She made tea. As they sat in the elegant upholstered chairs Hannah had bought for the shop so that customers could sit and read, she told Tom that Michael had died in Auschwitz, the same Auschwitz she had spoken of before, months back.

"A concentration camp. In Poland. Near Cracow. More than one camp: three, four camps. Here they murdered us, Tom. Many, many thousands. Here they murdered Michael. Here Leon died in the gas chamber. He had typhus, so they put him in the gas chamber."

Tom managed not to say anything trite. It was all part of knowing that the Germans, the Nazis, were pretty bloody awful. He thought he may have been told something by Uncle Frank about concentration camps. It was to do with a decision not to erect a bigger fenced-in yard for the chickens. Uncle Frank had said—did he?—that the bigger you built a yard, the more chickens you wanted, like the Germans and their camps. Maybe he was talking about POW camps.

Hannah sat with her legs crossed, sipping her tea. Her massy hair was longer now than when Tom had first met her, with more gray. She spoke calmly but was not, as Tom could see, in the least calm. She gave him a few details of her arrival at Auschwitz. Her husband, Leon, had been sent in one direction, she and Michael in another. The officer in charge, the one with the white gloves, SS, had spoken to her. He had asked her—

"'SS'?" Tom interrupted.

"An SS officer. You know the SS?"

"Not much. I'm sorry, Han."

"Don't worry. Horrible. This officer was among the worst."

In Auschwitz, she and Michael were set aside. She was in a daze. She lost consciousness for a minute. In that minute, Michael was gone.

"To where?" said Tom.

"'To where?'" Hannah bent over and put her cup and saucer on the floor beside her. "To be killed, Tom. To die."

"But why, in heaven's name?"

Hannah raised both hands and let them fall to her lap. "Tom, do you know nothing about the war?"

"I do, Han. But up in the islands. That's where we were, in the islands, fighting the Japs. My uncle Les was on the Kokoda track. Mum's brother."

"Okay. But in Europe, Tom, the Germans put all the Jews into camps and killed us. You understand? Millions. Not only in the camps. In towns all over Europe. Millions."

"But, Han, why? That's what I don't get."

Hannah nodded. She looked away. Her hand drifted up to her bare throat and softly kneaded the flesh there. When she looked back at Tom, she simply said, "So, he was gone."

She reached across and patted Tom's knee. "You like the shop?"

"Of course. It's beautiful, Han."

"When I can't be here from three to six, Maggie will look after it."

Tom nodded, but was aware that not enough had been said about the boy, about Michael. He said, "Darling, I'm sorry about your boy. I truly am."

"Yes. Well."

Hannah stood and let her gaze wander up and down the shelves. She thought she might say: "And your boy, Tom. He can't be with you." But she didn't.

"Then, 'Hannah's Bookshop'?"

"That's best," said Tom. "Hannah's Bookshop."

When Teddy Croft came an hour later to pick up the signboard, that's the name Hannah provided.

. . .

Tom gave the brass of the shelf railing a rub with a rag soaked in a light oil and showed Hannah how to slide the ladder along. Then he headed back to the farm to tend to a hundred things, such as nailing down the new sheets of iron he'd left only temporarily fixed to the roof of the dairy. "We're going to have some weather," he said. Hannah said she'd come to him after she'd seen her students.

But she had something to tend to before she left the shop for the flute and the piano. She took an oblong of stiff paper, craft paper, the color of parchment, sat at the counter and wrote a single line of neat Hebrew script with black ink and a steel-nibbed pen. She taped the paper to the window, close to the door and beneath the prayer she had posted months earlier. Horry Green didn't speak Hebrew and couldn't read Hebrew script. His wife was Church of England, and naturally enough, didn't speak Hebrew, either. Certainly the five Green children, who were well aware of their father's Jewish heritage but had been raised as pagans, knew not a word of Hebrew. That took care of all those in the shire who would have even recognized that the sign was in Hebrew. And so Hannah's first choice of a name for her business remained known only to her: bookshop of the broken hearted.

CHAPTER 14

The river ran due north from the Alps before turning west on the inland side of the ranges, then north once again until it found the Murray. The Hometown valley, formed where the river changed direction, took most of its stormy weather from the east, the moist wind hurtling down from the mountains as clean as if it were running along a fixed channel in the sky.

Those like Tom, obliged to form an idea of what weather was on the way, took a pale blue sky in the east as the harbinger of a storm: an odd portent, but don't ignore it. Tom was up on the roof of the dairy with an electric drill and coach screws as soon as he got back to the farm. He paused in his work and gazed east and saw the black storm with a golden haze around it powering over the hills. Small drops rattled on the iron. Before he'd fitted two more screws the rain came down in a blinding torrent. He worked in the downpour at some risk—electrocution—to fasten the remaining screws, then detached the drill from the extension flex and hurried down the ladder. Beau, drenched, was fretting below. He whistled the dog along as he ran to check on Jo and Stubby. Rain shouldn't spook horses with any character at all, but Tom had spoiled the creatures by stabling them in every storm. Now they were galloping up and down their paddock in hysterics, blind Stubby with the fit upon him cannoning into Jo and squealing. Tom shrieked above the roar of the rain until Jo came to him at full tilt, pulling up just short of a collision. Tom hurried both horses into the shelter of the stable, Stubby letting go with a high-pitched keening like a bird.

"Shut up! You're inside, you moron!"

Beau, thinking it was required of him, nipped Stubby on the fetlock and had to endure the bafflement and ignominy of Tom's boot.

The cows: Tom herded them into the dairy. The reek of wet beast was rich. The rain on the iron roof was like a crescendo heralding an implacable god who was ready to announce the end of everything. The water ran across the dairy floor up to the height of Tom's ankles. Beau barked at the flood, bit it, quickly looked to Tom in case this was also something punishable.

A cow is a tyrant of a certain sort, and all dairy farmers entertain fantasies of murder. The sheer unendingness of the milking routine. Even Tom, who loved the beasts, sometimes imagined shooting the lot of them. Water lapping his shins, he battled to keep the stainless-steel milking pails from floating away even as he worked the teats.

He stopped to listen. The racket of the rain had increased, impossibly. As he waited with his head raised, the noise took a new leap. Tom thought, *Nothing can survive this*. The flow on the concrete floor had almost reached his knees. At that moment the old, demented ram burst into the dairy and charged Tom. It was not malice, just panic. Tom managed to get in a punch forceful enough to subdue the ram.

"Get into the workshop!" he shouted. "Jesus! What's wrong with you?"

Tom grabbed a handful of fleece and urged the ram to the workshop, and inside. The floor at the back of the building was raised high above the ground. Tom pushed and prodded, installed the fool of a beast out of the flow of the water, returned, exasperated, to the milking. He had to get the woollies in the slough paddock to higher ground. The slough would fill with water and become a lake up to the fences and beyond.

He heard his name called, or probably didn't, a trick of the drumming rain . . . But no, there was Hannah beside him, shouting into his ear.

"Jesus!"

"I'm here!"

Her lovely green dress was plastered to her body. Her hair looked like sea wrack. Her shoes of stiffened green felt were sodden and muddied.

"I can milk!" she shrieked.

"What?"

"Yes! I can milk!"

"Get inside!"

"No! I can milk!"

"You can't! Go inside. Get dry."

"Yes! I can milk!"

He knew enough of her obstinacy to accept that she would do exactly what she intended at any given time. Her idea that she could milk was insane. But he had to get to the drowning woollies, and gave way.

The density of the downpour was absurd, not rain but a waterfall. Tom called Beau to him, told him in a shout that they wanted the woollies.

"Get 'em up, Beau!" Overjoyed at the opportunity to exercise competence, Beau ran and balked and turned and leaped and drove the woollies to one gate and through it and to another and through it until four hundred sheep had been forced onto the higher ground of the hill paddock with the other two-thirds of the flock. They formed a thick collar around the base of the bushy gums, except for the ning-nongs, the dumbest of the flock, left out in the flood from the sky.

The water flowed unimpeded through the grass. The entire farm was a river. The house was raised two feet above the ground but Tom worried that two feet might not be enough. And God, the chooks. They'd have enough sense to roost high, wouldn't they? Tom hurried with Beau to the hen shed, where the chooks, under the generalship of the roosters, had found the topmost shelves of the coop. They would be saved from drenching by the projecting roof Tom had built a month earlier. They looked tranquil.

The orchard would be okay. The trees were past blossom and wouldn't suffer any harm once the water ran off.

In the dairy, Hannah on the milking stool battled to hold a ten-pint pail steady with her feet while she worked unavailingly on the teats. She had filled half of one pail in thirty minutes. The cows looked at her askance. At the first sight of Tom, they raised their wet noses at the scent of the trusted and familiar.

Hannah made some sort of complaint.

"Pardon?"

"Cooperate! They won't cooperate."

Tom took her place on the stool and demonstrated, Hannah's face beside his so that she could hear. "A tiny bit too firm, they don't like it. Don't twist your hands at all. You get the feel after a while. Just for the moment, they don't care for you. But they know when you're trying your best. They do."

Hannah eventually finished her pail while Tom filled the remaining eight. Wrecked though she was, Hannah's eyes still glittered with the joy of instruction. She kept calling comments back to Tom as she went about her botched milking. Nothing carried; the crash of the rain was deafening. But he smiled. He couldn't think of a time when he'd loved her more.

Tom stored the pails in the refrigerated chest. Indoors again, they showered and dressed, Hannah in Tom's trousers and jumper with a raincoat and sou'wester and rubber boots a few sizes too big for her. Tom would have preferred her to stay indoors, but she imagined herself a big help and must be allowed to go with him when he dug a channel at the back of the house for the water to drain away. And as a matter of fact, she was a help. She took the spade and cleared the channel of soil as Tom swung the mattock. Using a spade with a steady swinging action, taking a full load of soil with each motion—that took practice. So where, when? In that camp, that terrible place, what was its name?

The rain had abated, but not much. Looking up to the hill paddocks, he could see the flow running through the barley grass and phalaris with a freight of twigs and leaves, small branches, also a sheet of corrugated iron from the old derelict bird blind Uncle Frank had built up above the hill paddock fence. Frank had given bird-watching a shot for a year or two when Tom was a kid.

When Tom had dug the channel to the side of the house and was ready to turn the corner, he glanced down toward the floodplain and saw the astonishing sight of two complete houses bobbing distantly in the river. He called Hannah.

"Look at that!"

"Aiee! Tom!"

"They must've come loose at Sawyer's Flats. That'll be Nev and Poppy's place, and Scotty Campbell's. God almighty!"

"Aiee! My house, Tom. Will it go into the river?"

"No, no. Nothing from Harp Road. You're a mile from the river."

"The shop, Tom. The water will go into the shop!"

"Maybe yeah. Can't do anything just now."

.   .   .

THE RAIN STOPPED at dusk. Hannah and Tom fed themselves on left-overs and went to bed at eight. The storm had drawn all the strength from Tom's body and he was desperate for sleep, but Hannah chattered without pause. The experience of the storm had left her as high as a kite. She lifted Tom's eyelids with her fingers whenever he gave way to the longing for unconsciousness, squeezed his cheeks, slapped him lightly. She wanted to talk about Dostoyevsky, about *Crime and Punishment*, also Turgenev, the favorite of Russian readers among all the towering geniuses of the nineteenth century, more than even Tolstoy, Tom, more than even Chekhov.

He was aware that Hannah was making free with him as she babbled. Fine by him, but it had to unfold while he slipped into a potent sleep of rising water, flotsam, and of his wife-to-be swimming, swimming with an elegant overarm stroke.

.   .   .

IN THE MORNING after the milking, a tour of the farm, Tom and Hannah searching out damage. Not so bad. The rain had fallen like something biblical, but with only moderate winds. The workshop, with the old ram roaring on the platform at the back, had come through well; so had the garage that housed the two tractors and the forklift. The drainage channel had done its job. The woollies needed a good breeze to dry them out, but no harm done. The horses Tom kept stabled to save their hooves from the water and muck in the highway paddock.

.   .   .

THEY DROVE TO Hannah's house in Harp Road for some dry clothing and then to town. People from all over Hometown had been drawn to the shopping strip as the place where stories of the storm could be traded, complaints voiced (the weather bureau), expressions of amazement spoken. People said: "What the hell?" and "Never in my life" and "We were due." Connie Cash held forth on the savagery of nature: "I looked at that cloud coming down the valley and I said, 'You wicked bastard.' You were standing beside me, hon. You heard me."

Connie's husband, Duke, endorsed what his wife had said.

"'You wicked bastard,'" Connie repeated. And, "Nev and Poppy. Where's their place? Halfway to the Murray!"

"Nev and Poppy," said Duke. "Scotty Campbell. Halfway to the Murray. Nev and Poppy are with Poppy's auntie on Hell's Ridge, Scotty and Di are with the Pastors. They'll be wanting that insurance to come through. Didn't touch us, but. The water parted up the hill and went both sides. Couldn't believe it."

"On both sides," said Connie. "Little bit got under the lino, not much. And what about your shop, Hannah? Have you had a look? All the shops—Dennison's, Russ Burnett's, Jenny's, Lawson's—bad, bad damage. Bad. Your beautiful books!"

Hannah said, "I haven't seen."

She and Tom made their way to the bookshop, followed by Connie and Duke, prepared to stand as witnesses to the devastation. Hannah unlocked the front door. The shelves gleamed. Hannah stepped inside. She clapped her hands.

"Tom, can you see?"

"Looks okay," said Tom.

"Can you see?"

"I'll have a squiz out the back."

The shire land sloped downhill toward the dozen shops and the flood had surged under rear doors. But Tom had erected a fence at the back of Hannah's shop, sinking the hardwood palings a foot into the clay according to Uncle Frank's painstaking method, and so the flow had been forced away.

"Bit of good luck," said Tom.

And Connie, "Will you look at that?"

Duke, "I'll be buggered."

Juicy, who'd come along to help Hannah lament, said, "Tommy, if you didn't bury those planks, fuck me. Sorry, Hannah. But you see what Tommy's done? Water couldn't get under. That's engineering, my friend."

Hannah grabbed Tom and squeezed. Embarrassing for some watching on, not for Tom.

Others heard of Tom's fabulous foresight and came to gaze in admiration. Tom explained that he'd put up the fence to make the back look good; he hadn't been thinking of a flood.

"But you sunk the palings," said Juicy. "How many blokes would think of that? Eh?"

It was while these people were gathered around the engineering marvel that was Tom Hope's fence that Hannah made her announcement.

"Okay, so this man I will marry. Everyone comes to the wedding—everyone."

The wedding had not been made public yet. Those in the gathering held on to their good wishes until they were able to feel confident in

Tom's reaction. It was widely accepted that Hannah was at least a bit mad, and no wonder with Hitler and all that, so anything she said about marrying Tommy was maybe nuts. Best wait for verification.

But Tom smiled and nodded. "Yep," he said.

Slaps on the back. A hearty shaking of Tom's hand by Juicy Collins, Duke Cash, and Arnie Priest from State Rivers. Connie kissed Hannah.

"When?" asked Juicy.

Tom was vague. Then could Hannah answer the question?

"Soon," she said. "Open the shop. After that, soon. September."

CHAPTER 15

⸎

DECEMBER 1944

In Northern Poland in the valley of the Vistula the earth begins to
harden in late November. By mid-December the snow stays where it
falls without melting. Within a further month, the rivers ice over up
to Danzig on the Baltic Sea. Late in 1944, Hannah and the women of
the slave army were sent from the Stutthof camp to the eastern floodplain of the Vistula to labor with picks and shovels in the frozen earth.
Their task was to excavate trenches deep enough to balk Soviet tanks.
The shoes they were given were made of coarse wood and the feet of
all the women bled each day. If Hannah permitted herself to wish for
anything, she thought of soft leather and woolen socks.

One team started to the left, one to the right. The trenches were to
be three meters broad, fifteen meters long, two meters deep. If one
team reached halfway before the other, the four women of that team
were permitted to wait. But they were not to sit. They rested on their
picks and shovels, huddled close for the sake of warmth. The team
of a Lithuanian woman by the name of Judith, built like a circus

strongman, always finished first. Her face was bright red in all weathers, even brighter in that time of ice and snow. She showed off her muscles to the SS guards when they asked her, baring her arm and flexing it. Indomitable at the digging site, at night she wept bitter tears for her father and mother and little sisters. None of the other women wept. Most had lost parents, sisters, brothers, but it was only Judith who remembered as if it had happened a few hours ago. Even Hannah had ceased to shed tears.

Then one morning Judith failed to wake at dawn and was pronounced dead where she lay by the doctor of the slave army, a Polish medical student of limited competence. The SS officer commanding the wandering slave army of twelve hundred, Oberführer Schubert, came to the tent out of curiosity. He wanted to see Judith's corpse stripped so that he might satisfy himself that she was female. She was. He allowed Hannah and two helpers to bury the body, at Hannah's request. It was a big concession. The many women of the slave army who faltered along the way were shot dead and were carried a short distance from the roadside and left in the snow.

· · ·

HANNAH HAD DEVELOPED a skill of her own with her tools. She had studied Judith. But she knew the pick and shovel and the miserly rations would kill her soon—kill all of them. From the Polish doctor who was not really a doctor and from one of the *kapos* she learned that the Germans were close to defeat. The Russians were advancing from the east with tanks and big guns and a million soldiers in uniform. She was quite sure that Oberführer Schubert would shoot all of the women of the slave army when the Russians drew closer.

Maybe he would shoot himself, too. Every so often he would stand at the lip of the trenches watching the women while a junior officer held a huge black umbrella over his head. He never said a word. But what would he say? "What's the point?" Or: "Go home, for God's sake, it's all over." Or: "Today I'm having you shot, don't ask why." His face was gaunt and gray. It was too much to believe that he was wrestling with his conscience. He had served at Auschwitz. What would be left of his conscience? Hannah sometimes looked up at his face. He allowed her to meet his gaze. If he'd asked her to speak, she would have said, "You killed my son. I hope there's a Hell and you go there."

.　.　.

THE WORST DAYS were the days of blizzard. The wind and snow came down on the slave army from the Arctic. The canvas of the tents was stiff with ice. The horses were draped in blankets, but not the women. They died each day by the score. Some froze upright, still holding their tools. Those living wrapped themselves in the rags of the dead. They bound their clogs, bound their hands. Looking up from the bottom of the trench pit, the world was white. Digging was impossible. Hannah and the three women of her team hugged each other and turned in a circle, stamping their feet.

.　.　.

THEN ONE MORNING, the women of the slave army decided to die. Two days had passed without any food from the kitchen wagon. All over the camp, without any previous discussion, the women stayed in their tents wrapped in their bedding. A collective decision in the corporate mind of the oppressed: time to die. The soldiers would come and fling them all from their tents into the snow. Then they would be compelled to shoot each woman because not one would find her feet and pick up a shovel. Waiting for the end, Hannah imagined heaven for the first time since childhood. Bright stars in a blue sky and her celestial body free of pain. The air of eternity had a vanilla taste.

It was not the soldiers who came, but Marika from the kitchen wagon, a fair-haired girl of eighteen from Budapest who had been sleeping with the cook. She stood in the midst of the women and told them that the Germans had gone. They had taken the three wagons and the six horses and gone. The soldiers had assumed that they would shoot the women before departure, but Oberführer Schubert said no. They were gone, all of them. Marika added: "There is no food."

The Lithuanians had been the most competent women of the slave army, and all were dead. Leadership fell to Hannah. She said that they should walk east and hope to meet the Russians. The objection was raised that the Russians would rape them. The Germans were monsters, sure, but the Russians had uncontrollable appetites; not quite monsters but bad enough. Hannah dismissed the complaint. What else were they to do?

·   ·   ·

WITH THE COMPLICITY of the heaven Hannah had pictured, the blizzard abated, then ceased. She doubted there were any Germans left on this side of the Vistula and felt safe enough shuffling east on the open road with the eighty remaining women of the slave army. It was her hope that they could raid the farmhouses abandoned by those fleeing the Russians. She'd seen plenty of deserted farms as they had been marched westward.

. . .

THEY MET ETHNIC Germans and Poles heading the other way in horse-drawn carriages. No fuel for motor vehicles. The Poles and Germans passed silently, but with faces in which disdain could not be completely concealed. A few of the smaller children held their noses and made waving motions with their hands, as if to fan away the stink. Abandoned cars and trucks littered the road. The women searched each vehicle for food. A bag of ten hard sweets was divided up, two minutes per sweet by strict count in the mouth of each woman.

. . .

THEY FOUND THE first farmhouse at the limit of Hannah's strength. Hewn timber, two stories, a steeply pitched shingle roof. It seemed to be empty, but wasn't: A bedridden old man inside began screaming abuse. Hannah ignored him to concentrate on the larder. And dear God—a full ham, potatoes, carrots, green apples, salted beef, hazelnuts. It was agreed that dietary rules applied at other times in other places and the entire ham was carved, the potatoes and carrots eaten raw, the beef shared out, the hazelnuts demolished, the apples—eight of them—divided up among eighty. They fed the old man, even as he hissed at them. The rest of the family had apparently abandoned him. It was suggested by some that the old man might be better off dead, but Hannah said no.

. . .

AND IN THE farmhouse they remained.

There was wood for the stove and three fireplaces and materials for makeshift bedding—curtains, tarpaulins from the farm's workshop, horse rugs. As if overwhelmed by this sudden comfort and warmth, five of the women died within two days. Hannah found herself digging once more.

Two cows were tethered in the milking shed, Holsteins, lowing with hunger and the discomfort of full udders. They were milked by Frieda, the oldest of the surviving women, who'd grown up on a farm in Hungary. She showed Hannah how to go about it, but her instruction was curtailed by her death after a brief coughing fit.

The food quickly dwindled. In one of the fields, a solitary goat was left running about—a big billy. A team of women chased him with carving knives and an ax. It took, finally, ten would-be butchers to corral the beast. He was held down while a woman with a carving knife straddled him and stabbed him wherever she could, again and again. The billy struggled free and for days evaded capture, watching the women in his dire exhaustion through his eye slits. When he collapsed, he was beheaded with multiple blows of the ax, inexpertly chopped up, and served stewed for days on end.

After the debacle of the billy goat, any further killing of animals—the cows—was never a realistic solution. It was suggested that half of the women should take to the road again to search out other deserted farms. By the middle of January, after three weeks on the farm, Hannah and twelve of the original eighty were all that remained. They lived on milk and turnips, a small mountain of them in the cellar. The old man was still alive, still vile.

The snow had stopped falling but the fields were white, other than the vivid patch at the site of the billy goat massacre and the red dotted lines that mapped the progress of the unfortunate beast after his initial stabbing. Hannah, bundled up against the cold, developed a habit of sitting in the seat of the tractor in one of the sheds for an hour each day. It was a period she employed for thinking of nothing: for blankness. If she were to live and if the war truly came to an end, this is what she would do. Sit and think of nothing. She would read no more books. She would avoid art of any sort. She would not cultivate her mind. Nothing in books was true. Art was not true. The truth was Michael burned up at Auschwitz. There would be no more children.

On the first day of February, the Russians came. The old man slapped one of the soldiers on the face, and was immediately shot dead.

CHAPTER 16

Tom's verdict on *Crime and Punishment* was that nothing could redeem a man who'd murdered two women with a hatchet. "It's a good story," he said to Hannah, "but if you knew this Raskolnikov, there's no hope for him. There's no use Sonya coming to see him in jail. He's a basket case."

Hannah gave him *Down and Out in Paris and London* and *1984* and he finished both books in ten days. The pace of his reading had picked up. He thought *Down and Out* was terrific, but *1984* far-fetched.

Hannah enjoyed watching as he read; she barely cared what it was she'd given him. Or maybe that wasn't true. She did care. But the way he held a book in his hands, and the frown of concentration on his brow, kindled love in her heart. She wanted to stroke him as he read. The altering expressions on his face were like cloud shadows passing over a landscape.

. . .

THE BOOKSHOP OPENED without any great fanfare; just a full-page advertisement in the *River Tribune*.

Hannah Babel and Tom Hope
announce the opening of

HANNAH'S BOOKSHOP

Ben Chifley Square, Hometown

Our Shire's only bookshop

Open 9–5 weekdays, 9–12 Saturdays

Fully stocked with Classics and
the Best New Books of every variety

7,500 Titles!

Come and browse, enjoy a cup
of tea or coffee—free!

Opening day coincided with the annual Hometown Hospital Stall Day, sixty card tables and trestles piled with articles that the people of the shire had prepared to donate over the year. The Hospital Stall attracted a big crowd to the King George VI Lawn and the Coronation Memorial Rose Garden opposite Ben Chifley Square. Never any concern about weather; it had not rained on Hospital Stall Day in the thirty-two years of the event. Also celebrated on this day: the Shire Ferret Show, important in this ferret-loving region where the quicksilver blonde was first bred. The results of the rabbit hunt were announced at the ferret show, a yearlong contest between Queenie, with the blond ferret, and Bobby Hearst with his Mauser. This year's tally: Queenie, 211, not counting kittens; Bobby, 247, only counting confirmeds. Bobby was every year's winner. The *River Times* regularly sent a photographer: Bobby and Queenie cheek to cheek, Bobby looking smug, Queenie bitter.

. . .

FAIRGOERS WANDERED ACROSS to Hannah's Bookshop in a mood to spend something on literature, perhaps. And a few of the ferret people from Fisher Reserve, when they could tear themselves away. Books were sold; Enid Blyton more than most; a number of Noddys, Famous Fives, Secret Sevens.

. . .

MOST OF THE customers were women. Some would take a book from the shelves and turn it about with a savoring expression. Others held the books a little anxiously, as if picking up a volume might count as a commitment to purchase. Bessie George, who, like Tom, managed her farm single-handedly on what the early settlers from Yorkshire called "the big moors" west of the town, had no such scruples; she went through the Agatha Christie titles like a chaffcutter and brought a bale of books to the counter. A nurse from the hospital, a hefty middle-aged woman called Lilly with a hank of red hair on the top of her head that flared like a beacon, came to the counter with a hardcover: *War and Peace.* She plonked it down with a look of defiance that only a veteran of the wards can summon. "Been meaning to read this for years," she said. "Now's me chance." It was as if she'd prescribed herself a hard-to-swallow medicine that would nonetheless do her a world of good.

At one point a shriek came from somewhere in the shop and a woman in a tartan beret hurried up to Hannah with a book held in both hands. "*Swallows and Amazons*! I read it thirty years ago when I was a littlie. Hell's bells!"

Not all visitors to the shop had come to buy. Many were simply curious to see what a bookshop looked like. The town had a library until recently, financed offhandedly by the shire, so people knew what to expect when stacks of books were packed together on shelves; but the library had closed after the flooding, and had never had the luster of Hannah's shop. It sat next to the ES&A Bank branch at the bottom of Veronica Street, above the overflow. Everything at that end of the street had filled with water in the flood, up to the lightbulbs. All the books went to the tip, and Ern Murdoch, the librarian, aged and frail in a gray cardigan, retired to be cared for at a home in the city, as he might have done ten years earlier. Even when there'd been books, it was nothing like the number kept by Hannah.

But did Hometown need anything this flash? Seven thousand five hundred titles? Nobody asked Hannah that question, but she could sense it. She could sense, too, that women were more at ease with the abundance than men. Perhaps women were happier by habit and temperament with the prospect of immersion. The men, all of them, shook their heads as they gazed at the shelves. So many books. It was like looking at the blocks of the pyramids sitting on the sand on a daunting day one of construction.

The curiosity of the visitors extended to Hannah herself. Those who knew Tom—quite a few about the shire—took a dim view of a middle-aged foreigner luring him into marriage. That Tom could be lured, had been lured, was taken for granted. It was conceded that Hannah Babel was a striking woman for her age, but the gray hair— oh, dear. Also, she was crazy. What saved Hannah from actual disdain was the story that had spread of her heroic efforts at the farm during the downpour. Tom had told Bev and Juicy; Bev and Juicy had let other people know. So, okay, good, she was ready to get her hands dirty; ready to roll up her sleeves. But, what, forty-five? And Tom around thirty?

．　．　．

TOM WAS ON hand from ten-thirty to closing time at midday. He was pleased with the trade for Hannah's sake. At the same time, he felt like a goon in the shop, ringing up sales, ushering customers round the shelves. He was a farmer; before that, a boilermaker and electrician. And okay, he could turn his hand to another dozen trades, but no jack-of-all-trades added "bookshop proprietor" to his list. Thanks to Hannah, he knew who Dostoyevsky was, also Turgenev (he was forty pages into *Fathers and Sons*) but really, clodhopping about this beautiful shop with its antique tapestry and lovely framed pictures and rugs from Kabul? He was a fraud. An hour before he appeared in the shop, he had been covered in muck, rounding up the sheep, shouting at cows, putting his fingers to his teeth to whistle up Beau, and now he stood with a big smile telling farmers' wives where to find the Georgette Heyers. In a shirt and tie. Polished shoes. Black slacks with a pleat down each leg. If you loved a woman, this is how you might well end up. Dear God. At midday, he kissed Hannah good-bye and skittered back to the farm with a hundred things to attend to.

Hannah saw off the last two dawdling customers, turned the sign to CLOSED, and was left alone with her gladness. The shop had sold thirty-seven titles, about half of one percent of the stock. To break even, pay the rent, the bills, Hannah would need to sell fifty titles a day. Since her busiest trade would be restricted to Saturday mornings, this was most unlikely. It didn't matter. Happiness ran in her arteries and veins and reached every part of her body and being.

Do you see how things can turn out? Do you see that the world is big enough to make certain things possible? That thirty-two years ago the German Student Union could hold a rally in Opernplatz, Berlin, and burn twenty-five thousand books, many written by Jews, the students rejoicing in their festival of loathing, and now this, in Hometown. Hannah's bookshop of the broken hearted, a thing of beauty.

Her father had listened to the news on the radio at the apartment in Budapest near the Chain Bridge, Hannah and her sister Mitzi, a year older, beside him on the sofa. "They are burning books. Why this madness? The students are burning books." He'd wrung his hands and pushed his thumb against his wedding ring, as he did at times of distress. Hannah had closed her own hands over his and calmed him. Silver showed in the stubble on his cheeks and chin and the round lenses of his spectacles had misted over. His lips had moved silently. A prayer of forgiveness, Hannah guessed; her father went through life dispensing forgiveness even when it was especially uncalled for. He was by profession an accountant who employed a staff of ten, but his vital life was entirely devoted to literature. The apartment was filled with shelves in almost every room; they fitted around doorways, around windows; an exasperation to Hannah's mother, Magda, who spent half her life up a stepladder with a feather duster. Each book, to Eilam Babel, held its place in the worldwide narrative, a single story told by thousands of voices. He had favorites—Moses Mendelssohn, Tolstoy, Aristotle—but he never spoke of them as giants among the less accomplished, rather as leaders. In the same way as Hannah, he didn't approve of colonies on the shelves and forced all authors to live together in a literary kibbutz.

Hannah closed her hands over her father's and spoke words of comfort to him, but comfort didn't save him. He died in a camp up north when his heart gave out. Hannah's mother and two of her sisters,

Mitzi and Pasqual, were hanged for theft in the same holding camp; Deate was beaten too badly to survive; Moshe was sent to a labor unit and was said to have died of hunger. None of them reached Auschwitz. It was 1948 before Hannah learned the fate of each member of her family. Her father's library was gone when she returned to the apartment in 1945. She might have thought: *So what? Did books save my father? Did books save anyone?* Or, instead: *He loved the books, I loved the books, one day there will be a shop and I will stand behind the counter and sell.*

. . .

THE BOOKSHOP MIGHT have opened in Budapest after the war, except that Stefan was too busy to pay attention and the Communists were too nosy about titles. That, she couldn't abide. But even here in Hometown, Australia, the censors must be accommodated. Her solution was to display a block of wood where a banned title would have been shelved. On each block (Tom had made them to her specifications) she attached a label: *Borstal Boy* is banned in Australia. Apply at the counter for a summary of the story. Or *Lady Chatterley's Lover*. Or *Eros and Civilization*. The summaries were in Hannah's head. She intended to rattle off the comings and goings recorded in the banned books for anyone with enough curiosity.

. . .

SHE CAME TO Australia with the bookshop still in her imagination and thought: *How much farther can I go? This is where I stop.* A very long way west of Budapest, of Auschwitz. She had read enough to know that we cannot speak of things that are "meant to be." If her long journey from

Europe to Hometown, to Tom Hope, to the bookshop of the broken hearted was meant to be, then *Mein Kampf* was meant to be, and the cleansing, the säuberung of the students in Opernplatz were meant to be.

She said: "Too bad about that." Hannah's happiness was great enough to embrace contradictions. It was without doubt meant to be, this bookshop that would bankrupt her, this love for a man who would one day notice her gray hair and her wrinkles more keenly than he did now. Too bad about that. For now, a little taste of paradise.

CHAPTER 17

The all-important trifle. Tom said, "In the country, Han, at every wedding reception. And sausage rolls."

"Who can make it?" said Hannah. She was baffled by the importance placed on the trifle. It sounded disgusting.

"Bev's going to make the trifle. She's famous for trifles."

Hannah said she would watch. If a trifle was like this, more important than God, she would have to make it herself for Tom sometimes.

. . .

Bev, in her immemorial pinny, with a pocket at the front for her Turf Filters and matches pointed at the array of ingredients on the table.

"Your sponge, your swiss roll, okay? You'll slice that up and layer the bottom of your bowl with it. Then you'll pour in your sherry and let the sponge soak it up. You don't want to be miserly with the sherry, Hannah my love. You want that sherry taste to go right through the trifle or you might's well be eating something for a kid's party. Big swig of sherry. On top of the sponge, your layer of sliced peaches. Then your jelly, port wine—layer of that. It's all layers, Hannah—all layers. Next your custard, nice deep layer. Another layer of peaches, another layer of jelly, raspberry this time, another one of custard, good and deep. It's a big bowl, you can see that, big bugger of a bowl, clear glass every time, a pottery bowl's no good, you've got to see your layers, right? Right. And on top, my love, the cream. Now this is proper cream. This is thick, thick proper cream. You won't need to whip it. Thick, proper cream. And how you'll finish up is this. You'll sprinkle some grated chocolate on top. It'll be dark chocolate. Milk chocolate, don't bother. It'll be dark chocolate. That's your trifle."

·　·　·

NOT ONE BUT two giant trifles were produced; with everyone in Hometown invited to the wedding and reception, two trifles would be barely enough. The sandwiches were left in the hands of Juicy's long-suffering wife, Kay, and a team of offsiders. Shy though she was, Kay wished to be involved, and wished to dress up, and wished to watch Hannah take her vows, and wished to cry without restraint. Huge platters of sandwiches would be required. Tomato and cheddar, tomato and ham, tomato and lettuce, tomato and sliced egg, tomato and curried egg, curried egg by itself, pickles, pickles and ham, gherkin and egg. Other helpful women of the town baked ginger fluffs, passionfruit sponges, vanilla sponges, apple turnovers. The sausage rolls were left to Tom's sisters, who were staying with Tom at the farm. Bev's advice: "Don't hold back on the sausage rolls. An acre of 'em'd be about right." The salads, of course. Patty and Claudie would also take care of the salads. Hannah offered a couple of recipes that included things like roasted eggplant. The recipes were accepted graciously and ignored.

. . .

HANNAH WAS INSANELY busy in her own kitchen the night before the wedding, fashioning traditional Hungarian dishes sufficient to feed the Red Army. Tom called in to offer his assistance and was told to go away and stay away. First one glass of an expensive shiraz, then another—and three more—kept Hannah willing until after midnight, when she fell asleep on the kitchen floor. She woke at four and telephoned Tom.

"Tom, my darling, I am a drunkard. Don't marry me."

"It's okay."

"You're too good for me. There, I've said it! You should marry—who is she? The girl with the bosom? Sheila? Who works in the grocers? She is crazy about you."

"'Sheila'? Darling, what are you talking about? Go back to sleep."

"I've seen her, the way she looks at you. Is her name Sheila?"

"Darling, Sheila is sixteen. Go back to sleep."

"All this Hungarian food! Who will eat it?"

"Everyone. You have to get some sleep, Han. Go to sleep."

The toothbrush? In God's name, where was the toothbrush? She cleaned her teeth with toothpaste smeared on her fingers and slept in her bed until nine in the morning.

. . .

WHO COULD HAVE asked for better weather? A bluer sky? Bev had helped Hannah get herself ready; a gown from Budapest, originally purchased for Stefan's sister's wedding ten years earlier. Maybe a little too close to crimson for a wedding, maybe a lower neckline than was polite, but gorgeous. A bouquet of violets, tied with a purple ribbon that Hannah's sister Mitzi had once worn, found in the Budapest apartment in 1945.

Tom was in a new dark blue suit, a new blue shirt, and a horrible fawn tie with yellow diagonal stripes—what in God's name? This was not the tie he'd said he would wear. Hannah led him into a room off the area set aside for the ceremony and gestured for Juicy Collins, in a plain red tie, to follow them. "Change ties," she said. "Be quick."

Horry in a plaid sports coat inquired quietly, when bride and groom had finally taken up their positions before him, "Good to go?"

And then it got fancy. "Mrs. Babel has requested that we start out with a poem," said Horry.

The crush inside the building was near enough to hazardous. The people of Hometown and its region had taken "All You Can Eat and Drink" on the sign pinned to the public notice board as an inviolable promise. But there was a feeling that it might apply more fairly to those who'd taken the trouble to view the service. Pretty warm outside; warmer inside. The news that a poem would be read was greeted with groans, just a few.

"This poem," said Horry, with an eyebrow raised to warn against any further dissent, "is by—by Sappo. That's 'Sappo' is it, Hannah? Your handwriting's a bit tricky."

"Sappho," said Hannah.

"'Sappho.' Just the one name?"

"Yes."

"And it's short. Not quite sure what it's called. Hannah?"

"The title is the first line."

"Is that right? Same as the first line?"

"Yes."

"So that'd be, 'It's no use'?"

"Down to the comma."

"What, 'It's no use, Mother dear'?"

"Yes."

"Doesn't leave a lot. But right you are. Right you are. The poem's called, 'It's No Use, Mother Dear.' Presumably about weddings and the like. Here we go: It's no use, Mother dear, I can't finish my weaving. / You may blame Aphrodite, soft as she is, she has almost killed me with love for that boy."

Horry read the poem with the same hushed and singing cadence he employed when quoting odds in the shopping center. When he'd finished, he continued to study with a puzzled expression the sheet of paper on which Hannah had written the lines. The crowd couldn't tell if it was over or not.

"Yeah, well, that's it, apparently," Horry finally allowed. "'You may blame Aphrodite, soft as she is . . .' That will be the goddess, apparently. Aphrodite. One of your favorites, is it, Hannah?"

"Yes, it is."

"Sappho. Not familiar with the lass. But there you go. Now, we're here for something else, and that's the marriage of Tom and beautiful Hannah. Not the first time for either one. Third time for you, Hannah? Third time. Second time for Tom. An old saying: 'Hope springs eternal.' Anyway, let's push on."

Vows were taken; promises were made. Tom stood straight and tall and said that he would love Hannah no matter what, and care for her and comfort her until his life was over. Hannah said the same, but in a whisper, her eyes averted until at last she looked up at Tom, took his face in her hands, and kissed him on the mouth. She let out a cry more of anguish than joy—"Tom! Dear God!"—and kissed him again. If Tom had studied for a year, he could not have made a more stoic figure—stoic, stern, sober. Yet at the end, pronounced husband and wife, he permitted himself to smile. First to his wife, then he turned his head to the crowd and shared his—relief, would it be?—his relief with the people of Hometown. They responded.

"Good on yer, Tom!"

"Good for you, mate!"

"Well done, Tommy!"

And intended for Hannah: "Happy times, dear!"

Outside, at the top of the steps, Hannah was commanded to throw the bouquet.

"You must give me back the ribbon. It's from my sister."

She turned and tossed the bouquet high over her shoulder. It was caught by Sheila with a leap that would have done credit to a fielder bringing down a hook to fine leg on the cricket field.

"The ribbon!" shrieked Hannah.

Sheila picked up the bow and brought the purple ribbon to Hannah. A few minutes earlier, she had murmured to her mother, with sincere loathing, "She's too old for him." But now she was lit by the festive glow of the day and found she could forgive Hannah. By way of contrition, she whispered, "Your dress is nice," as she returned the ribbon.

. . .

The Country Women's Association had declined official involvement in planning the wedding reception since it was a private rather than a community affair, but that was just Marg Barrister with a stick up her backside. Most of the women from the association knew Tom and were ready to help. Tom's choice of wife? A problem, overlook that.

Bev and Kay and a number of offsiders sped from the Mechanics Institute down the highway to have everything ready at the farm before the hordes descended. Vic Viney hired from his studio in

Healesville had snapped any number of pictures at the service and would want a hundred more outside, so the ladies could enjoy a full half hour to warm the food and set the tables. Four nine-gallons up from the pub, a dozen bottles of bubbly, sherry, brandy, advocaat, Pimm's, whisky—and wine, at Hannah's insistence, but a waste of money, only the booze hounds would drink it. Lemonade and raspberry and lime soft drinks for the kids. Three refrigerators on loan were plugged into double-adaptors on the back verandah and Kay had hooked up in Tom's kitchen an old electric stove from the shed for the sake of four extra hot plates and the oven. The food would be served on benches and tables indoors: The idea was you filled your plate with chicken and lamb and T-bones and veggies, carried the whole heap outside, and sat yourself in one of the chairs hired from the Masons and the Returned and Services League. Six kids from Hometown High—fourteen and older, arguably legal—had been given five dollars each to pour drinks throughout the afternoon and evening.

Goodwill toward Hannah mounted hour by hour, since it was accepted that the happy abundance of food and drink was the expression of an exotic, European sensibility. And what do you think? Do Jews eat pigs? Look at this: two sucklings roasting over the coals in cutaway forty-four-gallon drums. A Jew who wouldn't let being a Jew get in the way of serving up suckling pig was a wonderful person.

The band was Gearchange: Angus Mac on bass guitar, Col Fast on fiddle, and his two sons on drums and steel guitar. Tom had nailed together a stage of untreated pine in the middle of the backyard with the idea of introducing Col Fast's band, Gearchange, in the early evening. But for a hundred bucks, Col was willing to commit his boys to eight hours of performance and the music started while the roast meats were being carved. Jenny Kitson, channeling Patsy Cline in a black sequined dress, threw herself into "The Wayward Wind" with a plangency that won Bev's deep approval, tears in her blue eyes as she bustled about the kitchen with a Turf between her lips and a meat fork in her hand.

· · ·

IN THE ABSENCE of a father or mother on either side, Patty took the role of senior relative. At five in the afternoon, with a flock of white cockies forming a rowdy gallery in the thistle gums, she called for attention with the traditional tap of a fork against a champagne glass.

"If I could have your attention!"

Children by this time were running wild. Mothers called them to order: "Kevin! Georgiana! Get yerselves over here! Now!"

"If I could have your attention!"

Patty offered a compact speech in which she did not refrain from telling Hannah she was a bloody big improvement on Trudy. Tom, unexpectedly asked to say a few words, and with no bridesmaids to thank, simply said that he was a happy man. He mentioned briefly that he was "learning the classics" under his wife's tutelage. Hannah declined to speak at first, then bowed to the pressure of the crowd.

"Very well. Very well."

She kissed Tom on the cheek before standing, and spread her arms in an embracing gesture toward the very large number of people who'd made the trip from town to the farm.

"Thank you for coming here," she said. She always had a natural huskiness to her voice, more exaggerated today with emotion.

She had come to Hometown, she said, because she was sick of Europe. "They wanted to murder me. I wasn't so special. They wanted to murder all the Jews. Even after the war. Here, nobody wants to murder me. I love the Australians."

And then: "Eat! Drink!"

When she sat down, she whispered to Tom: "I shouldn't have told them that, do you think?"

"It's okay, darling. And it's true."

"Australians, they don't want to hear about murder. I don't know why I said it. But I am sick of Europe, Tom, yes. Budapest, I love; but I'm sick of it. I want only to be with you. That's okay?"

"That's okay. That's good."

Hannah's only European friend in Australia had made the trip up from St. Kilda, George Cantor, dapper in old age, a superb head of silky white hair, kippah pinned at the back of his head. He shuffled up behind Hannah and whispered in her ear, "You are very beautiful, my love. But stupid. No murder at the wedding."

Then Kay Collins asked if she could say something. "I love this fellow, this Tom, our Tom. I love Hannah. I want to sing a song."

. . .

A GAUDY SUNSET extended itself over the western hills. Rupe Stevens and his wife had undertaken to milk the cows and Tom was free to dance with his bride while the colors in the sky deepened and disappeared. He shuffled competently through Jenny's rendition of "Tennessee Waltz" and Jim Reeves's waltz-time ballad, "He'll Have to Go," but it was a trial. The more Hannah drank, the friskier she became. She wanted Tom to take her to the bedroom, and had to be persuaded to consider how that would look.

Past eight in the evening, under a sky teeming with stars, the guests started to wend their way to the line of cars parked along the driveway. The diehards sat in small groups on the verandah holding their glasses with a defiant resolve. The women among them were not yet ready to resume the ordeal of the household, while the men were closing in on that teary stage of lost love and loneliness. The food was gone, except for what remained of the salads. The trifles? Not a morsel left. The Hutchinson kids from the Catholic ghetto on the wrong side of the tracks, appetites adapted for unrationed banqueting, had licked the big glass bowls clean.

Tom was called away to chase a gang of kids out of the highway paddock. Hannah said, "No, stay here." But the matter was urgent: Stubby would go crazy and run into a fence.

Hannah stared at the patch of darkness into which Tom had disappeared, accepted in a distracted way the good wishes of more people departing. A distress had grown in her that she hoped to fix in bed with Tom. She left the last of the guests and walked all the way up to the boulders in her high heels; she spread her hands against the gritty face of the tallest one. The big moon coming up in the east turned the stone the white of bone.

She said, "Forgive me. I am not even on the continent where you died. Forgive me. I couldn't stay there anymore. One day they smile at you in the street, the next day they hang you from a lamppost. I couldn't stay, my darling boy."

CHAPTER 18

The Russians were cheerful. They had won the war. Not quite, but any time now. The Germans were retreating and would soon be trapped in the cities of their homeland, blown to blazes by Allied bombers. The soldiers—all from the east and not, in fact, Russians but Siberian Mongols—were gleefully happy and hoped to hunt the Germans to their final refuge and slaughter every one of them. It was carnival time, a happy time, and thank God for the senior Russian commanders—sophisticated and astute—who knew how to restrain their gleeful Siberians. The Russians commanders allowed the Siberians to rape ethnic German women but not women who had escaped from the Nazis; particularly not Jewish women who'd suffered in the camps. They did, of course, but they were not supposed to.

The women in Hannah's care, their number reduced to eight by illness and death and departures, were not raped. Those who were ill were sent to a Russian field hospital for treatment. The senior officer commanding the Siberians in this small corner of Poland saw to that. He was a Moscow Jew by the name of Zalman; an educated man, committed, austere. He'd seen the camps that his Siberians had liberated. He told Hannah (their common language was German) that it would eventually be revealed that the Nazis had murdered not hundreds of thousands of Jews, but millions. He was not sentimental about those millions; he was merely stating facts. His great mission was not to show how vile the Germans had been, but to uphold the authority of the Party. He wasn't a political officer, yet he behaved like one. He said to Hannah, "If you were in our army, I would watch you like a hawk." There were quite a number of women among the personnel of the Rifle Division commanded by Lieutenant Colonel Zalman. They were not armed. They worked as typists, as secretaries, in food preparation. They were from the east, like the field soldiers, and had an Asiatic look, but were not Mongolians.

Zalman was austere in his demeanor, yes, but he had a taste for informed discussion. He came to the farmhouse every second evening for dinner with Hannah. They avoided politics. Hannah, as Zalman saw, was likely to say things that were too satirical for his taste. Instead they discussed literature and philosophy. His learning exceeded hers, but she didn't embarrass herself. She intended to ask him for a safe-conduct pass before he moved on with his Siberians—something that would permit her to move at will in the Soviet-liberated lands and to return to Budapest. She studied Zalman's serious face over the superb meals prepared by the women from the east and asked herself if he had ever known laughter.

He poured out Plato with such sincerity that it made her smile. She said one night, "Plato wanted to get rid of people he didn't approve of—isn't that right? Actors, writers. He wanted them shot."

Zalman held up a censuring finger. "There were no firearms in Ancient Greece." He had the most beautiful eyebrows Hannah had ever seen on a man—perfectly shaped, and with the luster of some gorgeous animal's coveted pelt. His lips were red, but not in the way that the lips of the stricken can redden in an unhealthy way. No, Shmuel Zalman's lips were red as wine in betrayal of some hidden complement of the sensual running in his blood. Hannah was sure that he wanted to sleep with her but couldn't admit it. Their humorless discussions over the best food anywhere in Poland were actually feasts of unconscious seduction. She didn't want the seduction to go any further.

. . .

IN EARLY FEBRUARY 1945, Zalman and his Siberians were ready to press on toward Berlin. Tanks had arrived, many of them. The soldiers climbed onto the tanks, ten or more holding on to each structure, even straddling the cannons. They shouted out war cries as they departed.

Zalman watched with Hannah. "They are very bloodthirsty people," he said. "They fought us for years. We Russians are their natural enemies. Now, they want to kill Germans. If I told them that the French were our enemies, they would kill Frenchmen."

Zalman intended to say farewell to Hannah the following morning. It was arranged. He had been encouraging her to live in Russia, even as he was writing her a pass for safe travel in Russian-controlled territories. He said he could fix it. But he didn't appear at the farmhouse the next morning. Hannah feared something bad had happened, and it had. She learned from one of the cooks from the east that Lieutenant Colonel Zalman had been arrested and was being taken back to Russia. The cook spoke Russian at the same barely competent level as Hannah. For what reason had Lieutenant Colonel Zalman been arrested? The cook said: "Political."

. . .

HANNAH, HAVING HEARD that the Russians were now in Torun, to the south, persuaded two of the remaining women in the farmhouse to attempt the journey to the city. The prospect was that they could catch a train once in Torun and find their way back to Hungary, which was also under the control of the Russians. It was a dangerous thing to do. Zalman had gone, and with him the protection he had given them. Even at the farmhouse, they might be raped any day. They might be raped every day. Most of the Siberians had gone away on the tanks to kill Germans, but more Soviet soldiers would come, maybe as bad as the Siberians, maybe worse. Out on the open road, the danger would be even greater. The Russians had advanced so rapidly that some Germans had been caught behind the leading units of the push to Berlin—Zalman had told Hannah this. Some were still to the east, on this side of the Vistula. And not only Germans, also units made up of Soviet soldiers who had deserted two years earlier to fight with the Germans. Those deserters were effectively already dead—they wouldn't allow themselves to be taken prisoner. To fall into their hands would be a catastrophe.

But Hannah and her two friends—Hette and Eva—took to the road with enough food for a week in hand-stitched fabric bags. They feared the deserters, they feared the Germans, they feared the Soviet soldiers. But staying put was worse. If they walked down the roads of Poland to Torun, they were at least facing their fate. Captivity, rather than making them timid, had emboldened them. They had seen their fellow prisoners selected for the gas chamber in Auschwitz; they'd seen women they had lived with as intimately as family fall to their knees on the road, seen them shot by the SS. Now they marched down the road to Torun. Ready to accept whatever the absurd world sent their way, and yet, hoping above all to live, to prevail, to walk the streets of Budapest.

But a week's food would not see them to Budapest. The farmhouses they came upon on their journey south had been stripped bare by the Soviet soldiers, who were well in advance of the supply corps and had to feed themselves. Hannah, Lette, and Eva muddied their faces and hair, hoping to appear too wretched to rape, and approached the camps of the soldiers to beg for food. They were lucky on occasions; at other times they had to run like Olympic sprinters, hoisting their dresses to free their legs. They at least had reasonable footwear, taken from the corpses of refugees along the roadsides. They'd learned quickly to undress the corpses because some of these once desperate people had edible stuff concealed close to their skin—fragments of wheat biscuits, bones, potato skins—preserved by the winter chill. Most of the dead had been shot by retreating German troops or by the units of deserters, but some had succumbed to illness. Hannah counseled restraint—better not eat anything from someone who'd died maybe of typhus.

They left a piece of animal hoof behind discovered in the rags worn by a girl who seemed to have been stricken by some disease or the other. After about twenty paces the three of them turned as one, ran back to the girl, and chewed on the hoof by turns.

.   .   .

IN TORUN, HANNAH found the main hospital, now run by the Soviets, and, in Russian, offered her services and those of Lette and Eva as bandage folders and cleaners to a harried doctor. He said, "Yes, yes," thrust them toward an appalled nurse, and rushed away. The nurse was one of the Asiatics. She told the three women that they must shower and disinfect themselves and provided them with coarsely woven underwear and ugly gray dresses. The three women didn't say so, but they were not about to stand under shower outlets. Not after Auschwitz. They scrubbed themselves with warm water and washed the grime from their hair in a bucket. The disinfectant they ignored.

. . .

AND SO BEGAN the three months, March until the start of June, that the three women spoke of as their Polish vacation. The work dried up within a week of their arrival at the hospital. As the Soviet troops raced through Germany toward the Berlin prize, Torun quickly became too far from the fighting for casualties to be sent back to the hospital. Hannah, Lette, and Eva mopped floors at a slow pace, bathed the bodies and brushed the teeth of soldiers who were either unable to use their hands or no longer had any, and helped out in the canteen. The food came up from Georgia and Azerbaijan. An administrative error had resulted in an allocation of food for three hundred patients and three hundred staff. In fact, there were ninety on the staff, including doctors, and seventy patients. Hannah ate herself into a stupor on Georgian raspberries. Breakfast, lunch, and dinner each comprised three courses for staff and patients. In five years of war, nobody had eaten that well. The great hope was that it would take a year to capture Berlin.

. . .

THE THREE WOMEN had been assigned an apartment in a building dating from the seventeen hundreds and that was said to have been the property of a wealthy German family up until a few months back. The Germans had filled this part of Poland with their own nationals over the past century, but they were all gone now. The apartment was equipped with modern plumbing and a magnificent kitchen tiled in blue and white. If it had been known that the apartment was so attractive, it would have been assigned to far less lowly folk than Hannah and her friends. All sorts of things had been left behind by the fleeing Germans—wardrobes filled with garments, ornaments, pictures. Even the larder was well stocked, not that Hannah could be bothered with opening cans of walnuts soaked in red wine; she was too well fed. But she did try on the garments. Before a tall mirror supported by carved porphyry figures of nymphs, she stood admiring herself in a long coat and hat of black fur. The shoes were too big for her—the madame of the house must have had feet like pontoons—but the dresses were about right. She went walking in the streets of Torun dressed in fine clothing, even the fur coat, not actually required in late April. Her hair had resumed its massy form, shining from the application of the German family's shampoo. The city had barely suffered any damage from the German occupation; many buildings were from as early as the fifteen hundreds, there was also a castle built by the Teutonic knights. Fine city walls still stood. Hannah hummed tunes as she strolled, accepting the surprised glances of Soviet soldiers as approving.

. . .

BUT IT'S NOT a life, filling your stomach with food three times a day, wandering a foreign city in the clothes of your enemies. It's not a life, but something vacant going on in perpetual dusk. Hannah did not feel confident that there was anything you'd call a life waiting for her in Budapest, where Leon would not be, where Michael would never bring her a picture book and plead with her to read him the words as he once had. Once.

Nonetheless, she told Lette and Eva one morning that she would be taking the train to Berlin, then another to Budapest. Lette said, "God help us, we will go with you. We have only the one travel pass." Eva agreed at first, then changed her mind. She was having an affair with a Russian anesthetist three times her twenty-one years. He wanted to take her back to Moscow, divorce his wife, and marry her. Eva said, "I love him." Hannah and Lette shrugged. The anesthetist was an attractive man and full of Russian nonsense. No sense arguing.

CHAPTER 19

Apart from Bev and Kay, almost everyone thought of the marriage of Tom and Hannah as mad. But people enjoyed seeing them together in the shop, as they were a few times a week. They came to enjoy Hannah in particular. She told them stories about the storytellers, also her personal theories concerning the private lives of writers: that Agatha Christie had been a nymphomaniac as a younger woman and that William Shakespeare had enjoyed a Jewish mistress. Many other theories. As the weather grew warmer she kept a chamois under the counter to pat her face dry without ruining her makeup and offered each customer a glass of lemon squash with ice.

Seventy books a week she sold, sometimes eighty, ninety, including the five-dollar romances and the Lone Wolf westerns she stocked for Juicy Collins's brother, Aubie. All of Hannah's money had been invested in the stock—thirty-five thousand dollars. At seventy books a week—Hannah was too vague to do the sums, so Tom did—she would be bankrupt in about a year. Hannah nodded when Tom, with the figures in front of him at the kitchen table, told her the bad news. She said, "I'll sell the Fragonard drawing to Victor in Prahran, and the De Chirico. They are worth more than the whole shop."

"But, Han, you can't run a business like that. You've got to have more coming in than you're spending, not the other way around."

"So you think I should close the shop? I won't. And Maggie. This is the best thing in her life. I can't." Maggie was the girl who looked after the bookshop from three-thirty onward while Hannah was teaching her students. Fifteen, crossed in love, she came recommended by Joan Swan, the high school English teacher. "Take her mind off things." She shone in her role as shopgirl and was besotted with love for Hannah.

"And when you don't have any paintings to sell? What then?"

"Then is then. Tom, we can't close the shop. Do you see? We can't."

She had paid out the lease on the house in Harp Road; Tom had hitched up the tandem trailer to the ute and moved her furniture to the farm. Everything except the Steinway: A professional piano handler came up from the city with two helpers and coddled the instrument all the way to its new billet. The big living room of the farmhouse had a smaller room off it that served no purpose at all—a sofa and arm-chairs that were never used, an oak secretary, more of Uncle Frank's paintings. That space would become the living room, and Hannah would teach in the big room.

Tom watched her sometimes with her students. Their parents drove them out to the farm, then accepted a cup of tea while they waited; or Hannah would pick them up from Hometown. At the Steinway, she stayed on her feet while the students played. She inter-vened by bending over and reaching around the child. She never lost patience; never said a harsh word. She might rest her hands lightly on a child's shoulders and speak softly, encouraging a slower tempo. "You see what we need? Friendship. You and Henry Steinway. Perfect friendship. Later, you can say rude words if you wish, in ten years. For now, 'Pleased to see you, Herr Steinway. I hope your sons are well. Pleased to be sharing this time with you.'"

.   .   .

UNDER THE ONE roof and wed, what had delighted Tom in Hannah delighted him more. He looked down the hallway and saw his wife reading *The Age* on the kitchen bench—she read newspapers standing up. As she read, her feet played out tiny dance steps, her body unwilling to remain still. It stirred him to see her. One afternoon after her students had gone, she called to him from where she was reading: "Tom! Mr. Whitlam! An intelligent man!" The federal election of 1969 was just past; a close-run thing, but not quite a victory for Hannah's favorite. "I voted for him! Clever Hannah!"

She kept up her commentary of gleeful disdain in front of the big AWA television Tom had picked out at great expense from Vealls in the city. She groaned and covered her face with her hands during the *ABC News* and *This Day Tonight*, implored Bill Peach to cut loose in interviews. It was all personal. She watched *Pick a Box* without complaint but *Bonanza*, a favorite of Tom's, she scorned utterly. Pa Cartwright and all of his sons were plainly homosexual, she said, and should be allowed to say so.

The moon landing enthralled her. She closed the bookshop on the day of the landing and invited everyone she knew who didn't own a television to come to the house—thirty people, including kids. She was too excited to sit. Tom's enjoyment came more from Hannah's childlike excitement than from the fuzzy stuff on the screen. Why did it mean so much to her? When he asked, she said that it was an adventure that did not end in murder, a good and uncommon thing. "Vietnam, horrible. But the moon, Tom, the moon!"

. . .

YET A PART of her he couldn't reach. She turned her eyes to him sometimes and she was a thousand miles away. He was nothing to her then,
a stick figure. She would look away, raising one hand in a tired gesture.
Once she said, "Tom, go somewhere else." He knew she meant for an
hour, only an hour, but it was as if she'd struck his face. Nothing in
him could take it calmly; he looked at the slump of her shoulders and
wanted to shake the mood out of her. He'd go outdoors to the store
shed with his stomach knotted. Shuffle up and down in the darkness
where nail holes and rust holes let in fine rods of golden light. He
thought of leaving, just in the clothes he wore. Came almost to the
point of it. Knew it wasn't possible. If he walked away it seemed the
flesh of his body would unwind from his bones.

After the mood, she would sleep close to him, grappled to him.
This was her apology. No words, just the holding. Her body still
remote, even as she clutched him. When she came back, her desire
made her violent and clumsy and she hurt him physically: seizing the
flesh of his neck and wrenching at it, taking his hair in handfuls.
He never uttered a sound. He forgave everything—but held back. He
didn't stroke her shoulders, didn't kiss her, because she would pull
away and he would be on the rack again.

Then he was left for a day or more—until her tenderness truly returned, and her humor—to ask himself if she really loved him as she
said. He knew she did; he only had to think back to Trudy to be sure.
Trudy, who for a time had said, "You're beautiful when you fuck me,
Tom Tom," who'd sometimes let him take her beyond herself. But
she'd lost interest. He'd once tried to kiss her neck as he stood behind

her on the verandah. He could recall the expression on her face when she whipped her head around; the surprise and anger.

Hannah didn't look at him like that. Only it made his stomach knot, made him think of walking away when she withdrew to the place he couldn't reach. He said to himself, *I'll get better at it. I won't worry so much.* But he would.

So they were together, properly together, except when they weren't. And Tom knew, as if he was altering inside his skin, that certain things he'd once said to Hannah could never be said again. "How was it for you inside the camp?" He couldn't ask a question like that again. Nor anything about her boy. He had drawn too close to her to imagine that he could learn anything by asking her to speak of Michael, of Auschwitz. He saw that silence must be allowed its dominion.

.   .   .

HANNAH'S EPISODES OF absence were balanced by other occasions when she spoke happily of her life in Budapest; of her mother and father and sisters and brother; cousins, in-laws. She had to be in the mood, but once she got started and spoke of her family (never of Michael, however) she was everywhere: with her uncle Arkady for a minute or so, then in her early childhood being taught by a governess how to appliqué fabric shapes to a bedspread with tiny stitches. "*Governess*, okay, but not really, she was expected to do everything, kitchen maid, laundry maid. She was only twenty, maybe twenty, younger it could be, black hair that reached half down her back, and her father was supposed to be a Greek, of that I doubt, she was not Greek by looks. My mother found her selling *pogácsa* at the railway station—biscuits made with yeast, on top some cheese—a baby in her arms. My mother, Magda—softhearted, Tom, she questioned the girl, who had nothing and lived nowhere, her father was in Romania, her mother had died running away to Hungary. The baby was not hers but her mother's, so she said. But a Greek? No, no, the Greeks are not like Helena, she was Kalderash, Romany people, Gypsies, but at that time Hungary didn't want any Gypsies so she said she was Greek. After two years she disappeared, for me tears and tears, she was kind to us, my sisters, me. I think my father paid her to go away. My uncle Lem was maybe doing things with her. You know?"

And Shabbat, the Sunday of the Jews, and Saturday, the family gathered at the table on a Friday night, special bread, prayers, her father's hand on the crown of her sister Judith's head with an invocation and a blessing, all the food prepared in advance because after a certain hour the Jews could not cook. "A craziness," said Hannah, "but my father, Eilam Babel, honored Shabbat, my mother didn't worry so much."

Other uncles and aunts, more than Tom could keep in order, a certain Uncle Viktor with a birthmark on his cheek in the shape of Czechoslovakia, a vivid spot exactly where Prague would be found; Abigail, Hannah's father's eldest sister, who took on the role of wife for both her husband and her brother-in-law, Aaron, two children to each, all very amicable. Cousins popped up to perform in Hannah's tales: Daniel, the eight-year-old math prodigy; Susan, lame with polio, taken in her wheelchair to the top of a hill and allowed to accelerate down; Noah, the movie fan who wrote love letters in English to Hollywood actresses and received polite replies.

When Hannah talked of her family members she quarantined them from the holocaust. She told Tom just the one time that all of her family had perished, including all of her in-laws, everyone, thirty-two of them. She had in-laws from her second marriage still living in Hungary, yes. She wrote letters. But when in her gay mood she told of

Noah with a note from Norma Shearer beneath his pillow, or of Susan exultant as her wheelchair bounced down the hill, she kept them on this side of a thick black line. And Tom was happy with that. He didn't know what to do with mass murder.

· · ·

HE DIDN'T KNOW, either, what to think about the money Hannah sent to her in-laws in Budapest—Stefan's sister, Antoinette, who'd crawled out of a cellar on the day the Russians came, not a word heard from her between 1944 and 1945. "Her mind is gone, poor thing," said Hannah. She was filling out an international money order in the post office; a second money order for Stefan's grandmother, Golda, now eighty-five, cared for by the family of her former maid during the Nazi occupation.

"Stefan was the one who was crazy?" Tom asked. "That was him?"

Hannah said, "Crazy, yes."

"But you loved him?"

"Of course. Very much."

Tom nodded. "Do you miss him?"

"I miss him. Yes, that's true."

And the question that he'd wanted to ask when Hannah had first told him of Stefan, but hadn't: "Maybe you wish I was a bit crazy, like Stefan? Do you?"

Hannah looked up from the money orders and gave her husband fuller attention. "Tom, you are reliable. It's a good thing to be reliable."

"But better if I was a bit crazy."

"No, no, no," said Hannah. Meaning, of course, *Yes.*

Hannah's thriving tribe, her family of geniuses and loons—Tom was fascinated. His growing up in Mordialloc had been . . . modest, he supposed, matter-of-fact. His father, Gus, out in the backyard mowing the lawn, would pause and stand with his gaze fixed just above the rooftops, taking in the farthest part of the sky. As if his dreams were a kite, wrenched free from his controlling hand and now no more than a speck in the remote blue. His mother, Liz, puzzled out the *Sun* crossword each day, sitting on the back step, if the sun was out, with a cup of tea and a Craven A. She had a welt on her right calf from a burn she'd suffered one Guy Fawkes night as a kid, and in her concentration she'd reach down and scratch it lightly with the end of her pencil. "Come and give me a hand here, Claudie love." Claudie, the clever one. "Six-letter word, third letter *n*, last letter *y*, means 'conceit.'"

A modest family. Self-contained, apart from the outlier Uncle Frank. Tom had never known ritual gatherings around a table except at Christmas.

He hadn't realized that there was no Christmas for Jews. He said, "What?"

"Tom, we are not Christians. No, no. It's okay. I can make a good Christmas for us. In Buda, sometimes we had a little Christmas. Sure. Presents, Christmas cake. One time a tree with lights. Mostly Hanukkah—that's for Jews, Hanukkah. Cakes at Hanukkah, too. Games. About the same time, Christmas, Hanukkah."

"Jews don't have Christmas?"

"Tom, it's for Jesus, Christmas. Who is Jesus to the Jews? A nobody."

"Truly?"

"Tom. Listen to me. This Christmas, we will have Hanukkah at the same time, in the same house. We had rabbis in my family. I have the power to declare that we can have Hanukkah and Christmas in the one house."

In the spirit of the coming season, Hannah urged on Tom a new book, *A Christmas Carol,* the novel that his uncle had read to him; a few passages of it, at least. Tom finished it in three days. He enjoyed it more than any of the other novels Hannah had foisted on him. He was a man who approved of happy endings. In life itself, you didn't get the chance to choose an ending; but if a writer could give Bob Cratchit a Merry Christmas, then that's what the writer should do.

CHAPTER 20

⌒

The valley and the river took in one of everything: a swamp below the overflow where the mudeyes bred and black swans battered their way through the rushes; a cataract that ran over fluted basalt by the Tennessee diggings; a seventy-yard breadth of deep current named the Mississippi Hole by an American who'd mined at the diggings; miles of fast, narrow-flow water where the spinning gums on one bank and the self-seeded walnuts from Matty Croft's old stand arched over the stream close enough to touch.

· · ·

THE RIVER FEATURE nearest Tom's place was what was known as the granite bridges. Not really bridges but a place where the water ran shallow over ribs of granite that lay beneath the skin of the floodplain. Upstream lay the Mississippi Hole; downstream the fast water below the spinning gums.

Some hours after midnight, two weeks before the Jewish-Christian celebration being prepared in Tom Hope's household, the figure of a small boy stood by the granite shallows on the west bank of the river.

He wore torn clothes, shirt and shorts, and carried a single leather sandal in one hand. He stared out across the flow of water, his body slack with the weariness that comes over children with a powerful, fixed purpose, unheeding of the need to rest before the point of complete exhaustion.

After two days of travel by train and on foot, this was the site he'd been seeking—the crossing below the farm. Over those two days no sleep, no food, and, before he'd reached the river and scooped up some water, nothing to drink. When he'd commenced his journey, food and drink hadn't been a consideration. It was the same now. The tension in his expression, his eyelids barely flickering, was far too mature for his small stature. He had the look of a fully grown madman.

The boy plunged into the river and waded forward, holding his one sandal above the water. He seemed to disdain the caution that would have better served the fording of a river in the dead of night. When the flow rose to his waist, he pushed on, striving for balance. He kept his gaze fixed on the bushy mirror plants on the eastern bank that glistened in the moonlight. By steady degrees he passed the halfway point, and farther, until he was close enough to the overhanging branches of the mirror plants to lunge and seize hold with his free hand. He allowed the current to swing his body into the bank, transferring his grip from the branch to the rushes, and crawled to safety. Free of the current, he sat down in the water and rushes and gulped in air. He'd barely breathed while crossing, as if he'd been swimming underwater, lips sealed, cheeks puffed.

He'd torn his shirt and shorts climbing through barbed wire fences as he sought the course of the river, and he'd torn them again in Henty's paddocks. He'd torn his skin, too. Trickles of blood, some hardened, some fresh, ran down his arms and legs, one on his neck. He crossed the highway, then walked along on its left verge until he came to the gate of Tom's farm. Barely a dozen steps along the driveway, he heard Beau bark and his face relaxed in a smile. Within seconds, Beau emerged out of the darkness, his body shaking in a fit of delight. The boy fell to his knees to hug the dog. "I'm bloody not going away," he said to Beau, keeping his voice down. "I'm staying here, bloody well. I'm not going away."

.   .   .

HANNAH, WITH HER phobia of darkened, concealed places, must always sleep with the curtains open. The windows faced west and at this time of night—after three, by Tom's bedside alarm clock, the milking clock—the bedroom was lit by the moon. Tom made out a small shape shaking his bare shoulder. A moment or two of bafflement, then:

"Petey?"

Hannah's body stirred against his.

"Petey?"

The boy stood still, arms straight at his sides, the single sandal clutched in his hand.

Hannah had now come to consciousness and was blinking at Peter in confusion.

"Who?" she said.

"It's just Peter," said Tom. "I'll take care of it." And to Peter: "Petey, pass my under-junders from the chair."

Tom lifted his legs and pulled on his underpants beneath the blanket. Then climbed out, knelt down, and embraced the boy, who remained stiff.

"What's the story, old fellow? Come out to the kitchen. Let me see you in the light."

Tom drew on his trousers and singlet and with a hand on the boy's shoulder, went down the hallway to the kitchen and switched on the overhead light.

"Strewth! You're a bit of a mess for a fancy bloke like yourself. Been climbing through fences?"

Peter nodded. In his expression there was a bleak patience, as if a certain amount of this and that would have to be endured.

Tom ran the kitchen tap onto a tea towel.

"It's come to this, has it, old fellow? Reduced to one shoe."

He knelt and took the sandal from Peter's hand, then dabbed at the scratches. The freshest scratch he patched up with a Band-Aid from the medicine box. He washed out the tea towel, wrung the water from it, cleaned up Peter's face. A powerful surge of longing rose from his chest into his throat and he had to fuss more with the tea towel than he needed to, allowing himself to regain control.

"Don't imagine your mum knows where you are?"

Peter didn't respond.

"Didn't think so. What do you reckon? Something to eat? Some brekky? Toast and eggs? You sit at the table and I'll see what we've got. Be a catastrophe if we were out of eggs, eh? Chooks laying twenty a day, shouldn't run out, you'd think."

Peter sat at the table, maybe a fraction less overwrought. Tom first served him a tall glass of cold milk. As he sipped it, he glanced around at the familiar and unfamiliar features of the kitchen. What he thought of the various new ornaments here and there he didn't betray.

Tom said, "You want to tell me how you got here, old fellow? Give me a few clues?"

Peter said, "Train."

"What, you came by train? From Newhaven?"

"Three trains."

"Three? Bloody hell! What, up to the South Gippy line then into the city? To Spencer Street?"

"Yep," said Peter.

"Then what? Train from Spencer Street to Cornford? Is that it?"

"Yep."

"Came into some money, did you? Cost you three or four dollars, all that travel."

Peter said nothing. Then when Tom gave him more space for an explanation, he said, "I didn't pay."

"Well, I didn't think you did, old fellow. And you walked from Cornford?"

Did he? Twenty miles?

"Walked," said Peter.

Tom let the boy eat his eggs and toast without questioning him any further. He sat at the table, leaning back with his arms folded, his gaze on Peter. More questions would come shortly, of course. Peter would know this. He understood, surely, that Tom was providing a decent sort of pause before he had to reveal difficult things. But then Peter called a premature end to the pause. His eggs and toast were only half eaten.

"I don't want to go away," he said.

Tom didn't nod. But he moved his head slightly to show that he'd heard what had been said.

"I'm bloody not going away, Tom."

Tom said nothing.

"Bloody, I'm not going back to Jesus Camp. Bloody well."

"Whoa! What's all this swearing? Where's that come from?"

"Nowhere."

"Nowhere?"

"I don't know."

"It's okay. Better cut it out, though. Finish your brekky, old fellow."

Peter returned to the eggs and toast, but mournfully. He ate two or three mouthfuls then put down his knife and fork.

"Sorry," he said.

"For what? The swearing. It's okay, Peter. Better cut it out, though."

"From Trudy."

"What do you mean?"

"It's from Trudy."

"The swearing? No!"

Peter nodded his head in emphatic insistence.

"From your mother? I'll be damned. Truly?"

Peter crossed his heart.

"Well," said Tom with a shake of his head, "she's changed."

Peter's gaze suddenly moved to the door from the hall, behind Tom. Tom turned his head and found Hannah in her black silk dressing gown. The look on her face was too involved for ready interpretation. Maybe some disapproval. But concern, too.

"Peter's made his way here by himself, Han," said Tom. "From Phillip Island. No tickets. A junior hobo."

Hannah crossed the kitchen to the sink then gestured for Tom to come to her.

"You must take him back, Tom," she whispered. There was an insistence in her voice that Tom found awkward. Not pleasant.

"Yeah, I know. Give me a bit of time."

"I'm serious, Tom. He must go back."

"Well I'm not taking him right this moment, Han. Okay?"

"No"—Hannah made a face of exasperation—"no, not this minute. But he must go back."

Tom was painfully concerned that Peter shouldn't hear this exchange. He put his finger to his lips. But a glance over his shoulder told him that Peter was aware of what was being said.

"Han, go back to bed. Please, just leave it to me."

Hannah searched his face. "You can see I am serious?"

"Yes. But go back to bed. Leave it to me."

. . .

Tom put Peter to bed in the spare room—once his own room—after overseeing the cleaning of teeth and the washing of hands and feet.

"We'll talk after you've had some sleep, Mr. Traveler. Okay?"

"But, Tom, I'm not going back. I don't want Trudy. I don't want Gran. I don't want Pastor."

"We'll have a chat in the morning, old fellow. You get some sleep, okay? Pals?"

"Pals," said Peter, not with the conviction and confidence of times past.

. . .

Tom waited in the kitchen for a good half hour—time enough for Peter to have fallen asleep. He glanced into the spare room, and it seemed to him that the boy was out. He took the telephone into the bedroom and plugged it into the second socket. Hannah was wide awake, her eyes glittering in the moonlight. Tom turned on the bedside lamp to search for the number of Jesus Camp in his notebook. Hannah watched intently.

It was Gordon Bligh who answered, the pastor. His voice was muffled. He would have been woken from sleep.

Tom identified himself, apologized for calling so late at night, and explained that Peter had turned up at the farm.

"How?" said Gordon Bligh.

"He took a few trains, and walked for a ways. I want to speak to Trudy."

Tom was told to wait.

Trudy came on the line minutes later. She sounded sullen.

"What's he doing there?" she said. "You better get him back."

"I'll get him back. Is that what you want?"

"You better."

"You've been out looking for him?" asked Tom. He had his doubts.

"Yes, of course. Talk to Pastor."

Gordon Bligh came back on the line.

"We'll collect him."

"No. No. I'll drive him. We'll be there about midday."

The phone was given to Trudy.

"Do what you want," she said.

Gordon Bligh again: "Have Peter back by twelve o'clock."

.　　.　　.

HANNAH TOLD HIM that he had done as he should. Tom shot her an angry look. He undressed and climbed back into bed, but with no more than a half hour until the alarm went off, he didn't try to sleep. Three trains and a twenty-mile walk? Did anyone doubt where the boy belonged? Hannah put her hand on his back. He reached around and removed it.

.　　.　　.

BEFORE SHE LEFT for the bookshop at eight-thirty, Hannah found the carton in which a few of Peter's left-behinds were kept, including his Hometown primary school uniform. She ironed the shorts and the shirt. No footwear was on hand other than Peter's old thongs. She knew that the boy would be gone by the time she returned to the farm in the afternoon but had the tact to avoid saying anything as pointed as, "Good-bye." She took an opportunity that came along to place her hand on his shoulder, briefly. She wished the touch to convey much, much more than it possibly could.

. . .

PETER REFUSED A second breakfast. A glass of milk, only. He was broken in defeat. He knew that Tom would take him back before a word was spoken on the subject. He sat slumped at the kitchen table while Tom said his stuff, hearing but not listening. The law, what the law says, by law I have to take you back to your mum, by law to Jesus Camp, the law. If I had my way . . . I wish I could keep you, I wish I could keep you here, the law . . .

"So you see the problem, old fellow?"

"Mmm."

"The law."

"Mmm."

"It's hard, isn't it? It's hard, old fellow."

Peter raised his chin, but looked away. A door flew open; rebellion stormed in. He wanted to hit Tom in the face, to burn the house down, burn all the farm. It ran mad in his blood. Then it was gone; a foray, nothing more. He was broken in defeat.

. . .

ON THE LONG drive, Peter had not a thing to say. Tom strove to engage him, but saw that the boy's heartache was too much for him. He quietened down, all the while trying to find that one thing that would make a difference; that one comment that would throw a great light forward. And there was one thing he could say, but must not. He could say: "I want you with me at the farm. Nothing will stop me." That was what the boy had come to hear.

CHAPTER 21

It took a couple of days before Tom got past pausing in his work to sigh and shake his head. In all that time, Hannah barely looked him in the eye. Then on the Sunday more than two weeks before Christmas, Tom glanced up from his Hungarian fare and said, "He'll do it again, Han."

Hannah nodded. "He should be with his mother," she said.

It was the first hateful thing Tom had ever heard Hannah utter. "That's what you think, is it?"

Hannah lifted her shoulders and let them fall. "What can I say, Tom?"

"Han, you could say that it's a sad, sad business that Peter can't live with us. It's a sad, sad business that he can't be where he wants to be. That's what you could say."

Hannah said, "Yes. I could say that. Do you want me to, Tom?"

Tom didn't reply, and the rest of the lentil soup meal was eaten in silence. It was a season of daylong labor on the farm and Tom thanked his wife for the meal, excused himself, and headed outdoors. Where had he seen that, the husband standing up from the table, saying something poisoned by formality, and heading outdoors? In his own home, as a kid.

The screen door opened. Tom turned at the sound to see Hannah standing on the back verandah, her face made ugly by her emotion.

. . .

SHE CAME QUICKLY down the steps, held Tom by the front of his shirt with both hands and wrenched at him.

"I won't do this, Tom. No. Look at me."

He looked. But it was one of those times when he experienced himself, his being, as distinct, singular in the world, and he could barely summon what Hannah was to him. He didn't hate her, he didn't love her, and he was as cold and clear in the head as a warrior who has taken up a weapon to face an enemy he knows he will defeat.

Hannah said, "Tom, be kind to me. I won't do this. I don't want these stupid things. Look how hard your face is!"

She turned and went back into the house, and Tom walked to the shed for the tractor. A problem with the gearbox. He would be glad to be alone with the problem. He didn't care if she packed up and went back to Harp Road, to Budapest. But let the gearbox be fixed.

He worked alone and with a profound contentment. He heard the leaves of the cider gums that the northerly picked up from the ground falling with a tapping sound on the iron roof of the tractor shed. And he heard the breeze itself, every so often a stronger gust like a voice raised in an argument. It was a spring that was causing the problem— a small metal spring, worn away on one end and unable to hold reverse gear in place. Tom held the worn spring before his gaze and studied it. Then he went to a wooden crate and sorted with his fingers through hundreds of bits and pieces from another tractor, spares, until he found exactly what he was looking for—a gearbox spring pretty much the size he needed. He fitted the replacement spring, nudged it into place, and it released a satisfying *click*. He tried the action of the gears. Perfect. Perfect. He smiled and nodded, happy in his work. His mind was free and cold and clear. He didn't give a thought to his wife; he didn't think of Petey suffering at Jesus Camp.

Hannah came into the tractor shed holding something made of fabric by its corners, displaying it. She was smiling.

"Tom, see what I found. I was looking for my tea towels in a box. Do you see how beautiful?"

And it was gone, like that, the anger that had in some way trans-formed itself into such a feeling of freedom. He was back in the arena, Hannah facing him under a bright light. In his wife, not a trace of the distress and vexation of thirty minutes earlier. He wasn't sorry that his contentment had gone. He couldn't have Hannah and be free in that way. This was where he must be, in the arena.

"It was in a box, Tom, the one with the tea towels. Mixed up with them, I don't know. Do you see how beautiful, Tom?"

"Yes, I see. It's beautiful, Han."

It was a cushion cover. The appliquéd shapes depicted a woman in loose eastern clothing playing a musical instrument. A man sat lis-tening.

"My cousin Susan made it, Tom. Who had polio. You see this woman, playing the dulcimer? You see how beautiful she is, all done with shapes of cloth? And the man, who is a king, you see how his face is full of desire? How could she do that? She was so good, stitching in her wheelchair, Tom. And the tree, you see it's a cherry tree, the little cherries? It was at the apartment when I came back. Three things left, and this."

Tom nodded. He was still holding a pair of needle-nose pliers. The gearbox sat on the bench.

"Han," he said, "I love you. I can't stop. I can't."

Hannah nodded. "Yes, I know," she said. "Tom, this I will put up on the wall. With a pin in each corner. It can't be put on a cushion. It would become ruined. Do you see?"

. . .

ON THE SATURDAY before Christmas, the twenty-second of the month, Hannah searched out an ornate candlestick holder, a *hanukiah* (as she said), in one of the unpacked Harp Road boxes. She placed it on the kitchen table at dusk and fitted nine candles. With the lights out in the kitchen, she lit the elevated central candle and used it to ignite the first candle on the left. One candle would be lit on each of the following days, until all had burned. Tom was told to sit at the table, and he did, arms crossed, legs crossed. He could not have been more uncomfortable if his wife had been about to reveal herself as the High Witch of the Continents. Hannah, seated, her back straight, hands folded on her lap, sang a song in a sweet, flute-like soprano. The singing took years off her appearance; she could have been sixteen. Her eyes shone in the candlelight. She raised her chin as she sang and every so often put her hand on her heart. Tom's uneasiness faded as he watched and listened. He thought, as he had in the past, that he could never come to the end of her transformations. And look, now, as the song concluded, such a shy, pleased look on the face of Hannah, who never gave the least indication of shyness.

. . .

CHRISTMAS CAME, A day of great heat after a few days of milder weather. Light in the sky from four in the morning when Tom rose for the milking. The leaves of the cider gums out back moved in the motion of the air; the usual signal of a blank blue sky daylong.

.   .   .

THE DAY PROPER, after the milking, began with a dreidel. Hannah called Tom to the kitchen table after he came in from the cows. She explained the rules; she explained the Hebrew markings on the dreidel. Tom had twelve cherry liqueur chocolates; Hannah also had twelve. Tom made the right call time after time. He had all of the chocolates within a half hour. They drank brandy from sherry thimbles because it was Christmas and Hanukkah, ate all twenty-four cherry liqueur choc-olates, and went back to bed to roll around and kiss. Later, in a ram-shackle state, an exchange of presents. From Tom, a wooden jewelry chest with a brass clasp and cedar inlays, including a Star of David on the lid. He had worked on it in secret for three months.

"Tom, so beautiful! The star, Tom. Dear God, forty-six years, nobody has made me such a gift."

From Hannah, an embroidered shepherd's smock based on a pattern from Cornwall she'd found in a book. Pleated. A thing of beauty, the stitching in fine green wool. It had been made by Thelma Coot of the CWA, a genius with needle and thread. Beautiful, yes, but also ridic-ulous. Tom tried it on and with the best will in the world could not promise that he would ever wear it outdoors.

"Once a year, Tom, wear it for me. Just for me. At Christmas."

Well, once a year. Tom wore it all of Christmas Day to show it to its maker, Thelma Coot, a widow with children and grandchildren in Perth, who came for Christmas dinner along with the childless Nev and Poppy, no one special in Hometown to pour gravy with, and after the recent flood, no home.

Nev said, "'Jesus wept' and well he might. What the hell's that, Tommy?"

And Thelma: "It's a Cornish shepherd's smock, you ass."

"Is it, but? Listen, Tom. Don't show up wearing that. The sheep'll be over the highway to Henty's searching for safety."

Hannah had set the *hanukiah* on the Christmas table. She invited Tom and the guests to sit at their places, the table spread with a crisp white linen cloth, and served the roast chicken and veggies and gravy that Tom had prepared. There were colored tissue hats in the shape of crowns, bonbons, whistles. On the record player, an LP of carols commencing with "God Rest Ye Merry Gentlemen."

"For this, my father would weep in heaven," said Hannah. "Four Christians at my Hanukkah table."

"Hold on," said Neville. "I'm no Christian. Not on your life."

"Yes you are," said Poppy. "We were married in church. Makes you a Christian."

The decorated Christmas tree in a big terra-cotta pot had been draped with electric lights rigged by Tom, a transformer switching phases on little fifteen-watt bulbs painted red, blue, and yellow. Two electric fans played a breeze over the gathering, riffling the tissue of the party hats. David the canary, normally restricted after hours to an alcove beyond the shop's little kitchen, had been brought to the celebration; he treated the breeze of the fans as a type of adventure playground, darting through the currents and issuing a racket of approval.

Hannah, in the best of moods, sang Hungarian folk carols and chirruped away like a featherless David. When the time came for the pudding, she danced it in from the kitchen with little hopping steps and pirouettes. After pudding, performances. Each guest was required to sing something, recite something, read something—their choice. It was a Hanukkah innovation of Hannah's Budapest household. Neville offered a transpontine version of *The Face on the Barroom Floor*—no gesture was considered too extravagant. Poppy, half a shandy from collapse, drew lipstick faces on her knees, held up her skirt, and wiggled her legs in a way that caused the boy face to kiss the girl face. Thelma, a foot-washing Baptist before her husband died, a little lapsed since, sang "Santa Claus Is Coming to Town." Hannah sang, in Hungarian, a Christmas song that included peculiar birdcalls. And Tom, exposing a comic gift he'd kept from the public until now, read the "Doreen" poem in Uncle Frank's copy of *The Songs of a Sentimental Bloke*. Uncle Frank had read to him from the same book, on occasions. In place of Frank's tropical phrasing, Tom gave the poem a contemplative reading.

And then, from nowhere, Vietnam. Where it was located on the globe, nobody other than Hannah had any clear idea. It had been announced that more Australian conscripts would be sent there, wherever it might be. Nev, made merry by liquor and primed to toast all those dear to him, provided the opening.

"To Terry!" His nephew, Terry, had been called up. "Off to fight the little yellow heathens." As he raised his glass, he added, "Vietnam."

Hannah, giving it a few seconds' reflection, sauntered through. "'Off to fight.' And this is a good thing?"

"It's what he wants."

"Is it? It's not what the little yellow heathens want."

The antiwar demonstrators on the radio and television were widely disdained in Hometown: creatures of a culture from somewhere else— a foolish culture, also annoying. So, a hush. Hannah appeared to be, inconveniently, one of the annoying people.

Tom braced himself. His wife would say more, he was sure of that.

Neville, not conceding he'd done any harm, said: "Just a way of speaking, Han. Joke."

"Well, when it comes down to it," said Thelma, "they're still human beings, the same as you and me."

Thelma spoke as if her words might be happily accepted as the final comment on the subject, for the sake of keeping things cordial.

"Cuppa?" said Tom. "Interest anyone in a cuppa?"

"The Vietnamese, they are the traditional enemies of Australia?" said Hannah. "You have been fighting them for thousands of years? They want to take away your land? Pardon me, I don't understand."

Tom murmured, "Dear God."

"The Russians do," said Neville. "The Reds. They're backing the Vietnamese."

"Oh, the Russians," said Hannah.

Poppy said, "Well, that's enough of politics."

The party petered out. The three guests thanked Hannah and Tom for their hospitality, Nev with special enthusiasm since he needed to show that he was not wounded in his pride, which he was. Thelma and Poppy pleaded to be permitted to help with cleaning up, washing up, but Hannah said, "No! Are you mad?"

Alone with the mess, Hannah said, "Tom, believe me, I didn't want to embarrass you. But Vietnam, Tom. The Americans are making a nightmare. Do you see?"

He didn't. But maybe he'd listen more closely when his wife came to him with the newspaper in hand while he was clearing the channels in the orchard; came to him to scold the Americans, scorn Billy Mc-Mahon.

"Ai, Tom! What are they doing? Listen to this."

What he wanted to say was: "Hannah, you did embarrass me. Everything you say embarrasses me. Everything you do. But too bad about that."

. . .

Too BAD, BUT in a different way, about his present to Peter. A crafted box like Hannah's but with crossed fishing rods on the lid. It had been returned in the mail with a note from Pastor Bligh informing Tom that presents were not given at Christmas in Jesus Camp. Pastor Bligh pointed out that Christmas presents from Tom had been returned the previous year. So for future reference, no presents. Yours sincerely.

CHAPTER 22

Peter took off from Jesus Camp again after midnight on the last day of January 1971. He'd been kept in a room by himself since the first time he ran away and Pastor had rigged a makeshift alarm on his door fashioned from tin cans. The idea was that any movement of the door would set the cans rattling. Peter was supposed to keep to his room all night; a chamber pot was provided if he needed to wee. But it was no great feat to thwart Pastor's alarm if you were patient, and Peter had been patient.

. . .

He had money this time. He'd been pinching coins from the trouser pockets of the men of the congregation while they slept at night. Not from the women—they were more alert to a missing five-cent piece than the men, Peter had noticed. He'd slip out of his room when everyone was asleep, very late at night, and go from hut to hut in what was known as "the dwellings." Doors were left unlocked in the dwellings as a token of trust. As silently as a spider, he'd creep his way into bedrooms and glide a practiced hand into a pocket. The men were all permitted to keep twenty-five dollars per week from the wages they earned at their various occupations out in the region; three dollars for individual purchases—mostly tobacco and treats for the children. Sixteen families lived at Jesus Camp (a further two hundred lived in their own homes in the broad area of the church's catchment area), so that made for a decent harvest of coins. Peter took only five-cent and ten-cent pieces—coins that would be less noticed in their absence than twenty-cent and fifty-cent coins. He carried a total of four dollars and thirty cents in coins when he left the Jesus Camp compound and hurried over the bridge, heading for the railway station. If a car were to come along while he was crossing the bridge, he'd see its lights in the distance before the driver would see him. And he'd slide under the timber rails and hang down from the planks until the car passed. He'd thought it out.

.　.　.

HE'D ALSO THOUGHT out getting himself onto the train, which wouldn't leave the station until seven in the morning, late enough for Pastor to have missed him. Pastor would drive his Chev to the station and tell the stationmaster to be on the lookout for a boy by himself. But the stationmaster would never see him. He'd sneak into a carriage and hide himself until the train began moving.

.　.　.

HE HID HIMSELF at Anderson Station, as he had last time, in the tall grass just beyond the platform. He thought, *I'll see Tom, but I won't see the lady. I'll see Tom by himself. I'll tell him I'll kill myself if he takes me back to Pastor and Trudy. Bloody well.* He felt in his pocket for his paper bag of coins. He didn't intend to spend his money on train tickets unless he had to; he knew how to hide in the toilet when the conductor came around. But if he was caught, he'd pay. Tom had said it would cost three dollars to go all that way to Spencer Street and then to Cornford. So he might have enough to buy a sandwich at Spencer Street, and a piece of fruitcake. Maybe a bottle of Passiona.

It would be a long wait for the train. He lay flat on his stomach with his cheek against the grass and thought about Tom. He was worried about him. The lady at the house was old. Peter felt strongly that it would be impossible for Tom to do proper things with a lady who was old. Fishing, things like that. Fixing the engine of the tractor. It was awful for Tom to be with that lady. Peter had entertained over the past two weeks a remedy for Tom's situation. It had come to him. The lady must go away. Tom would say: "Petey's back now. You have to go away."

The only thing was, the people you didn't like never went away. Trudy and Gran never went away. At Quiet Prayer in the church when people bowed their heads, Peter prayed for Trudy and Gran to go away. And Pastor—Pastor most of all—but when he opened his eyes, they were still there.

Pastor said, "What you say to God is a measure of the person you are." Peter didn't know what Pastor meant by that, but he sort of did. Pastor meant secret things. Peter wanted Trudy and Gran and Pastor to die, and that was secret. He didn't like them. He didn't like Jesus Camp. He didn't even like Jesus. Trudy said, "He rescued me." But Jesus didn't make her happy. All day she was in a bad mood. All day she pulled at her hair and said she wanted it to grow. The women and girls of Jesus Camp were supposed to have their hair cut by Meredith every fortnight. The boys, though, never went to Meredith. Pastor didn't care about the boys' hair, he only wanted the girls and the women to have short hair. Trudy said, "I'm not going to Meredith," and then Judy Susan made her kneel in the big field behind the dwellings and pray for inner peace.

Judy Susan was Pastor's wife. Every Sunday at Big Worship, Pastor told the congregation, always more than two hundred, some of them standing under the new extension of plywood at the back: "I bless my God for Judy Susan. We all bless Judy Susan, who makes our church glow." Judy Susan, at the front of the congregation, close to Pastor, would turn around smiling with her hands clasped under her chin. She was a very pretty woman, much younger than Pastor, and was permitted to wear her silky red hair very long. She was Pastor's second wife. Peter particularly disliked her. Pastor never raised his voice and never hit anyone, but Judy Susan did. She told Peter almost every day: "I can see right through you, bad boy." She liked to pull his ears and stamp on his toes. If Pastor was nearby, he'd say: "Leave the boy. He's trying his best." Which was not true. He was not trying his best. When Judy Susan asked him if he was trying his best, he said, "Yes, bloody well." Then he'd get a slap.

.   .   .

HE SLEPT FOR minutes at a time. But he was awake when light came into the sky and the stationmaster started work. He saw Pastor's Chev pull up. Trudy and Gran were with him, and Judy Susan. Trudy called out: "Peter! Wherever you are, come here this minute!"

Peter could see the four of them clearly. Pastor was making motions for Trudy to keep quiet. The four of them stood around talking to the stationmaster, Clarrie. They looked up the track, and down. Peter smiled. Did they think he'd be standing on the track? Didn't they know he'd be hiding in the long grass? Didn't they know that the train would pull up right next to the long grass? Didn't they know that he'd open one of the doors on the hidden side just before the train started up the track to Nyora and climb in and hide in the toilet? He squirmed on his stomach in delight and sang to himself in his satisfaction: *You can't find Peter, You can't find Peter, No matter if you look, You can't find Bad Boy!*

People were waiting on the platform for the train, not many. A man in a suit and hat carrying a gladstone bag. A mother with a baby and a little girl. Peter thought he'd get in the carriage they chose. People would think he was with the mother.

The train arrived with a long screeching of brakes on its down journey. It would go on to three other stations then come back on its way to Nyora. Peter would change at Nyora for the next stage of the trip through Koo-Wee-Rup and Dandenong to Spencer Street. If Tom said he couldn't stay, he'd live on the train. Instead of killing himself, he'd live on the train. This one and others. He'd go everywhere. He'd pinch food, he'd sleep on the seats. One day when the train was going across a river, he'd jump out and drown himself. Before he jumped out, he'd go everywhere.

When the train stopped, Pastor and Judy Susan and Trudy and Gran walked along the platform looking through the windows of the carriages. Six carriages, and they looked in the windows of each. Peter could see what they were doing. The place he'd chosen to hide was on a hump. He could see through the carriages. He laughed because why would he get on the train when it was going the wrong way? It made him feel free and happy to watch Pastor being stupid, and Judy Susan. He sang softly to himself, "Bad Boy, Bad Boy, no one can see . . ."

A little later, the train returned and stopped for a minute just short of the station. Then came a clanking sound and the train gave a wriggle and moved forward slowly until it was at the platform. Peter watched to see which carriage the lady with the baby and the little girl chose. He left the tall grass and crept along the line of carriages on the far side of the platform, hidden from Pastor. The carriage doors were old-fashioned and they opened with the turn of a brass handle and swung outward. Peter heard Clarrie call in his shouty way: "Service to Nyora! Change at Nyora for Dandenong. Service to Nyora!" Just as the train began its forward movement, silent at first, Peter leaped up and seized the brass handle. He made the door swing open then held on for dear life until he could struggle his way into the carriage. The woman with the baby and little girl peered at him in alarm. Two other passengers, men, came to their feet. Peter sat opposite the lady, the mother, smiling brightly. He said nothing. The little girl stared at him with admiration and deep suspicion out of wide-open brown eyes.

The man in the suit and hat with the gladstone bag rose in his seat, studied Peter with a smile, then came down the aisle and sat heavily next to him. He placed his bag on his lap, lifted his gray hat to show courtesy to the mother. He was too close, and Peter attempted to make more space between himself and the man. But as soon as he'd gained a couple of inches, the man shoved himself over, right up against Peter. His head was too big for his hat. It sat a long way above his ears, as if he were trying to be comical. He was a big man all over, too big, as if he'd been lumped together out of one-and-a-half normal men. His smile, as Peter saw when he stole a quick look at the man's face, was not a smile, just a strange set of his lips.

When the man spoke, as he did after a few minutes had passed, his manner was cheerful enough.

"Off to the big smoke, lad?"

Lad was a term that Pastor used. Peter hated it. He made no reply but only turned his head to look out the window. His instincts told him he was in trouble.

"Traveling light?"

Peter didn't know what "the big smoke" was and he didn't know what "traveling light" meant.

"What's your name, lad?"

"John," said Peter.

"Just John? John who?"

"John Hope."

"John Hope is it? Be the right thing to give you me own name, wouldn't it? That be the right thing?"

A harsh authority had come into the voice of the man, despite his friendly tone. He appeared to expect approval from the mother, perhaps also from the daughter. Whenever he spoke to Peter, he only addressed the first few words to him before glancing over at the woman in her summer dress.

"Luke Shutter," said the man, and he held a soft, white hand out to Peter. Reluctant to touch the man, Peter thought it best to accede.

"So," said the man, "you're John. John Hope. Not Peter Carson from Pastor Bligh's camp."

Peter blushed. But he shook his head.

"I think you might be. I think you might be little Peter Carson, on the run."

Peter shook his head, more emphatically.

"I spoke with the pastor on the platform. Asked me to keep an eye out for a lad about your age by the name of Peter Carson."

Peter made a lunge across the man, but was grabbed and pushed back down on his seat.

"That's what I thought," said Luke Shutter. He looked over at the woman, as if sharing his victory. The woman, her baby in her arms, freed one hand to draw her daughter closer. The brown eyes of the daughter grew even larger in wonder. Peter's right leg was thrust forward after his attempt at escape, touching the knee of the girl. The mother reached out and pushed Peter's knee away, and as she did, a spasm of revulsion distorted her face.

"Now, young Peter, next station's Woolamai. You'll be getting off there. The thing is, how? Nice and quiet? Be best. I'll tell you what I've got in this bag, lad." Luke Shutter patted the gladstone bag on his lap. "Handcuffs. Leg irons. You don't want to be carried off the train in handcuffs and leg irons, do you? Eh? Like a crim from Pentridge, eh? What do you think? Eh?"

Peter said, "No," in a voice muffled by humiliation.

"No. Course not."

The eyes of the little girl were now fixed on the gladstone bag.

.   .   .

PASTOR WAS WAITING at Woolamai, and Trudy, Judy Susan, Gran. It must have been their guess that Peter would jump the train at Anderson, somehow. Luke Shutter opened the carriage door and hailed Pastor, who threw back his head and brought his hands together in a loud clap. He strode to the carriage door and took Peter from his captor.

"Mr. Shutter. I thank you from the bottom of my heart."

"No trouble at all, Pastor."

And Luke Shutter lifted his hat.

Pastor watched the train depart, raising his hand in response to Luke Shutter's wave from the open window of the carriage.

"Now," said Pastor to Peter, "this is no good, lad. This is no good, is it?"

Trudy had her hand on Peter's neck. Judy Susan stood on the other side of him, itching to get her fingers on his ears by the looks of her.

Gran stood with her arms folded, shaking her head. It seemed likely that she could go on shaking her head for an hour to show her disappointment.

Pastor said, "In your pocket. What is it?"

The paper bag of coins made a visible bulge.

Peter said, "An apple."

Pastor reached into Peter's pocket and found the bag of coins. "What's this?"

Judy Susan took the bag from Pastor before he could look inside. Her instincts must have told her that what she would find would significantly magnify Peter's offense, both to Pastor and God. And her.

"Money!" she said, staring down into the open bag.

She displayed a ten-cent piece, dropped it back in the bag, then showed a five-cent coin. She shook the bag so that the witnesses of this crime could hear the money in its chink-and-rattle volume.

"Thief!" said Judy Susan, and it was clear that theft, in her scheme of things, greatly exceeded the wickedness of hightailing it from Jesus Camp.

Pastor pushed his hand into his white mane. Trudy covered her gaping mouth, drawing in a deep breath. Gran continued to shake her head in sorrowful rebuke.

"Let's get him home," said Pastor, clamping his huge hand down on Peter's shoulder.

· · ·

EVERY SO OFTEN at Jesus Camp—and this was a shame—some child would require a thrashing. It was uncommon, maybe three or four times in a year. Pastor did not administer the thrashings, and certainly not Judy Susan; Pastor thought it prudent to keep a little distance between his wife and the exercise of her appetites. No, it was always Leo Bosk, who'd come to Jesus Camp from the Catholics. Four years as a Christian Brothers boy had taught him what a thrashing looked like. But more than his background commended Leo as a punisher, for there was no malice in him, merely an honest feeling of where his duty lay. And he was a dad himself, four daughters and a son at Jesus Camp, all of the kids models of good behavior, the rod never spared.

Thrashings were always supervised by Pastor with an eye to keeping the whole business in hand. Judy Susan was also permitted to look on. And the parents of the child suffering the thrashing, or in Peter's case, his one parent, Trudy, and his gran and his auntie Tilly. Punishment was normally carried out in the recreation room, where at other times the younger children played with Plasticine and pipe cleaners and colored wooden blocks. Pastor and Peter's family and Judy Susan sat in a semicircle on undersized play chairs, while Leo Bosk sat in a grown-up's chair with Peter across his lap. Peter's shorts and underpants had been pulled down to his ankles to leave his behind bare. Leo, in a jovial mood, as ever, said to Peter, before commencing the thrashing, "Well, Pete, it only goes to show—you don't have to be dead to be stiff. Bad luck to jump into a carriage with Mr. Lucas Maynard Shutter. Sells toupees these days, but used to be a copper." Without further ado, Leo Bosk brought down his thick leather strap on Peter's behind. The slap of leather on flesh rang out more loudly than might have been expected for those who hadn't witnessed a thrashing before—Trudy and Gran and Auntie Tilly. The three of them jerked in their small chairs. Peter, his arms hanging down limply, convulsed with pain but didn't cry out. The blows then followed rapidly. The dose was to be ten strokes. Peter writhed at each blow but kept his lip between his teeth. His behind was bright red by the time Pastor raised his hand after the eighth stroke.

"Ten," said Pastor. "That's it." It was his way to subtract one or two strokes from the dose, pretending that the full complement had been issued. But these reprieves didn't please everyone; sometimes even the parents protested. On this day, it was Judy Susan who raised an objection.

"Eight," she said.

"Ten," said Pastor.

"Eight by my count," said Leo Bosk.

Trudy came to her feet quickly. Her face was wet with tears and her lips wobbled in her effort to control them. "It was ten!" she said. She strode to Peter, lifted him to his feet, and hoisted his underpants and shorts up to his waist. Then she faced Pastor and Judy Susan.

"I don't agree with this, Pastor. I have to say I don't agree. It's not right to hit the boy. It makes me upset."

As she spoke, Peter lifted his face—like his mother's, wet with tears. He'd been able to stifle cries of pain, but not the tears.

Pastor nodded, his white hair a mess after he'd buried a hand in it while the thrashing was in progress. It was important to Pastor Bligh to rein in any appetite for revenge. His God did not sanction revenge among those who loved Him. A struggle, sometimes, to keep clear of vengeance. A good struggle.

"Trudy my dear, none of us takes any satisfaction in this," he said. "Not me, not Tilly, not Judy Susan, nor you, and certainly not Peter. But consider this. Proverbs twenty-nine: fifteen. 'The rod and reproof give wisdom, but a child left to himself brings shame to his mother.'"

Pastor raised himself from his child's chair with surprising ease; at seventy-seven he might have been expected to struggle. He stood before Peter, took his face in his hands, and tilted it up so that he could look down into the boy's eyes.

"Are we mates again, Peter? Because I would go much further

than this to see you in the arms of Jesus. Much further. Are we mates again?"

Peter said nothing. Nor would he. Pastor stood between him and Tom. Trudy, in time, would let him go. But Pastor—no. Not ever. In Peter's gaze burned implacable enmity. And in Pastor's gaze, as he held Peter's face in his two hands, also the relish of enmity; most welcomed. If Pastor'd been compelled by circumstances to set a burning brand to the timber stacked around a tethered Peter, he would have done so. He knew it. And Pastor accepted the weight of sorrow that would fall on him when he touched the brand to the kindling. This would not be vengeance. Be clear about that.

CHAPTER 23

NOVEMBER 1945

The ancient locomotive seething at the Torun platform was supposed to draw twenty battered carriages to Anhalter Bahnhof in Berlin. If it could. Hannah and Lette had been waiting hours for the arrival of the train, together with hundreds of Russian soldiers and fifty or more civilians making a belated attempt to escape from the Soviet occupation. The Poles, some with children, looked daunted, as if they expected the Russians to throw them off the train along the way, or shoot them; a well-founded fear. The Russians were boisterous, reckless with their firearms, firing at ravens in the trees beyond the station. They were drinking not vodka but slivovitz, a clear plum brandy of the region. Among the soldiers were a number who looked like dwarves, all wearing the same unit insignia. The language they spoke between themselves was not Russian. Hannah hoped with all her heart to find a carriage free of the soldiers; they looked savage and drank more freely than the other Russians.

.   .   .

HANNAH AND LETTE had dressed themselves for the journey like magazine models. They wanted to look special, inviolable. Dressing in this fancy way would normally have guaranteed trouble, but with the handwritten travel pass from Lieutenant Colonel Zalman, they calculated that they would seem untouchable, maybe the mistresses of big shots, and would be left alone. Unless a document written by Zalman was more likely to cause strife, considering that he was now probably dead, shot for whatever absurd transgression his masters had dreamed up. Would the Russians this far from Moscow know that Zalman was a traitor? Hannah thought, with a shrug: *I hope not.*

A skinny boy in the official uniform of Polish Railways announced in a faltering voice that all passengers must now enter the carriages. The boy's uniform was far too big for him and must once have belonged to the corpse partly covered by a blanket on the floor of the *poczekalnia*—the waiting room.

Hannah hurried Lette along to a carriage just behind the engine— as far as she could get from the soldiers. She chose the smallest of the five compartments—only seating for four. It was a carriage that must once have been first class and still retained vestiges of a happier era: the plush blue upholstery, which was not yet as badly torn as might have been expected, lanterns above the seats; here and there an antimacassar on a headrest; small pullout brass trays on which a cup and saucer could rest. Hannah might have spread her belongings over the remaining two seats to discourage others from choosing this compartment, but she didn't, believing herself to be the sort of person who would not behave in such a greedy way. And she told Lette to refrain, too. Two soldiers threw open the compartment door with a crash, gazed with aroused curiosity at the two women, heaved their kits up on the baggage rack. As soon as the soldier next to Hannah had seated himself, he attempted to put his hand up her dress. Hannah slapped his hand and threw it back on his lap.

"You speak Russian?" she said. "Good. Can you read? No? Listen to me."

She read from the travel document issued by Zalman. When she came to the end of what Zalman had written, she added, with emphasis, something of her own: "'If any harm comes to the bearer of this pass, I will know and my vengeance will be terrible.'" Melodramatic, but only melodrama would ever get through to uneducated Russians.

But not these Russians. The soldier snatched the document from Hannah and spat on it. Then handed it back. An animated argument followed between the two soldiers in a dialect completely unfamiliar to Hannah.

Lette eased herself to the far side of her seat. Hannah cleaned the spittle off the document with her handkerchief. The train was now in motion, but at no more than walking pace. As soon as it had cleared the platform, it stopped. The soldiers dropped their argument and listened. A voice was calling something in Russian, difficult for Hannah to catch. But the two soldiers went into a rant of disgust, full of Russian oaths that Hannah recognized regardless of the dialect. The door was wrenched open and a soldier, a junior lieutenant by his insignia, more refined in appearance than his comrades, shouted in clear, educated Russian: "Find your kits, brothers! We're getting off!" He departed down the corridor, shouting the same command at each compartment. The soldier who'd spat on the travel pass bent down with his kit over his shoulder and kissed Hannah on the mouth with force and a prod of tongue. At the door, he said something in his dialect. Hannah understood the word: *sweetheart.*

Minutes later, the train started again, empty of soldiers.

The journey settled into the monotony of the passing countryside, verdant, flat, sunbathed. The catastrophe of the war was not so evident: in the villages a few burned-out dwellings, a shattered farmhouse in the fields. But outside one village hours to the west of Torun, bodies lay beside the rails at regular intervals, suggesting that these people— all in civilian clothes, a number of children among them—had been shot at the doors of moving carriages and pushed off the train. Freshly killed—maybe no more than a couple of days earlier. Surely not ethnic Germans? They would have made their dash for Germany nine months ago. Hannah gazed down at the bodies without revulsion, but with an unsettling anger. Why the need? The war was over. A train in the east of Europe passes dead people left where they tumbled, and nothing is to be said, nothing is known. It exhausted her, this changing scene, evidence of the retreat of the Nazis in their defeat, sunshine on the fields of Poland, but then come the bodies, even children. It could go on forever: justice, beauty, murder.

.   .   .

LETTE HAD IN her hand—something. What? Like a small stone that she was turning about in her fingers. And muttering.

Hannah said, "What are you doing?"

Hannah had seen Lette at other times over the past months fiddling with this whatever-it-was. She'd never asked about it.

Lette shrugged, but kept it up.

"You, madwoman, I said what are you doing?"

The train, at its unhurried pace, passed through a small station where a group of ragged women stood holding hand-lettered signs in Polish written on paper, on cardboard. Women like these gathered at every station and on roadsides. Each sign asked if anyone knew the whereabouts of this person or that, this age, that age, send a letter to such-and-such post office. The futility of the quest made Hannah sigh each time. She didn't sigh this time because she was engaged with Lette's craziness.

Lette, in her fancy outfit, her felt cloche, her dress of bright yellow jersey, lipstick, small jade earrings, said, "None of your business."

Hannah reached out and took from Lette's fingers a white stone. She studied it closely. A vein of blue ran through the stone.

"What is it supposed to be?"

Lette said, "A charm."

"A charm? What charm?"

"From Kristina."

"Kristina who?"

"At the farmhouse. One of the Siberians. Kristina."

"The big one?"

"No. Not big."

"The one with the flat nose?"

"Yes."

"A charm?"

Lette took the stone back. "It keeps evil away."

"What?"

"It keeps evil away. She gave it to me because I fixed her toothache."

"Fixed her toothache? How?"

"A spell. A Magyar spell."

"What? Are you a witch? Where did you get a Magyar spell?"

"Our maid in Buda."

"Lette, we're Jews. We don't have spells. We don't worship stones. Do I have to tell you?"

"So what? Something from the Magyars, something from the

Siberians. Who cares? I was in Auschwitz because of being a Jew. I can't get a little help from the barbarians?"

Hannah dropped the subject. She knew why her friend was praying to stones. She wanted to find her husband alive, and the kids. By some miracle. By the miracle of the stone. Hannah would have nothing to do with it. Michael was dead. Not even his bones remained. Whenever she heard of miracles, a storm of disgust ran through her. *Don't talk to me of miracles. One person gets a miracle, a million don't.*

They changed trains twice—each time to a contraption more decrepit than the one before. But by fits and starts, they reached the ruins of Berlin. Cleared rubble was stacked high on both sides of the rail lines. The blue sky showed through the broken upper stories of buildings. The plundered capital of the Third Reich. It gave Hannah no joy at all. Hitler's egomania went this far. Berlin destroyed? For what?

. . .

A RESETTLEMENT AGENCY for Jews had been established in Berlin run by steely young men and women from Palestine, from Jerusalem. It was housed in an elegant building in Charlottenburg provided by the Americans, not so far from the Spree: pillars, colonnades, lawns, elms. The rubble of bombing raids hemmed it in on all sides; everything else in the neighborhood had been blown sky-high. If you looked north toward Charlottenburg Palace, you could make out, even from a distance, the damage to the structure caused by the 250-pounders falling from the RAF Mosquitos as they swept over the city from east to west. The Jews who came to the agency in tattered coats and threadbare dresses enjoyed a few moments of uplifted spirits when they reached the building. Surely this was a sign that impossible things could happen. Not one bomb had struck the building? Then there was hope.

The officers of the agency were highly motivated people and although capable of smiling, rarely did so during working hours. It was their task to find homes for any surviving Jews of Europe who came seeking help. The home that was commended to them was Palestine. Grow oranges, strawberries, tomatoes. Mix the sweat of your brow with the soil of your ancient homeland. Sit in the shade of the trees you raised yourself. There is no shade like the shade of a tree grown in Israel, the Israel that is to be. In the channels between the trees, freshwater runs. Dip your hands into the water. Wash your face and hands in the honored way. But you could turn the suggestion down if you wished. Tea and biscuits would still be offered; a home somewhere else would be found for you—maybe Vienna, if that's where you once lived. Maybe Berlin. Maybe Budapest.

.　.　.

THE YOUNG MEN and women of the agency had heard stories of suffering from Jews of twenty or more nationalities between June 1945, when the agency was set up, and November of the same year, when Hannah and Lette came looking for help. Whatever their feelings as they listened to the stories, they kept them to themselves. They had known of the camps before they came to Berlin from Palestine, and their purpose. They didn't yet know the exact number of Jews who had died in the camps and elsewhere, but they had an estimate close to the figure that emerged from painstaking investigation a few years later. They kept a disciplined space between themselves and atrocity. They'd been trained to think practically, and to say few words when the people who came to them spoke of their daydreams. "In Vienna, twenty-five of us, they can't all be dead, find my sister, find my mother." The only conceivable consolation for a past that had been destroyed was a future of safety, forever. And so, Israel. The orange trees, the shade.

· · ·

HANNAH HAD BEEN given an address at Anhalter Bahnhof by a young man, plainly dressed in a black coat and trousers, white shirt, and with a healthy glow about him. Quite handsome. He gave Hannah a slip of paper printed front and back and said, "Go here." Below the address, in four languages—Hungarian, German, French, and Hebrew—the words: *For your relief.*

Hannah said, "You are Jewish." A statement.

The young man said, "Of course," in Hebrew. They nodded at each other.

It took four hours to reach the address in Charlottenburg. The city was broken, a mess, and so many checkpoints. Who had papers to show at such a time? A few buses traveled short distances, no tickets required. Otherwise, Hannah and Lette walked. The most common expression on the faces of the Germans on the streets was one of sullen endurance. Even children wore that look. Also resentment. Of whom? Their Führer? The occupying forces? Perhaps simply for the misfortunes of life. Among the debris modest crosses had been erected, many of them. Some had names written on them in pen, in pencil, or etched into the wood; some were bare. The lettering of shop signs amid the rubble conveyed messages of a commercial life that could not now be imagined. LEBENSMITTEL FUR SIE. ALLES IST FRISCH. BILDERRAHEN. CHIROPODIST NACH VEREINBARUNG. KUNZ UND SOHNE BESTECK UND KERZENHALTER. People could be glimpsed in the debris—faces peering out of pits and hollows, eyes shining with hunger. Hannah saw a child who could have been Michael's double, and her heart stopped. She called in Hungarian: "Who are you?" The child ducked out of sight. Hannah muttered to herself: "What's happening in your head?"

. . .

AT THE AGENCY, an efficient young woman who spoke German with an accent took them to a desk, recorded their names and dates of birth, then, in a calm monotone, asked them about their experiences. "Auschwitz," she said. "You came in '44? From where? By what means? With your family? A husband, a child? Tell me about the selections. Your child was selected? I am sorry to hear that. And his name? And his age? Do you know the names of any women who were selected? Do you know where they came from?" The young woman wore small earrings, amber in a gold setting. It was an odd effect she created; a touch of allure—but here, asking about Auschwitz? So sober otherwise. Lette asked about her husband. It was a difficult question for her to ask. Lette had willed her husband to be alive for months and months. The calm young woman consulted a bound folder of many pages. She said, "Mrs. Rosen, we have nothing. I am sorry."

. . .

To BUDAPEST, THEN, if it was possible, and it was. Not so many soldiers making the Budapest journey, and only six carriages. The engine was even more ancient than those on the Polish line. It was as if the Russians had developed an affection for an earlier era of steam locomotion. Until you saw the Soviet big shots boarding at Leipzig, pickled beyond affection for anything at all. They called coarsely to Hannah and Lette and waved a bottle of brandy.

.   .   .

No MORE BODIES, thank God.

The countryside had returned to its priorities. In Bohemia, winter was gathering, the broadleaves almost bare. Beyond the grassy verge of the rail line, red deer in groups of four grazed close to safety on the fringe of the forest. Was it madness to imagine what Hannah imagined? In summer, a trip by train to the forest outside Budapest, a picnic, red wine, the sun striving through the foliage? Only without Michael. Only without Leon. Could that be imagined? Oh, for a moment, for two moments. Then, no.

CHAPTER 24

⁓

March each year, Tom sent the lambs to the Garland & Garland slaughterhouse, past the cemetery in a small homely town left over from the gold rush. He held them back this year to concentrate on picking the apples, the nectarines, the pears, all ripening freakishly at the one time. Orchards up and down the valley were producing no more than an average crop but at Tom's place the trees had gone berserk. Theories were offered. Tom's drainage and irrigation system, so carefully attended, had saved the roots from any damage in the flood. That was science. Witchcraft was also suggested. Hannah the Jew had fashioned a spell from Hungary, or maybe from a book of charms that Jews were known to keep under lock and key in their what-do-you-call-it, synagogue.

This, according to Pearly Gates, president of the Hometown branch of the Returned Soldiers League. Pearly's strain of anti-Semitism took in only primitive Jews (he'd seen one) who wore peculiar clobber, fancy hats, and not, for example, Sir John Monash, the finest soldier of the First World War and an educated man after whom a university had recently been named. A Jew like Hannah (such was her cunning) could keep a bookshop and still be primitive. It had to be conceded that

Hannah exacerbated Pearly's prejudice, well known in the town. He came into the shop one day looking for a Golden Book (*The Little Red Hen* was his choice, a grandchild's birthday) only to have Hannah tell him that she kept a black rooster on the farm that could speak Hebrew.

. . .

THE CES SENT Tom four pickers in February, said to be experienced but in reality hopeless; frightened of ladders, flies, doodle-bugs, spiders. They were all one family, Assyrians from Turkey, accepted as migrants because they were Christian and spoke English: mum, dad, and two daughters. The father, Hector, had been an engineer back in Turkey (he'd altered his name and those of all his family at the suggestion of an immigration officer). He wore a beard that reached his chest and spent lunchtimes and smokos sharpening a knife with a twelve-inch blade. He kept a small black whetstone in his pocket for the purpose. And to demonstrate that any male Assyrian, even an engineer, knew how to use a knife, he skewered an apple on a branch with a throw of fifteen yards.

The daughters, Sue and Sylvie, fourteen and fifteen, went about the picking languidly, singing along with the Partridge Family on a transistor radio tuned to 3XY. The mother, Sharon, labored long and hard, but it took her five minutes to climb a ladder. And her picking technique was rubbish. In a day, she might fill a single bin rather than the four expected. At night they all four slept in the spare room. They removed Uncle Frank's paintings from the walls of the room and pinned up pictures of Turkey, crewelwork embroideries of traditional Assyrian designs, portraits of The Beatles, Mick Jagger, David Cassidy. They had to be roused at seven in the morning for breakfast, an entire sliced loaf, a dozen fried eggs.

The other picker was Bobby Hearst, who worked two weeks each summer for Tom. Up in the boughs of the apple trees, he sang and giggled, took a bead on "gooks" with an imaginary M14, and called ribald suggestions to Sue and Sylvie. Tom had to tell him that it was the custom of fathers in the land that Hector came from to cut the throats of young men who flirted with their daughters. Although with Hector, it was difficult to know exactly what the knife meant to him. He was more a philosopher than a janissary, leaning on his ladder as Tom checked the quality of the pears in his bin to speak about the inner life of trees. "They are creatures, same as you, if you understand. The fruit, this is the children. When I take the fruit from the tree, I say sorry. The tree tells me, 'It's okay. But plant the seeds.' In this world, Mr. Tom, how long we have been here? One hundred thousands of years? Trees, millions, millions of years. Millions." A civil engineer in Turkey, Hector had lost his job when the government listed him as a subversive. Tom, smiling, asked if Hector was indeed a subversive.

Hector shrugged. "Who can say?"

. . .

HANNAH PICKED APPLES when she could; maybe for an hour from five to six after her last student. Still plenty of heat in the sun when she climbed up into the foliage under a ludicrous straw hat the size of a Mexican sombrero—one of those occasions when she chose comfort over style. She picked by herself in the grove of Gravensteins that Uncle Frank had grown for some Austrians in Melbourne, who used it to make Obstler brandy, a big thing in the region of Austria they came from. She chose that grove to keep out of earshot of Bobby's war on phantoms. And it soothed her to be up in the foliage. She needed soothing. That thicket of thorns between herself and Tom, his love for the boy, his hope that Peter would come to him and stay. Hannah's heart was not a parliament; instead, three or four despots shouting at each other. And the loudest of the despots roared: *You will leave him. If the boy comes, you will leave him. But what insanity. I'll run from this man I love so dearly, this Tom? And live a life by myself? I will. I know it. I will.* Yet all the while pleading with Tom in words she never uttered: *Don't bring the boy here. Don't bring him. Don't bring the boy.*

. . .

UP THE LADDER one afternoon Hannah paused, and in that pause allowed herself to recall another orchard. She might have let her thoughts drift as she did now on other afternoons, but no. Why more willing this day? Only that she'd been brushing tears from her cheeks up in the apple tree. Only that the soldier had been weeping that day years past when she and Eva and Lette traipsed, starving, through Poland and found a shack in an orchard where they sheltered themselves from the winter. Eva, who knew, said, "It's a cider hut. In here they put bad apples for cider. With marks on them." The hut was bare. Eva and Lette huddled in their scraps of clothing on the earthen floor. Hannah went to look in all the places where food would never be found but against reason might be found, and found nothing. Until she did. High in one of the trees of the naked orchard, an apple: an apple that could not possibly be an apple because it was November and the harvest was four months past. And yet. Hannah climbed into the boughs and higher and with care plucked the yellow fruit as cold as a snowball, pushed it into her rags.

Before she could descend, a soldier, German, hobbled into view on the track below, struggling in his progress, capless, one hand held to his neck. A boy, fair-haired, sixteen, seventeen. He carried no rifle.

He stumbled and fell below Hannah's tree. She remained still, clasping a bough, barely drawing breath. The soldier, the boy, lay on his back in the blackening leaves gazing up at the clouds, sobbing loudly. Blood ran through the fingers of the hand he held against his wound. The escape of blood from his body kept time with his pulse. It had soaked the shoulder of his uniform jacket all the way down to the Wehrmacht Adler emblem over his breast pocket. He saw Hannah above him and let out a scream. He must have thought she was the angel of death in rags. His sobbing began again. He surely knew he would soon be dead. It wasn't the sobbing of a man but of a child, the mouth distorted, tears flowing. Hannah could see that his holster was empty and the idea came to her that she might climb down and comfort him. Then came another idea, more practical: that she might suffocate him. The sound of his sobbing would maybe attract Russians, because there must be Russians—who else would have shot him? And with Russians, you knew. They saw a woman, they thought of the obvious.

But no, she stayed where she was and watched the boy relinquish his life, sobbing until he stopped without any abatement. She continued to watch even when he was still, his eyelids no longer blinking, his mouth open in a rictus of grief. She climbed down, knelt by the body, and thought: *So tall for his age.* She left his eyes open when she might have closed them, feeling that the final gesture toward the dead shouldn't be hers because she didn't know him. She went through the pockets of the uniform hoping for food, a biscuit he might have carried, something. But his pockets were empty; not even documents; someone had already searched him; maybe the person who shot him. She rolled him over and searched his back pockets and found, dear God, squares of chocolate, *schokolade*, in a dark green wrapper. The German lettering on the wrapper read: *Unsere Jungs*. Our Boys.

Hannah forgot the soldier instantly, and hurried back to the cider hut with the yellow apple and the Unsere Jungs chocolate.

.   .   .

A BREEZE HAD come to the orchard. Hannah enjoyed its touch. Her wet cheeks dried. It seemed inconceivable that she would leave Tom if the boy came back. The breeze lifted the brim of her big straw hat.

This terrible obstacle to her happiness, just as the bookshop of the broken hearted was beginning to make its way. Better to think of success than the prospect of catastrophe. Hannah had recruited the CWA women to sell books out in the shire. They visited schools, service clubs, the regions' three libraries, and spoke at afternoon teas organized for the purpose of unloading books. The women earned half the profit for the CWA. This left Hannah with a skinny margin, but not too skinny. Selling books—it turned out, she could make her living. At about the level of a first-year post office clerk, okay. Nonetheless it thrilled Hannah. Look and see—a shop with a stock worth twenty-two thousand dollars, overheads, Maggie's pay. You could make your living. More than that, the writing of men and women of genius in the bookshelves of houses in the thirty-two towns of the shire, maybe *Such Is Life* sitting next to the folded pink sheets of the *Sporting Globe* on a bedside table, maybe a bookmark in *Middlemarch*. Okay, lots of nonsense, too—*Kisses at Midnight, Kisses for Breakfast*— but Hannah considered the nonsense at least in the family: Nina and her bosom in *Kisses for Breakfast*, her pancake brain smothered in sugar and clotted cream, was the cousin of Dorothea Brooke—you would admit it, if you were not such a snob.

Hannah had no sense of mission; no desire to convert the masses to art. But she kept count of the books she sold. Her target was twenty-five thousand, the approximate number of books burned in Berlin on May 10, 1933. At the moment she was selling around 110 books each week with the help of the CWA. So, four years, five years. The delight for her when someone emerged from a house in the town, from a farm-house twenty miles away and brought to the counter a book that the students had set ablaze: *The Trial, A Farewell to Arms, Civilization and Its Discontents, Women in Love, Anna Karenina, The War of the Worlds, Ulysses.*

Hannah was often surprised by who bought what. *Civilization and Its Discontents* was purchased by an aged woman with awkwardly applied lipstick who got about with the aid of two cane walking sticks. She was the grandmother of the Hometown GP, Bob Carroll, fetched out of Ireland in her widowhood. As it transpired, one of the first women admitted to Trinity College Dublin, back in 1910. The one copy of *Ulysses* went to Des Bond, a retired high school principal who'd come to live in Hometown with his wife for the sake of the trout fishing. He was reading his way through a list of classics from *Punch* he'd been holding on to for thirty years.

. . .

THIS WAS NOT Budapest, the big apartment off Andrássy, nor the smaller apartment on Nagymezö where she lived first with Leon and then with Stefan. Everyone who came and went there had read everything, mad people with mad politics and all of them dead now with all of their appetites. No one postponed reading books until retirement. Yet the Hometown people, the shire people were to be valued; very far from Bohemians, but dear to Hannah. Here, Adolf Hitler would have brayed in vain. Maybe. Days came when she wanted to throw open her arms in the doorway of the bookshop and say— Well, what? Something impossible, something offensively patronizing, such as: "God knows what's going on in your Australian heads, but I like you all the same."

· · ·

THE HARVEST WAS eighty-seven bins above the previous year; cannery prices were well up because of the flood. Spring lamb was also likely to be boosted; thousands of sheep had drowned. Tom factored the high fruit price into what he paid Hector, his family, and Bobby as an end-of-harvest bonus of fifty dollars. For the pickers, the bonus came out of the blue. Hector in his gratitude made his daughters dance a sort of Assyrian polka for Tom on the rusty soil of the orchard. He said that he would come back when his papers were recognized by the Australians and build Tom a dam. "You think I will forget? Never, Mr. Tom. Five meters deep, rammed earth, across the middle an iron bridge. Woo ho!"

· · ·

HANNAH MADE A meal with an Assyrian complexion for the final evening. Judging by the too-ready chorus of compliments from Hector and Sharon, with a few subsidiary words of milder praise offered by the daughters, the dishes were a failure. Considering the amount left on each plate. But the shared meal and the shared wine gave Hector an opportunity to more fully express his vision of a Turkey running with rivers of blood. It was not enough for the Turks that they'd murdered the Armenians—who may or may not have deserved it, who can say— but then they had to butcher the Assyrians? That was a day of evil;

many days of evil. But an army was being built, said Hector, a secret army, men who were shopkeepers by day and assassins by night. And the time would come, God would see to it, when Turks in their thousands died in their beds.

Sylvie the daughter said, "Oh, Dad, nobody cares."

Sharon said, "The *biryani*, Hannah! Too beautiful. The potatoes a little more time in the frying pan. Next time."

Hector told stories of massacres. His voice took on a chanting quality, as if something related to the sacred should be invoked for such tales. Bobby, who was also at the end-of-harvest dinner, lapped it up. He said, "Man, let me at 'em. Fucking Turks. Sorry." Sylvie and Susie teased him by pushing their breasts out and inhaling and exhaling deeply.

Tom looked at Hannah, and Hannah looked back. She had no stories of her own ordeal to offer. Her face was a mask. Tom could only hope that Hector's tales would not reach a point at which the Jews were added to the Turks as enemies of the Assyrian people. But no. Just the Turks. Hector did point out that Assyrians and Australians had a kinship in blood spilled by Turks. Gallipoli.

CHAPTER 25

Murder in the bush, murder in the big city—not the same thing. Most murders in the country occur in the afternoon, for one thing; in the city, at night. There's a greater candor to the country murder, enacted in the broad light of day. And its contemplation is brief and direct, the commitment arrived at casually. No tussle with the devil, and no great to-do when it comes to concealment. The deed and its consequences are grasped together, as if the murderer had muttered, gathering his gear, rifle, blade, "Might hang for this."

Bernie Shaw was a newcomer to Hometown; eight years at State Rivers on Hydro Road, transferred from somewhere down south. He'd come with his wife, Lou. No kids, but Bernie kept a big, dopey mongrel, Huey, that he and Lou adored. After years of comfortable domesticity, Huey had been led astray to Henty's paddocks by a feral from the tip, a genuine outlaw, half Huey's size but a big enough complement of pure evil in his heart for both of them. They went killing. Huey discovered an aptitude for it, until, his face buried in the hot guts of one lamb after another, he missed Henty's scent. A hollow-point .303 bullet carried his hind legs away. Henty strode down, cut the beast's throat, and read the information conscientiously inscribed on

Huey's tag, including an address. He returned the carcass to Bernie and Lou's house in Commonwealth on Australia Street, but at ten in the morning of a workday, only Lou was home. She screamed, she carried on, maybe not properly grasping that in sheep country a dog that went crazy in the paddocks was wearing a target.

Later in the day Bernie, in a suit and tie, turned up at Henty's house with a .22 and shot Henty's wife through the head at the front door, then shot Henty himself in the workshop, not once but five times, reloading after each discharge. He drove the half mile to Tom's across the highway to tell him what he'd done. Bernie had picked fruit for Tom during his annual holidays from State Rivers, off and on, paid work, not this year. But why choose Tom? Because he could be counted on to keep calm? Something like that?

Tom was up in the slough paddock tending a ewe that had gone loco, attacking other sheep without any clear motive. He heard his name called down at the house and raised a shout. A figure appeared at the gate in a suit and hat. *What the hell?* He watched as the figure negotiated the gate. Bernie Shaw, a rifle in one hand, suitcase in the other. Tom didn't think Bernie's rifle anything odd, not in this heavily armed shire. The suitcase, though. That was peculiar. And the hat and tie.

Bernie said, "Tom, I shot Henty and his missus."

"What?"

"Yeah, twenty minutes ago."

Bernie waved a hand in the direction of Henty's place. "Twenty minutes ago," he said again. "Both dead. You'll want to be letting Kev Egan know."

Tom looked at him hard. If Bernie had gone mad, that would explain the shirt and tie and suit coat, the polished black shoes.

"You shot Henty? You shot Juliet?"

"I did, yeah."

Tom had been holding the loco ewe by the fleece. It had a maniacal glint in its eyes. He gave it a slap across the nose, then let it go.

"Let's have the gun, Bern." He accepted the rifle from Bernie, drew the bolt. It was unloaded.

"Okay, show me," he said.

He strode with Bernie to the ute, leaving the rifle standing against the wall of the workshop. Bernie climbed in the ute's passenger side, brushing the seat down first, hoisting the cuffs of his trousers. He placed the blue suitcase between himself and Tom and rested his hand on it.

"Ready for the clink," he said.

Tom said nothing.

·   ·   ·

ONE NEAT HOLE between the eyes for Juliet. She had collapsed on her knees in the doorway, the screen door wide open. Juliet had been something of a rural beauty, smooth complexion, dark arched eyebrows. Murder had left an unattractive grimace on her lips. Tom let her remain where she was after feeling for a pulse and followed Bernie down to the workshop. Henty was on the floor with his knees up, his head and face a mess.

No pulse.

Shells lay scattered on the clean-swept concrete floor. Henty had been a fastidious man in his habits, despite neglecting his sheep. On shelves and racks along the walls of the workshop, lengths of timber were stored up off the floor, sorted according to length.

"Dead all right," said Tom. He'd been kneeling. Now he stood and put a hand on Bernie's shoulder. Bernie was on the short side and had to raise his chin to look Tom in the eyes. The tip of his nose was red and shiny, as if an alarm had been activated.

"Bernie, what in the name of Jesus?"

Bernie raised his shoulders a fraction, then let them slump.

"He shot Huey."

"Huey?"

"Our dog. Huey."

Tears rushed into Bernie's blue eyes.

Tom nodded, partly to show Bernie some understanding, partly in confirmation to himself that the man was insane.

"We're going inside to ring Kev," he said.

Bernie said, "Yep. Yep. I'm good and ready."

. . .

THE LAW TOOK charge of Bernie. Father Costello took charge of the souls of Augustus and Juliet Henty. A long line of cars with headlights on rolled at a walking pace from St. Benedict's on Federation Hill, down Alfred Deakin Way to Mercer Street, over Top Bridge and up Old Melbourne Road to the cemetery. Father Costello drove himself from the church to the cemetery in his old blue Fiat at breakneck speed (that was usual) and was waiting graveside in the Catholic sector when the mourners arrived. Among the mourners, the two Henty daughters, Bea and Pip, tall, fair girls with their mother's good looks, back from teachers college at short notice. Bea was bleached white by grief; Pip, the elder daughter, was cool, composed. Later, at the reception (the Mechanics Institute rather than the farm, which, after all, was a murder site), Pip spoke to Tom of her father's three thousand sheep, what was to be done. Did he know, did anyone know? Tom said he'd tend them for the short term. Pip nodded. "Do you want to buy them? Do you want to buy the farm? It's no use to us. I never liked it here. I like Glenferrie. Not here. That man, he's mad, is he? Who shot Mum?" After a pause, she said, "And Dad."

Tom said, yes, Bernie Shaw was mad. And he told her he didn't want to buy the farm.

. . .

OR MAYBE HE did. Over the month looking out for Henty's sheep, he thought, *It's not impossible.* The paddocks that stretched back to the base of the pasture hills were underlaid with a rich, humid soil that had washed down the slopes over the ages. That soil threw up moist grasses all year round. Henty, who hated sheep, had run only the minimum he needed to make them pay, but it was clear to Tom that the back paddocks could feed twice the number. Henty's five thousand trees—apples and pears, ill-tended, rarely pruned—perhaps. With the canneries paying high. Also, down by the oxbows Juliet had recently prepared a half acre for strawberries—an experiment that she was not fated to see through. So that, too—the strawberries.

Hannah said: "Tom, you want it, buy it."

They were looking about Henty's place in the evening a week after the funeral. The magistrate who would sit as coroner, Ted Beach, had called by earlier in his old red Riley to take a quick look at the scene of the murders. It was Ted who'd given Tom's idea of buying a nudge along. With Henty's sheep and his own, Tom would have enough hoof to give guarantee of supply and in turn get himself preferred status from Garland's. Same with the fruit: preferred status at the canneries. Ted had land of his own down the valley and knew what he was talking about. "Look to it, Tom. You'll thrive." Then added, "Unless someone shoots you. Ha! Unless someone shoots you, Tom."

. . .

SET BACK FROM Henty's house and sheds stood a two-story barn built by the Germans who'd farmed the spread in the decade after the Great War. A superb piece of work on foundations of hewn granite so solid that every upright, every spar, remained dead square against a spirit level. In 1928, the Germans, the Baughmans, sold up and moved to South Australia to join a bigger Lutheran community; crazy, because the farm was thriving. The barn was too big and too peculiar for the Sullivans, who succeeded the Germans. Or for Henty, who bought out the Sullivans in 1950. It had been built to cater to farming practices a little alien to local husbandry.

At ground level, it was divided into stalls and enclosures for the horses, but with offset entrances, so that the horses needed to negotiate a turn before they were free. The idea was that if the swing door of the stall had been left open, the horse would still stay inside rather than make the turn, until urged. The roost for the chickens was attached to a pulley and hook, and a rope over the hook lifted the roost clear of the barn floor, out of reach of foxes. A device had been fitted, also dependent on pulleys and hooks, that made sure the roost rose evenly. On the interior, the walls of the barn were paneled in pine planks of a quality that would, in this day and age (so Tom told Hannah), be reserved for furniture. Hay was stored on the second story—not a loft, but a fully built second floor with three trapdoors, the biggest for the hay; another for—probably—clean grain; another for silage, as Tom guessed. And look at this. Grooves chiseled in the granite-slab floor ran down to a gutter that emptied into a pit outside the barn, overgrown now.

"For what?" said Hannah.

"Slaughtering," said Tom. "Pigs, sheep; bullocks, could be. To let the blood run away. Good Lord. Thought of everything."

Stairs instead of a ladder led to the upper story. Hannah wanted to see. The ceiling above was of pine planks, the same as the walls. The space between the ceiling and the tiles was big enough to act as a strorage area with space to stand. Dust-covered, open-topped ply boxes, like tea chests but square, were filled with German magazines, German books, left behind by the Baughmans for some reason. Hannah hovered over them in a chirruping rapture, using her handkerchief to clean the dust from the magazine covers. *Jugend, Simplicissimus, Pan, Puck.*

"Tom, how can this be? These are art magazines, and satire. For a German farmer? Whose taste was this?"

"Don't know. I only know what Uncle Frank heard. Germans, four kids. Don't know."

"And the books, the books."

Carpentered into the front of this attic area, below the shallow gable, a mullioned window with a latch and hinges. The glass was crusted with grit. Tom worked through the rust of the latch with his pocketknife, forced the window open. He and Hannah stood with their upper bodies in the air looking out over the farm all the way to the river, the hills, the billabongs, the sheep in the lush north paddocks.

Hannah said, "We'll sell the shop. The new shop will be here."

"What?" Tom stared. "Will we?"

"Do you see?"

"No."

"Don't you see?"

"A bit. Do I?"

She was laughing. "Don't you see? The books." She gestured at the plywood boxes. "Tom, my darling, it's a sign."

"'A sign'?" he said. "You?"

Hannah famously did not believe in signs.

"Why not? My mind is changed. Signs are good. Signs are every-where. The sign of the Germans. 'Hannah, you pretty Jewish girl, use our barn for your books, please do.'"

Tom reached up under Hannah's loose red blouse and placed his hand on the small of her back. A ripple ran through her flesh. In Hannah, the world; in him apples and pears, the sheep, the points that needed resetting on the ute. But between them, a living current.

He wanted her to gaze at him in the way she had, as if she were too crazy for ordinary love; as if in sheer excess she might take his hand and bite it. She did, sometimes. He wanted it this way—that she had more power, more anger, more glee, greater ambition.

"Han," he said, "people won't come here."

"You think?"

"It's a farm. People won't come way out here to buy a book."

Hannah smiled. "I will make them."

CHAPTER 26

The people of Budapest, including Hannah Babel, came to understand that the Russians had the final word. Usually the Russians made their wishes so known behind the scenes that it wasn't necessary to say anything publicly. They were discreet even in such matters as murder. Bodies were never thrown out on the street but were buried quietly. So far as possible, the impression should prevail that the Hungarians were deciding their own future. The Hungarian Communists of 1919, who'd hoped for so much, had been allowed to return from exile in Moscow, to resume their careers. The Russians said, "Don't go crazy," and the gray-haired men and women accepted the suggestion, but with a certain amount of heartburn. A democratic election was held in November of 1945. It was not unrealistic to think that the people of Hungary would appreciate what the Russians had done for them in the months since the end of the war—broken up the big estates and redistributed the land to the poor—and so vote for the Communist Party of Hungary. But no. The Hungarians voted in a party of conservative, churchgoing peasants who approved of the land reforms but spurned the architects. Feelings were hurt. The Russians, from 1946 onward, dispensed with niceties and strove to establish a one-party socialist state. They succeeded. Of course.

.   .   .

HANNAH, BACK IN Budapest early in 1946, walked straight into the apartment on Nagymezö that had been her marital home up until 1944. No reason to imagine that the apartment would still be unoccupied, but it was. A beautiful place, nouveau, richly colored windows in the two bathrooms and the living room. Beautiful, except for the painful memories. Michael, Leon. Some of the household bits and pieces she'd left behind when the family fled to the countryside were there when she returned. Most, in fact. Only the two blue sofas were gone; the rugs; the wooden table from the larder. Even the paintings remained, until she sold three of them at bargain-basement prices in order to eat. When she tried to imagine some sort of plan, a future, all she could think was: *Futile.* The ambitions of obstinate, hateful men had picked her up and hurled her across borders, and now a new set of ambitious men had taken over the task. But at least she knew the Russians, understood them. They would not give Hungary back to the Hungarians. She would have to find ways to exploit them. An advantage was that she now spoke their language fairly well. Only don't reveal it too quickly. Choose your moment. They would be suspicious, and in a Russian, suspicion rouses the remedy of a prison term. She knew she must handle it carefully.

She came to know that a certain captain in the military contingent attached to the political wing was a little less adamant than his comrades; had been seen to smile. It was his task to go about with a 35mm Leica taking pictures of anti-Russian graffiti on walls, but he also enjoyed snapping pretty girls. Looking out through the window of a shop in Lipótváros, she'd seen him with his ruddy boy's face and wet pink lips hailing women in horrible Hungarian: "Russia! Ivan! Take nice pictures!" The younger girls hurried away, but the women allowed him to do what he wanted. They were looking for an opening, an opportunity to ask a favor, maybe Ivan could find them some stockings or a butter ration.

One of the lanes off Deák Ferenc Utca attracted patriots every night and the Russian captain went to the lane each morning to record the infamies. Hannah dawdled in the lane at the right time, applying lipstick (from Torun; also the beautifully modeled compact mirror) and dressed in a way that showed off her figure. The youthful captain appeared on cue, caught sight of Hannah, and jogged up the lane beaming all over his chubby face. She allowed him to blunder along in Hungarian for a minute or two before telling him in Russian that she spoke his native language. He stomped about on the cobblestones in a fit of delight. He wanted to take her to a café. Yes? Did she agree? She did. Tea and cakes, photographs of his wife and three-year-old daughter. And of an icon he'd rescued from the ruins of a church in Lódź, kept as a curiosity. Ha ha! Would Hannah pose for him? Not in the street, in an apartment he shared with another officer in Belváros. She would.

. . .

THE APARTMENT WAS surprisingly bright. Hannah had expected something squalid—a place away from the barracks where the captain and his comrade enjoyed the women they picked up. It was swept clean and dusted; dishes were drying on the sink. The floors were bare, but not raw. A portrait of Comrade Stalin hung above the varnished mantelpiece in the place that a crucified Jesus would once have occupied. Two neat rooms at the back, a narrow bed with clean white linen in each. The windows of the sitting room opened onto a street of shops and the traffic below. This housewifely tidiness was the taste of the captain's comrade, Vassily Vassilovitch, a shy, dark-haired lieutenant from a suburb of Leningrad. Hannah saw in him immediately the type of boy who endures painful thoughts of naked girls day and night, replete with declarations of love. She saw, too, that her cheerful captain would want to photograph her naked. She would decline, but would lounge about for him, perhaps pout. And when the time came, ask him to find a job for her in the Szabó Erwin Central Library. Her university qualifications would commend her, up to a point.

.   .   .

THE CAPTAIN ACCEPTED in good grace Hannah's refusal to undress for his camera. He photographed her in what he termed his "classic" style, but now and again asked her to look more "casual"—smoke a cigarette, gaze into the lens with her chin resting in one hand, a teasing smile. Vassily Vassilovitch bought her perfume—purchased or informally acquired—and cooked for the three of them. The fact that Hannah could speak Russian endeared her to the captain and the lieutenant so completely that force was never a threat. The Russians were permitted to kiss her on the cheek, fondle her hand, but further than that—no. She heard everything there was to hear about Ivan's family, about Vassily's parents and his lame sister, consoled them when they wept (all the time), toasted Comrade Stalin with beer, brandy, vodka. They danced polkas and waltzes—the gramophone and records obtained almost legally when Ivan Ivanovich tipped off a tobacco merchant about the coming state monopoly on cigarettes: The gramophone and records were the merchant's expression of gratitude for being given time enough to unload his stock.

. . .

A POSITION AT the library. What could be done? Budapest was governed by a municipal authority, itself governed by a Russian general. At the level of minor municipal appointments—librarians, for instance—the Hungarians could please themselves. No one-time fascists, no anti-Communists; otherwise, go ahead. The Russian administrators were more concerned with hyperinflation. Ivan spoke to a political officer who kept watch on the general's staff and on the general himself. The political officer was indebted to Ivan Ivanovich for procuring high-quality black-market coffee and Crimean cheeses. He told Ivan Ivanovich to send Hannah to the library on such-and-such a day and ask for such-and-such a person, who would put her on the payroll. She would be paid in rubles. Not very many, but better than the Hungarian rubbish. As for actually finding some way to occupy herself at the library—well, if she wished.

She did wish. Of the twenty library personnel, most held sinecures and had no competence with books. A few were passionately mad about the collection. Hannah aligned herself with the passionately mad while contriving to keep her wits. The chief of the library, an anxious, exhausted man in his seventies with a habit of sighing at the start of a sentence, told Hannah it would be her task to check the volumes for signs of wear once they were returned from the thirteen reading rooms. And to check, twice daily, that the books had been placed in their correct place on the shelves, which they never were. The library collection was superb, books in seven major languages and also in minority languages of the Austro-Hungarian Empire. The building itself was a neo-Baroque monstrosity. Once a palace, glitter and gilt and mirrors and varnished teak were everywhere. But surprisingly easy to get used to. Best of all, the books. She was happy to discover that the library had never been subject to a purge of Jewish authors. Hannah in white gloves turned the pages of pre-Renaissance manuscripts, some with finely carved pearwood covers, the illuminated vellum heavy in the lifting.

. . .

LETTE CAME TO Budapest to make her home after two years in Debrecen. The mourning for her husband was over and a new husband had taken his place: Isaiah, an architect. Almost impossibly, he'd survived the labor squads of Jews that the Hungarians and the Germans had worked to death in the last year of the war. Wife and husband moved in with Hannah, and in this way Hannah came to meet Stefan, Isaiah's nephew, twenty-seven years old, one of the few Jewish men of his age left alive in Hungary. He'd lived a feral life on the streets from April 1944 until the arrival of the Russians in early 1945. Handsome, confident, full of a violent, nihilist energy, he came to dinner at the apartment and sat humming songs from Hollywood movies. He shrugged when asked to speak, but then, without warning, began to babble.

Isaiah had asked a question about the intentions of the Russians when it came to the Jews. "Oh the Jews, the Jews, I met one the other day, the most elaborate fairy story he told me in his tallit and tefillin and his lovely little kippah. Even the Nazis had a more plausible yarn to tell. Even the Russians. I had to strangle him."

Isaiah smiled. "Nobody takes you seriously."

"No, no—don't take me seriously. Don't take what comes out of my arse seriously. Don't take my piss seriously. Nothing, please! Except this."

He picked up a banana from the fruit bowl—Lette had found two of them in the Armenian market.

"Please take my banana seriously. Of course! This is a very serious banana."

He was attracted to Hannah. He said he would marry her, take her on a honeymoon to Niagara Falls and throw her off. He was studying at the drama and film academy, but fitfully. "You know the best film you will ever make?" he said to Hannah. "The film you don't make. Plan everything first. Write the script. Find the actors. On the first day of filming, fire the actors and burn the script."

But in bed, he clung to her like a child. A gang had cut his back with razor blades to make him admit he was a Jew, which he was. He'd escaped, but the scars remained. Hannah soothed him. It was only in the dark that he could endure tenderness. She grew exasperated in the light due to his scorn for her insistence that there was better and worse in people. And especially his mimicking of her words of love and concern.

"I am Stefan Sweetheart," he said. "I am Hannah's sweetheart. Call me 'sweetheart,' and I'll call you 'my darling.' I am the darling sweetheart, and you are the darling sweetheart. But Lette is not the darling sweetheart. Lette is the dearest dumpling. Lette is the dearest dumpling of Isaiah. Plump and content."

Nevertheless, Hannah married Stefan. He said, "Well, we choose our fantasy, don't we? This is a nice fantasy, a marriage, a chuppah, a little old rabbi from Kecskemet with long gray whiskers. Bad teeth, but who can be fussy after the Nazis?"

He was a drunk, but not the worst sort. He didn't lash out. Instead, he sat with his bottle and amused himself by dreaming up schemes that appeal to teenage boys: building underground ant colonies for humans and melting the polar caps with atomic explosions so that Budapest could have a beach. Other ideas he chose for their offensiveness: Auschwitz could be turned into an amusement park. Lemonade would fall from the showerheads. Cakes would be baked in the ovens.

At times the marriage disappeared. Stefan would go missing for weeks. Hannah would search for him all over Budapest. She found him living in a shack on the riverfront, in an abandoned biscuit factory, in the ruins of a Jewish nursery. He was attracted to sites of dereliction; any place that breathed squalor, hopelessness. It made him happy in some way only he understood to have his feet in a puddle of mud with scraps of windswept rubbish forming heaps against broken walls. And Hannah thought: *Why did I marry him? I'm a nursemaid. What was the point?*

Maybe she thought he could be made new. Maybe he could be persuaded to wear a clean suit, attend the academy each day, set aside his bottle, feel love or at least a little warmth stirring in his heart. Hannah wrote his assignments, those that had to be completed on paper, wrote his scripts, but the filming she couldn't master. He was thrown out of the academy, a day of triumph for Stefan. He took up painting again for a few months—his first love. He painted Hannah naked three or four times a week. And girls he met on the street.

. . .

HANNAH FOUND HIM a position at the library; invented a position. He was to fashion a new catalog in Latin. He spoke Latin, of course he did, in its desuetude it was the perfect language for him to have mastered. No such catalog would benefit anyone, but at the pace that Stefan worked it would take him a hundred years anyway.

By good fortune, the work suited him. He immersed himself in past ages in the way he gave himself to dereliction, and Hannah realized for the first time that, for Stefan, squalor was an escape. Such relish of buildings in ruins, empty lots full of debris. And the past was an endless expanse of waste, of dead time where nothing could happen ever again. Hannah was right about the pace of his labors: He spent months creating entries for the ten volumes of a fifteenth-century study of the soul's anatomy.

. . .

SHE ADDED WATER to everything he drank, tiny amounts, secretly, and in this way, by slow degrees, reduced the quantity of alcohol that entered his system. It surprised her, but did not bother her, how readily she adopted deceit as a tactic.

An odd effect of Stefan's being more conscious at any given time was that he became involved with a gang of desperadoes from the university and the arts academy, old friends who had staked everything on getting rid of the Communists. The apartment became the meeting place of these boisterous people. Lette and Isaiah, who saw trouble ahead, moved out. Isaiah told the students they were mad if they'd thought the death of Stalin would change anything in Eastern Europe. "Do you know who comes after Stalin? More Stalins!" Hannah was sure that Isaiah was right, but she lent herself to the moment, permitted herself to soak up the glee of Stefan's friends, prepared meals for ten and fifteen people at a time, let her waist be encircled by the arms of exuberant young men who relished the idea of taking her to bed (that she did not permit) before they went out to murder their enemies.

But why did it matter to Stefan, the revolution? Democracy, this is what he wanted? When Hannah questioned him, he became uncharacteristically coy. "Well, you know, a little liberty, who can complain?" The high delight in his eyes when he hurried out the door with his friends carrying hessian sacks full of bottles that would become Molotov cocktails.

November 4, 5, 6, 1956—that was his life. Three days. And when he came back to the apartment on each of those nights he made love to Hannah like a crazy person, after many months of barely touching her. He'd climbed onto a Soviet tank with Milan from the academy and helped him spike the muzzle of the cannon. Heady days! And then he was dead, carried back to the apartment and stretched out on the kitchen table, a hole the size of a billiard ball in the white flesh of his breast.

Hannah closed his blue eyes, kissed his lips, walked through the maelstrom of the battling streets to find a rabbi. After Kadesh, Paul, the leader of Stefan's cohort, honored him with an epilogue. "The bravest of us. Nothing stopped him. A warrior for freedom."

Hannah, watching, listening, said to herself: *That's it for me. No more husbands. All they want to do is die.*

.   .   .

THE RUSSIANS HAD their victory. A puppet government was installed. Within a month, the furnace of revolution had cooled. People said: "This is our lot, then. Live with it." Those who couldn't live with it were shot or imprisoned.

.   .   .

THE LIBRARY REOPENED after a short interval. When Hannah returned, she spent more and more time reading in the stacks. She thought, *Life, I don't care. Books, so much better.* She read through every-thing from the Renaissance, and later: eschatology, the exploration of the New World, manuscripts on bird life. By some quirk of admin-istration, she continued to be paid rubles, both her own salary and Stefan's. After a further three years of indulging her sinecure, she made up her mind to migrate. To somewhere. America, it could be. England. France. Australia? Now there was a coincidence. She'd been reading an article in the *TLS* about the fiction of Patrick White. Was this a sign? No. But then she decided it was, and began enquiries. With her languages and her qualifications in music, she could teach high school children in Australia, so it was revealed. It would take years, she was warned. Years and years. Best get started. Australia. Really? All she knew of it was Patrick White. Oh, and kangaroos.

CHAPTER 27

Hannah bought a used FB station wagon and drove it about the state gathering boxes of books, sometimes five hundred volumes at a time. She was aiming for a stock of thirty thousand, which the new shop would easily accommodate. When had she been happier?

. . .

THE BOOKSHOP IN Hometown was sold to Andy Coombes, the dentist, who intended to set up a fishing emporium with a complement of books about trout and cod. Maybe a couple of copies of *The Compleat Angler* to give the collection a bit of class. All this for his retirement, still ten years off; the shop would be tended by Kerry O'Connell in the meantime, famous in the shire as the man who landed a five-pound rainbow with a twisty on a three-barbed hook.

. . .

BIGGER THAN ANY vehicle she'd driven, the FB. It thrilled her. Her little Austin was gone, traded in, she didn't miss it. In Templestowe she purchased the entire library of an Italian scholar who'd died six months earlier and carried it back in the FB in two trips. His grown-up children said, "Take the books. You want to pay something, one hundred dollars." He'd been a professor at Milan University before his kids brought him to Australia on retirement. Everything was in English, his teaching language. His ex libris plate read, in English: *Emmanuel Vittorio del Pierro owns this book.* In Italian, too, and a woodcut of a skull with long hair.

. . .

SHE WENT EVERYWHERE, the countryside vivid after the autumn rains; even in the far northwest. Tom came with her just the once, to a deceased estate in Nagambie. He was insanely busy on the Henty farm and with all the carpentry at Hannah's new bookshop. Hector and Sharon took over the running of Uncle Frank's property in a shared-profit arrangement. They lived in the Henty house. The two girls, Sylvie and Sue, went off to high school each day, singing together in their sweet, soft sopranos as they waited for the bus on the highway: "These Boots Are Made for Walkin'," "Yellow Submarine," "Raindrops Keep Fallin' on My Head."

The new bookshop, the German barn, would stock on the upper floor the secondhand books that Hannah had fetched from far and wide. The new books from the Hometown bookshop would be stocked on the ground floor. Tom built the shelves from the store of cedar timbers he'd used for the old shop. These shelves were taller than the first lot; Tom had to install running ladders on both the ground floor and the upstairs. He set Hannah to work polishing with beeswax the aged pine timber of the wall and floor, all of it free of knots: good, clean bright planks nine inches wide. One afternoon, dripping wet after dealing with a suicide pact by twenty sheep to drown themselves in the river, he found Hannah sitting on a saw bench lost in a novel. She looked up and smiled. "Tom, you've been swimming?"

He lost his temper with her for the first time. Did she think this was a holiday camp? Did she think that the shop would ever open if she sat on her behind while the floor waited for her to finish a chapter? She recoiled from his anger, as if she'd been about to spread her arms but now had to take two steps back.

"Tom, I'm sorry."

"Well, I'm sorry, too, Han. I'm sorry I can't rely on you to hold up your end. That's all I'm asking. For you to hold up your end while I hold up mine. We're not in Budapest with your arty friends. This is bloody Australia!"

She had to laugh. "'In Budapest with your arty friends'?" The laughter came bubbling up and spilled out almost in Tom's face. "Tom, dear Tom, I'm sorry, sorry, sorry. Oh, goodness!" And the laughter came bubbling up again. Instead of hurtling forward in his anger, Tom stopped himself and smiled. He saw what she meant.

Hannah jumped up and kissed him.

"My 'arty friends,'" she said. "Madame Babel and her arty friends."

"It makes me sound like a yokel, doesn't it?"

She held him close. "Madame Babel and her arty friends invite you to the opening of her arty bookshop. Her bookshop and Tom's— Tom the cocky. He'll wear his work boots for the occasion and say, 'Gor blimey!'"

"Australians don't say 'gor blimey.' Cockneys say that. You ignoramus."

"Oh, so you're a cocky but not a cockney! Silly Madame Babel. You should make love to me. You know? Why don't you take me inside and make love to me, Cocky?"

He did. Despite everything. Then returned to work on the bookshop in dry clothes.

. . .

As GORGEOUS AS the Hometown shop had been, the barn surpassed it. Hannah fixed her Hebrew signs to the glass door that Tom had installed, so this was still the bookshop of the broken hearted. Hannah took out ads in the literary quarterlies, *Meanjin* and *Overland*; in the *Age* book section, and in Rupert Murdoch's *Australian*. The CWA ladies remained as busy as ever on the bookshop's behalf. Hannah gave lyrical talks at all the schools of the shire on the benefit to the soul of reading. The students listened alertly, more because the lady was possibly mad and might do something interesting.

She kept the ads in *The Age* running for three months, all she could afford. Readers of the ads were made aware that the experience of browsing in the barn on the idyllic Henty spread would act as a gladdening agent on their hearts—words to that effect. A little excessive, but this was advertising, so.

. . .

THE NEW BOOKSHOP of the broken hearted opened without fanfare in the spring of 1971, just in time for the first visitors to go gaga over the antics of the new lambs. And astonishingly, they came. Better still, they bought books. The trip from the city had to be justified. There was a new taste abroad for Australian literature, and books by locals were emphasized in Hannah's ads: YOUR COUNTRY. READ IT. *Bring Larks and Heroes* and *Picnic at Hanging Rock* were both popular. And by a happy coincidence, the bookshop was conveniently close to such established tourist attractions as the granite bridges and the gold-mining sites at Mississippi Hole. Worth a look.

Maggie came to work full-time at the shop. As if to announce her commitment, she took up her gorgeous black tresses and bunched them on top of her head. And she wore her spectacles, which had been set aside while she'd waited for her absconding boyfriend to repent and return to her embrace. The boyfriend and his absence no longer tormented her. Hannah had to wonder whether Maggie had modeled her new self on librarians in Hollywood movies, and was maybe destined one day to loosen her hair, discard her spectacles, and win the heart of a handsome stranger.

. . .

AND THEN ON a day of sunshine and bird chorus came the letter from Tennyson and Moore, and the thriving structures of happiness and plenty that Hannah and Tom had labored to set in place faltered and fell.

CHAPTER 28

⁓

Pastor sent Trudy's mother, Monique, and sister, Tilly, to talk sense to her. She had been saying that her son must go to live with Tom. She said this was what Peter wanted, too, as he'd told Pastor.

Pastor said to Trudy, "Do you consider yourself incompetent? You're saying you can't raise your own son?"

And Trudy said, "Yes, I'm incompetent and I can't raise my own son."

Trudy's mother and sister knew that it would do no good to tell Trudy what Jesus had to say about obedience and families; Trudy didn't like Jesus these days. She was insistent: Peter must go to Tom. She had done a bad, bad thing in taking him away from Tom to start with. And the punishment must stop. It must.

. . .

WHAT TRUDY MEANT was the thrashing. Peter was thrashed weekly now. No other child had ever been punished so regularly. Compelled to watch, Trudy believed that she would do anything to stop the punishment, the strap. She didn't know what she would do to stop it, but she was getting desperate. Her entire life seemed to her a blunder—one long blunder. Away from the punishment room, nursing her distress in bed while her son was locked in another room with a bolt on the door, she whispered to herself: "That man loved you. Didn't you see?"

.   .   .

PETER ALSO WHISPERED. In his own narrow bed, he said: "I don't care." But he did. On punishment days, he had to put himself into a trance; stop believing that anything was real, even pain. It was easy to ignore Judy Susan when she twisted his ears and pulled his hair. He didn't care about her. He saved himself for his sessions with Pastor on the front pew of the church. Pastor sat sideways on the pew, his head turned toward Peter, legs crossed, his elbow resting on the upright part of the seat, chin in his hand. He smiled in a kindly way throughout each interview. Peter didn't respond to any question put to him. Remaining silent was the one pleasure in his life.

"Peter, do you know what it means to live in the love of Our Savior?"

"Peter, do you know how dark Hell is?"

"Peter, do you understand that Judy Susan punishes you out of love?"

It was Pastor's practice to set a piece of paper on the pew between himself and Peter. His questions were written on the paper, also arrows pointing to notes on the side of the page. Peter read what he could of the notes in brief glances. Does he know that he is being cruel to God? The comfort of J—remind him. And on this day the word *guardian* in a circle.

"Do you know what the word *guardian* means, Peter? It means I will be in charge of you. I will be your father."

What Peter would have said if he'd lowered his dignity and addressed Pastor was this: "You can't be my father because Tom is my father."

Pastor said, "There will be punishment. I know your backside is still sore from last Monday. It hurts more when your backside is still sore, doesn't it?"

Peter didn't reply.

"And, Peter, not ten but twenty. I won't tell Mr. Bosk to stop. It will be twenty."

Peter shrugged. At seven years old, he was intuitive enough to see that he was the winner every time Pastor gave him punishment. But this was no more than any torture victim grasped: There was no sense of triumph in it. It didn't stop the hurting. And it hurt a lot.

Pastor shifted on the seat. Peter noticed that he raised one finger on the hand resting on his knee. It was a sign of impatience, Peter guessed. Good.

"I want to tell you a story," said Pastor, "about the days before I found my brother in Jesus Christ." Pastor shifted on his seat again. "I was an engine driver for many years, Peter. Many years. I drove locomotives all over this state. Freight trains, passenger trains. Judy Susan was not my wife in those days. My wife was Margaret. She gave me two sons, Walter and Carlisle, from Margaret's maiden name. You know what a maiden name is, Peter?"

Peter might have shaken his head without breaking his vow of silence. He didn't.

"That's the woman's family name before she marries and takes her husband's family name. Margaret Carlisle. She gave me my two sons, Walter and Carlisle, as I said. My two boys were killed in their teenage years, Peter. They drowned in the rip at Kilcunda, one trying to save the other. Strong, handsome boys, clever boys. But they drowned in the rip at Kilcunda. Peter, do you know what is meant by a broken heart? Probably not. It is an ache in your heart that won't give you any peace. A broken heart. My heart was broken, Peter. Margaret's heart was broken in half. Then the nosebleeds came and Dr. Smithers down in Moorooduc sent my wife to a specialist. Do you know what a *specialist* is Peter? An expert. He found a brain disorder. My wife Margaret lost her wits and was placed in an institution. Jesus Christ came to my aid. Strong love, Peter. Strong love. When Margaret lost her battle, I took Judy Susan as my wife. But Jesus Christ I took as my brother. And, Peter, I will lead you to Jesus if it costs me my life. I will." Pastor prodded Peter's chest with his finger. "You can go."

· · ·

THE STORY MEANT little to Peter. It wasn't even true. Margaret was still alive. She worked in the kitchen, old and frail with only a few tasks to occupy her. And silent, except when she spoke to Peter. Not many words at a time but always gentle. There was nothing wrong with her brain.

What troubled Peter was the "guardian" thing. If Pastor became his father, he would kill him. Exactly how, he didn't know. But he would kill him.

· · ·

THE PUNISHMENT WENT ahead as scheduled. Twenty cuts with the strap. Mr. Bosk paused at fifteen, but Pastor nodded instead of stopping the thrashing. Peter bled. Trudy shrieked. Tilly seemed about to object, but in the end, kept quiet. Peter, for the first time, cried out as the final blows landed.

CHAPTER 29

❧

Eyre Heath Moore of Tennyson and Moore advised Tom in writing that his former wife, Gertrude Christina Hope, presently of Jesus Camp, Phillip Island, had expressed a wish to place her son, Peter Carson, presently of Jesus Camp, Phillip Island, in his, Tom Hope's, permanent care. Would Tom be further advised that Pastor Gordon Bligh, presently of Jesus Camp, Phillip Island, had made application to the Department of Child Welfare of the State of Victoria to be appointed legal guardian of Peter Carson on the grounds of the mental incompetence of the mother, Trudy Hope, herself presently in the care of Pastor Bligh at Jesus Camp, Phillip Island. No application for custody would be made by the child's father, Barrett Carson, who had died in Brisbane in October of 1969. If Tom wished to exercise his legal rights in this matter, Eyre Moore urged him to seek professional representation. Tom would find enclosed four letters written to him by Gertrude Hope over the past six months. The letters had been confiscated by Pastor Bligh, but had now been released on the advice of Eyre Moore. A total of sixteen letters written to Tom by Peter Carson, also confiscated by Pastor Bligh, were cited by Eyre Moore, but they had not been forwarded to Tom since they included unsubstantiated claims of a problematical nature.

. . .

TRUDY'S FOUR LETTERS were the one letter written four times. The first sentence of each letter read: *You will only see this letter if Pastor says it's okay.* Tom had postponed telling his wife of the letters (what they revealed wouldn't be welcome news to her), but now, sitting at the kitchen table at ten in the evening, he handed each of the five letters to Hannah, beginning with Eyre Heath Moore's communication, and proceeding to the earliest of Trudy's four.

> *Dear Tom,*
>
> *You will only see this letter if Pastor says it's okay. Dear Tom what a bad wife I was for you! You loved me deeply and I didn't care! But now there is something so important to tell you. It is this. I want Peter to live with you. It is not a good atmosphere for him at Jesus Camp. He wants you. He has tried two times to get back to you and now Pastor has locked him up first at night but now in the day too. Peter is so brave. I am proud of him. But Dear Tom, I am a bad mother and I don't take proper care of him but I love him only I am not such a good mother and things get all mixed in my brain because of the bad mistake I made you remember, when I left you not one time but two times and there was that horrible time with Barrett who I'm glad to say is is now dead in Brisbane. Peter loves you and I know that you truly love Peter, that's the only thing I properly truly understand, Dear Tom. He must be with you. I know that you are married again*

and I hope this is a happy, happy marriage for you this time. I hope that your new wife will love Peter, that is my true hope and that Peter can live a happy, happy life on the farm.

Your wife in the past times, Trudy, dear love

Hannah sat hunched in her chair. All that was vivid in her had drained from her face. Knowing what she would say, Tom readied himself.

"Of course the boy must come to you," said Hannah.

Tom said, "Yes."

"And I must go."

"No, Hannah. No."

"Yes, Tom. I will not live with a child. Not again."

Tom had hoped he could talk her round. He still hoped he could. She was too certain in things she said. Too dramatic. He would talk her round. He had talked her round a couple of times in the past. She would let him. She wouldn't carry this thing as far as leaving him. Pray God.

"Put it aside for now, darling. We'll talk about it tomorrow."

Hannah didn't reply. But had he ever seen her so gray, so haggard? He picked up her hand from the table and kissed it. Her fingers clenched.

"Pour me a drink, Tom."

"Scotch?"

"Brandy."

Tom poured the brandy, in pain. They had never discussed this, husband and wife: What would happen if Peter came back? Because they knew it would be the end of everything, that Hannah would retreat into a cave of wraiths.

She drank her brandy slowly, shuffled to the bathroom, cleaned her teeth. In bed, Tom held her close. He said: "Darling, my beloved, blessed Hannah. Never leave me." When he woke with the alarm at five—later, because Hector and Sharon handled the milking now—she was gone.

CHAPTER 30

APRIL 1966

She sailed from Bremerhaven for Melbourne in a Danish liner full of optimistic Dutch families. Nine weeks after embarkation, she was teaching the children of a town in the Mallee the songs of Schubert and Cole Porter. It was April of 1966. The children were sick of Schubert as soon as they heard him but quickly became enthusiastic about "You're the Top."

The Education Department provided a house for her on a dirt road that went out to the orchards. She was required to share the house with a highly strung redhead named Rhodie who cried in the morning before school and in the afternoon when she came home. She said that the boys in her classes were rude to her. Hannah said: "Slap them." Rhodie tried slapping, but wasn't good at it. After a fortnight of sobbing, Hannah marched into the poor young woman's most troublesome class with a Beretta pistol that had once belonged to her second husband. She placed it on Rhodie's desk and said: "Use it if you have to."

. . .

THE HOUSE WAS a little starved of furniture and ornaments. Most of Hannah's belongings were yet to arrive in Melbourne, including her piano. She tacked up three of her lovely Coptic appliqués of boys and girls with curly black locks carrying water jugs from a stone well. Thus encouraged, Rhodie drew from a huge wooden trunk a number of strange sketches of a man in a black helmet. Hannah was amazed by their originality, having expected in her snobbish way (as she conceded) sentimental renderings of young women reading love letters.

"They're by a man my mum knew before she got married," said Rhodie, gratified by Hannah's enthusiasm. "He's famous now."

Rhodie always remained at the school until five, attending meetings in her conscientious way and preparing lesson plans for the next day. Hannah came back to the empty house in the afternoons baffled by this latest landfall in her ludicrous journey through life. She sat on the back step with a gin and tonic, gazing out over the unfenced backyard with its giant peppercorn in one corner, its dusty patches of lawn. The weather was scorching hot every day. She enjoyed the heat, the only feature of her new home that had made her happy. The blue of the sky was many shades deeper and more insistent than anything she recalled from Europe. Her spirit was intimidated. She was used to gazing at beauty with her soul streaming toward the source, empty of every fear in her being. Here, baffled, daunted. Who owned this land? It was said that the local black people kept to a camp out of the town. She thought: *Let me see them.* But her colleagues at the school said no. The black people would tell her nothing.

. . .

Nevertheless, she went. Without much experience driving, she'd purchased an old car, an Australian car, with the steering wheel on the right, quite odd. A map had been drawn for her by Byron, a friend, less conventional than others at the school. "Show respect, I don't need to tell you." She crossed a big, dirty river lined with slumbering gums, the foliage a mess, like a woman who has risked the disaster of cutting her own hair. On the far side of the river, rough tracks headed off into the scrub. She took what she hoped was the marked track and became lost within minutes when it came to an end. Backing, she jammed her car between two gums with pale trunks. It was a simple matter to follow the track back to the road on foot but Hannah lost herself again and again. She laughed, then became afraid. This was the most implacable silence she had known in her life. Except when birdcalls broke it, and crashing sounds in the scrub. Then a hostile screeching like an attack of harpies, and a great number of white birds with yellow crests passed overhead. In the late afternoon, the sun still hard and bright, she was found by a family of the black people she'd been seeking. They stood in her path: two women; a tall, grinning man in jeans and a T-shirt; three barefoot children. She stopped in her tracks.

"What's happen, missus?" the man said. "You getting lost round here, eh?"

The children and the two women laughed, true mirth.

Hannah gestured behind her. "My car . . ."

They led her back to her car in ten minutes. One of the children, a boy, walked beside her chatting nonstop about the town of Mildura, the ice creams found there, the picture place, the cars. Along the way, one of the women stopped Hannah and indicated that she should remove her high heels and walk barefoot. She did as she was told. It was apparent that the black people, the Aboriginals, considered her a complete idiot, poor thing.

The man—the father?—freed the car from the two trees with ease. Hannah had imposed enough. She didn't ask to be guided to the camp. Should she offer money? She had carried her bag with her on her hopeless tramp along the tracks. Would it seem rude, a ten-dollar note? She held out the note. "For ice creams," she said. The man shrugged. The talkative boy took the money with a whoop of delight.

Hannah was urged to drive her car slowly, while the family followed. They kept just behind her until she reached the road. She stepped out of the car and shook the man's hand—he'd given his name as Jonathan—thanked him effusively, thanked all the family. Then drove home. Rhodie was in bed with Kurt, the German math teacher who'd come to Australia under the same arrangement as Hannah. Rhodie was mortified; Kurt, not so much.

On the back step, in the twilight, Hannah sipped her gin and tonic. The family had spoken their own language most of the time. The sound of it in her ears pushed into some back room with her Hungarian, German, Russian, English. Byron had told her that a party of Aborigines had marched to the German consulate in Melbourne after Kristallnacht to protest the Nazi treatment of Jews. On the step, thinking of the black man, she said, "Now I see." She thought of the white tribes of the world stepping off their ships to subdue people who were not white, and who had only a rudimentary understanding of firearms. Or none. Inside the house, Rhodie and Kurt were having a row. She heard Rhodie crying out, "Yes, but when, when, when?"

Hannah's employers sent her to Swan Hill, further down the river, after four months at the Mildura school. She was bitterly disappointed and phoned the Education Department. She ended up in the hands of a senior official who said simply, "You signed the contract, love." She had grown fond of Rhodie, and frankly doubted that the poor, foolish girl would survive without her. And she was fond of Byron, who had shared her bed, respite from his four demanding children and justifiably suspicious wife.

. . .

THE HOUSE SHE was given in Swan Hill was pretty much the Mildura house all over again. Peppercorn, parched lawn, no back fence to interrupt the view from the back step of paddocks taking on a green winter tinge. She shared the house with a young woman as neurotic as Rhodie, and just as pretty. This new young woman's name was Stephanie—Steph—and she used the same phrases in her arguments with her boyfriend that Rhodie had favored. "You're the Top" was once again popular; Schubert once again was scorned. A feeling of arrested motion troubled Hannah, not merely in the duplication of houses and housemates, but in the unawareness of the people. She liked Australians: good-natured, but not so much change from person to person. In Budapest on any day out walking, you knew you passed scoundrels, visionaries, tyrants, angels. Here, no. People always smiling, always cheerful. Too much. Often, her expressions were misjudged. She meant something wry, satirical; the Australians thought she was being nasty. And dear God, the Terylene. The women wore Terylene.

. . .

FROM SWAN HILL to Hometown, after five months. By this time Hannah's belongings had arrived, the piano most importantly. She was given a house a bit out of town on the road to the tip. The pretty first-year teacher with whom she was meant to share the house, Valerie, had a vexed relationship with her boyfriend and harrowing difficulties with the second formers. Nothing new there. With the best will in the world, Hannah couldn't find the optimism to negotiate the whole absurd business a third time. A month into the new year, she found the house on Harp Road and moved out. She didn't know if she could go on teaching. Her allotment was dominated by first formers. The boys were older than her son had been before Auschwitz, but in one child here and another there, she noticed mannerisms that brought him back with uncanny force and detail. On those days, a bleakness like the coldest day of a cold winter marched into her heart and her blood flowed like a torpid ooze.

She advertised for students. Piano, flute. Parents at that time had been roused by an unseen force to invest hope in their children's talents. They were avid to hear their son or daughter picking out Beethoven on a keyboard, Mozart on a flute. Hannah had more than enough students to support herself, if she should choose to give up teaching at the end of her contract. And she did so choose.

CHAPTER 31

He woke in the dark muttering to himself like a crazy person. He said again and again: "She'll come back." Anger took hold. What was she asking? That he turn away this boy who was desperate to live with him? She couldn't ask that.

His progress about the house always ended in the same way. He dropped down in a chair at the kitchen table and sat shaking his head, helpless. He saw shadow shapes in the kitchen, like the ghosts his wife had gone to live with. Hannah was his blood and breath. In the crowd of the world, they were both marked with the stain of meeting. He saw her among the shadow shapes and pleaded with her to return.

He went all over the town looking for her, then all over the shire. He carried a picture of her, head and shoulders. "Have you seen Hannah? Have you seen this woman? It's my wife." One afternoon in a place she would never have come to, a small town on the northern reach of the river, he saw her vanishing around the corner of the post office and left his car in the road to chase her. He called her name. Each time he caught a glimpse of her it was just as she was disappearing, rounding another corner, or suddenly on the other side of the road with a log truck in between. Then no more glimpses. He was losing his mind. He was seeing things. He asked the postmaster if there were any strangers in town, a woman of forty-six, pretty, long curly hair, a red station wagon.

The postmaster, in his bifocals, said, "Nope."

Tom said, "Can you see properly through those things?" He didn't mean to be rude, but it was taken that way.

He worked until late each day to compensate for the time lost on his desperate searches. Hector pitched in. He worked on both farms. He said, "Mr. Tom, she won't stay with this boy, this Peter. Okay? But listen to me. My civilization is three thousand years old. Everything has happened many, many times. So, we know. And I tell you this woman, this Hannah, she loves you. Yes, yes. I can see it. She will come back to you. Because there will be no life for her. So she will come back. The Nazis, fuck them for what they did."

. . .

HE HAD TO think of other things, of Peter. He drove up to Shepparton to see Dave Maine once more. Good news. Changes to the law meant Tom could legally be recognized as one of the adults in the boy's life with a valid claim to custody. Dave, in the same fawn suit he'd worn two years earlier, asked Tom to confirm that he and Trudy had been married all the time the boy lived with the two of them. Yes, they'd been married. And Tom had acted in the role of father, was that right? Yes, that was right. "If the mother is judged to be mentally incompetent, strictly speaking you're the next in line, Tom. By the new rules. You've acted in the role of father for five consecutive years. But your ex–old lady, Tom, it sounds as if this 'mentally incompetent' thing is self-diagnosis. Is that your impression?"

"I don't think a doctor has been involved, no. She's come to feel that this Pastor Bligh is a dud. She wants to get Peter out of the place."

Dave Maine paused to think, kneading the saggy flesh of his face with both hands. "You see, Tom, the law takes a dim view on self-diagnosis of this sort. Prefers a few learned letters after the name of the individual making the call. The child welfare people might attempt their own assay, or send this Gertrude, this Trudy, off to a clinic. Perhaps she's just exhausted. Well, ninety percent of the mothers of Australia are exhausted at any given time. Can't have them saying, 'I need a sleep, take the kid.' And why doesn't she simply walk out? She could bring this little Peter to you, hand him over, go on her way. She can't do that if she wants the whole thing stamped and dated, of course."

Tom nodded. "Dave, I reckon she's frightened of Bligh. But she won't leave Peter in his care. Herself, yes. But not Peter. There's some grit in her."

Dave Maine would make enquiries. And send notice to Trudy and Bligh that he had been retained by Tom Hope. But Tom, with no guarantee that any letter posted to Trudy would reach her, had Dave Maine draft the letter then and there and took a copy away with him. Three days later he left Hector and family in charge of everything and drove to Phillip Island, to Jesus Camp. He thought all the way not of Peter but of Hannah. *What if I knew I would never see her again? How could I love Peter? How would I do that?* He had heard the story of Hannah's boy vanishing. All around her, the huts and fences of a place made for murder. That grief in her heart, she was shorn of her hair. Every glance on that day seeking the boy, and the next day, for two weeks. Until a Polish wraith, a Jew in authority, three years in Auschwitz, told Hannah Babel that the boy, this Michael, had gone up the chimney. Nothing of him remained. Not a tooth, not a toenail. Tom said as he drove to Jesus Camp: "I'm sorry for your boy. But you must come back, Hannah."

· · ·

JESUS CAMP LOOKED deserted. Tom scanned the buildings and the grounds without seeing a soul. Then a child, a young girl in the shapeless green tunic of the place, appeared beside him from out of nowhere. She stood there, perfectly at peace, humming a tune. Tom asked her where he could find Pastor Bligh. The girl broke off her humming to say: "Pastor's in church."

Sunday. Of course. The girl pointed toward the church building, topped by its oversized white cross.

"Everyone's not here," she said. "Everyone's in Big Church. I don't go."

"Don't go to church?" said Tom. He'd crouched down to talk to her. She would have been six? Her hair was a thriving mass of dark curls, her eyes jet black. Hannah's hair. "Why's that?"

"From screaming," said the girl.

"Really? Why?"

"Things," said the girl. Without warning, she let out a shriek so loud that Tom sat back on his heels in alarm.

"Like that," said the girl.

"Yeah, that's a scream," said Tom. Then: "Mum and Dad?"

"Mum's in Big Church. She always sends me out from screaming."

"What's your name, sweetheart?"

"June."

"June, do you know a boy called Peter?"

"Yes."

"Is Peter in Big Church?"

"Yes. At the front."

"And Peter's mum? Is she in Big Church?"

"Peter's mum is Trudy."

"In Big Church?"

"Yes. At the front."

Tom strode to the church. June saw fit to follow. A hymn was being rendered—"How Great Thou Art." The volume increased when Tom opened the heavy timber door. The crowd within filled the church and its annex to bursting. The congregants stood shoulder to shoulder, some holding small children aloft, maybe for the sake of gaining a view of Pastor Bligh. Still keeping up with the hymn, people turned to look at Tom without any approval in their glances.

The church was spare in its ornamentation and art; walls and ceiling painted white, no figure of Jesus, a single vase of yellow chrysanthemums standing on an oblong table beside a white crucifix matching in miniature the one on the exterior. Rows of varnished pews on each side of an aisle ran down to two broad steps leading to what served as an altar, just the table with the flowers and the white cross, and a plain timber lectern. Arched windows of stained glass on each of the side walls depicted John the Baptist on a riverbank, and John's head on a big golden plate. The plate had been wrought in such a way that it could also have been taken as a halo.

Pastor Bligh in a white vestment stood at the lectern, big-framed, powerful. His thatch of white hair gave him a daunting Old Testament look. He was roaring out the hymn—no voice louder—head raised, arms outstretched. The accompaniment was provided by a Hammond organ played by a woman with hair as white as the pastor's, dressed in a jarring tunic the color of a mandarin.

Tom, taller than most, strained to see Peter and Trudy at the front but was thwarted by the congregants bobbing as they sang. The pastor, though, saw Tom. His gaze fixed itself on him. At the conclusion of the hymn, he signaled for quiet, and was obeyed.

"A visitor," said the pastor. "Mr. Hope. Mr. Tom Hope." Faces turned to Tom. "I'll ask you to wait outside until we conclude the service, Mr. Hope. If you would."

A commotion broke out at the front. Trudy and Peter had both come to their feet and were seeking Tom in the crowd at the back. Tom waved to make himself more visible. Trudy wasn't nimble enough to move herself through the pack, but Peter was. He dived and crawled and wriggled his way to Tom's arms, and was held high. The boy kissed Tom all over his face, like a dog in a transport of affection. Tom laughed and squeezed, but he was the only one laughing. The expressions on the faces of the congregants were puzzled, or else censorial. When Trudy had battled her way to him, Tom accepted her kiss. But dear God! Trudy, what a wreck, her eyes sunken in bruise-colored flesh, her hair hacked into untidy tufts.

"Tom, Tom, take Peter and run away," she whispered. "Take Peter and run."

The crowd parted for the pastor. "You'll come with me," he said to Tom, and led the way out through the annex to the open air. Peter remained in Tom's arms, his skinny legs wrapped around his waist.

The destination was the pastor's office, a fibro building with a double lock on the stout green door. The pastor applied two keys, swung the door open, and with some impatience waved Tom and Trudy inside. The walls were hung with framed photographs that depicted the pastor in younger years, posed beside locomotives and on the platforms of stations, and one in a boxing ring, gloves raised.

Pastor Bligh drew his vestment over his head and draped it on the back of an old-fashioned swivel chair. He stood in a short-sleeved blue shirt and braces, dark trousers, black shoes.

"Mr. Hope," he said. "Mr. Tom Hope."

Tom freed an arm from the boy and accepted the pastor's offered hand.

"I'd prefer to be clear straight off, Mr. Hope. If you don't leave the property, I'll knock your block off. I promise you that."

He said this with a broad smile, as if he wished to split the impact of his greeting between geniality and menace.

"You probably want to leave here with Peter. You can't. Peter stays here. Trudy stays here."

Trudy spoke up in a wretched, pleading voice: "Pastor, I want to go. I don't want Jesus anymore. I want to go."

"And I tell you that you will not go. I tell you that for one final time."

Peter turned his face from the pastor and tightened his grip on Tom.

"You can't keep Trudy and Peter here if they want to leave," said Tom. "They've both made it clear that they want to go."

Pastor Bligh, candidly unconcerned, lifted his chin and nodded. He reached down and opened a drawer of his desk.

"You probably don't know, Mr. Hope. Trudy signed a document before a doctor and a justice of the peace declaring herself incompetent to care for Peter, and requesting that I take on the role of guardian. This was—three days ago, Trudy? Three days ago."

Trudy let out a wail. "Tom, I didn't want to! I didn't want to!"

Pastor Bligh displayed the document he'd taken from his desk drawer, holding it up by the two top corners.

"Tom, I wanted him to stop hurting Peter. Tom, Pastor hurts Peter. With a strap. He hurts him."

Tom stared at Trudy's pale, drawn face, her lips weirdly distorted, downturned, as if arrested in the middle of a scream.

"What?"

"Pastor punishes Peter, Tom. With a strap."

A red mist descended. Tom lowered Peter to the floor. He took a step toward the pastor.

"Do you hurt this boy? Is that true?"

"Do I hurt Peter? No. His disobedience hurts him. His lies hurt him. His betrayal of Jesus hurts him."

Tom's hand shot out and grasped Pastor Bligh by the throat. Tom had never fought in his life; never seized a man in this way. But he was exceptionally strong. He could heave a full bale of hay from the paddock to the third stack on a truck; lift a red gum post and drop it vertically into the prepared hole.

"Now, you listen to me," he said. "If you hurt this boy again, I'll do you harm, Pastor. I promise you that."

He held the pastor by the throat a few seconds longer, for emphasis. Still enraged, he spoke brusquely to Trudy: "This has to be done by law. I've got a copy of a letter from Dave Maine for you here. Read it. The same letter's on its way to you by registered mail."

Tom turned to the pastor and struck him across the face with the back of his hand. The blow knocked the pastor two staggering steps sideways, left his hair disarrayed and his lower denture askew. He sat himself down heavily in the swivel chair and after a pause of a few seconds, hastily reset the denture.

"Is that enough?" said Tom. He seemed in a mood that could accommodate murder.

Pastor Bligh lifted a hand in concession.

Tom reached down and lifted Peter.

"This has to be done by law, Peter. You understand? It has to be right by law. I'll come back for you and take you to the farm. I'll come back. For now, stay with Mum. This man won't hurt you again. For now, stay with Mum."

Peter nodded in the grave way he had, his eyes level with Tom's.

To Trudy, Tom said: "Look after him. I'll be back."

He took a step toward the door, then in what seemed an after-thought, turned back and kissed his ex-wife on the forehead.

The little girl, June, was standing by herself on the path of white pebbles that led to the office. Tom paused to place a hand on her head of dark curls and thank her. Just as he reached the fence, June's ear-splitting scream arrested him. She was still standing where he'd left her, her gaze on him, clapping her hands together softly and slowly. "It's loud!" she called out to Tom.

CHAPTER 32

June's scream had been heard so often on the grounds of Jesus Camp that it no longer startled anyone. Pastor Bligh, staring out the window of his office to where Tom Hope's ute was parked, paid the girl and her madness no attention at all. He was waiting for Tom to climb into his vehicle and depart. His mind was made up. When the ute left, he said to Trudy: "There will be punishment." And then: "Remain here. Remain standing. Touch nothing." He locked the door behind him, obviating his command to Trudy, and strode to the church. The congregants hadn't left the building, hadn't even seated themselves. Nor would they, without Pastor Bligh's say-so. He made his way through the congregation to the altar, raised his hand, and spoke the prayer of completion. "You may depart," he said. He was aware that almost all of those present would have noticed the welt on his face, and the blood that had dried under his nostrils. He called to Mr. Bosk: "I'll require your services, Leo."

. . .

TRUDY'S SISTER, TILLY, and mother, Monique, were summoned to the kinder playroom. And Judy Susan, who had been told of the confrontation with Tom Hope and had ministered to the dried blood on her husband's lip with a damp cloth. Scarlet with anger, she declared that she would herself bring Trudy and the boy to punishment, accepted the keys from Pastor, and made it her business to deal out some advance slaps and ear-twists. "We will have two very, very sorry people in a few minutes," she said. "Don't count on tears. Tears will get you nowhere."

. . .

TRUDY HAD MARRIED Tom with no more than five minutes' reflection. Periods of protracted thought had got her nowhere, so she adopted the first thing that occurred to her, such as leaving Tom, teaming up with Barrett, ditching Barrett and returning to Tom, leaving Tom, joining the Christians of Phillip Island. Passing the kitchen, it occurred to her that she could duck inside and arm herself with the trimming knife she used in stints on the meal-preparation roster. Thus inspired, she shrieked: "Run!" and Peter took off, chased by Judy Susan. The congregants were still dispersing, among them a number of men and women and children who responded immediately to Judy Susan's cry of: "Stop that boy!" Trudy, at the same time, hurried into the kitchen, where Pastor Bligh's first wife, Margaret, was at work on the mutton. Trudy glanced at the knife in Margaret's hand, looked at Margaret, that seamed face blanched with regret, implored the woman wordlessly to yield the blade. Margaret returned Trudy's gaze, then averted her eyes, as if she needed privacy for a few seconds. She opened her hand and allowed Trudy to take the knife. Trudy slipped it up the sleeve of her green tunic and pulled the cuff down over her hand. By the time she stepped back into the chaos outside, Peter was being returned to the jurisdiction of Judy Susan by Nicky Mack, a brawny fourteen-year-old, who had the boy in a neck hold.

"Got him, Missus Bligh!"

Judy Susan congratulated Nicky and charged him with the responsibility of hauling Peter to the playroom, where his punishment awaited him. As a reward, Nicky would be permitted to watch the thrashing; act as a witness. Nicky was well pleased at the time. But not so much when later he was required to give a statement to the Newhaven police and found it difficult to remember anything except the blood.

· · ·

IT WAS THE pastor himself who bared Peter's behind for this session of thrashing. Leo Bosk, presented with the thick leather strap, realized that something was badly wrong. And was troubled. He had no desire to apply the strap to the livid bruises on Peter's buttocks, and he doubted that Pastor Bligh was in his right mind. He'd never known Pastor to involve himself with a thrashing in this way, had never seen him moved by anger. Leo, with the boy already writhing across his lap, spoke up for himself: "Pastor, we shouldn't."

"You say what?" said Pastor Bligh. "You say we shouldn't? I say we should, and will, Mr. Bosk! It's forty strokes."

"Pastor, no. No."

Judy Susan hurried over to remind Leo Bosk that Pastor's word was law at Jesus Camp and if Pastor said forty strokes or four hundred, it was his duty, Leo Bosk's duty, to do what he was told to do, and with force.

Leo said, "We've got rules. Pastor's word isn't law. We've got rules.

And I won't do it, I won't strap this boy one more time. Look at the mess I've made of him."

Judy Susan, a hearty enemy of disobedience in the camp, or anywhere, spat in the face of Leo Bosk. She seized the strap as if she intended to administer the forty strokes of punishment herself. But she'd failed to notice a determination of a different sort that had come to life in Peter's mother. Uttering one emphatic word—"No!"—Trudy strode rapidly across the floor to Pastor Bligh and plunged the blade of the trimming knife into his stomach.

The pastor, startled, threw his arms forward and wrapped them around Trudy, and for a short time they seemed to dance, Trudy held upright by the grip of Pastor Bligh as he staggered left and right with his face upturned. Then he was dead on the floor, the bone handle of the knife protruding from his gut. Leo Bosk quickly lifted Peter from his lap, then knelt by the pastor to see if removing the knife would revive him. Judy Susan stood trembling with her hands in her hair. Tilly ran through a scale of screams. Trudy's mother bolted. Nicky gaped at the spread of blood on Pastor's blue shirt once the blade had been removed. Trudy went calmly to her son and pulled up his underpants and shorts.

Peter glanced once, then a second time, at the dead pastor. Trudy whispered to him: "The police will be coming." And Peter nodded.

CHAPTER 33

The CWA people accepted Hannah's judgment on everything to do with the bookshop and book sales, partly because it was her shop and partly because she was brainy and a Jew and would therefore know how to make money. Also, she had suffered in the war, the awful Germans, and probably knew what she was talking about when she said that Tolstoy and Dostoyevsky and Turgenev had to be in every school library. She provided the women with summaries of books she was trying to get into libraries; summaries that they read aloud to secondary school librarians. But Maggie's authority—Maggie who was struggling valiantly to keep the bookshop of the broken hearted afloat—no, they didn't accept Maggie's authority at all. When Maggie gave them summaries, the women said: "Maybe." And they left behind, accidentally on purpose, Patrick White and Joseph Furphy and Rolf Boldrewood. Jane Austen they were willing to concede. They said: "We know what they want, love." Hannah had ordered fifty copies of *Where the Wild Things Are* for primary schools before taking her unscheduled holiday, but the ladies left them to languish. Too odd.

Maggie wept, in secret. When Tom came in, as he did three or four times a week, she looked up from the counter with the question on her face: "Any news?" But she knew. Tom's expression was always stern, or withheld. He said, "Good on you, Mag. You're a wonder." Or "Good on you, Mag, keep it up." But he never said, "Can't say much, Mag, aching heart." She wished he would. Because she would say, "Mine, too. Where is she? It's wrong. Why has she gone? We love her, Tom."

· · ·

SHE CAME TO the end of her tether. She took the opportunity on a Friday when Tom called in to pay her wages to plead for information.

"What?" said Tom. "Pardon?" This was the Friday following the Sunday of his visit to Jesus Camp. Since then, he'd been told by Dave Maine that his ex-missus had murdered Pastor Bligh. Allegedly. And that Peter had witnessed the murder, alleged murder. Tom's response on the phone to Dave Maine had been: "What in the name of Jesus Christ?" And then, "I'm going to get Peter. I'm going now." Dave Maine had said, "Best not. Wait. In fact, definitely not."

"Tom," said Maggie, "I don't know anything. Tell me."

A second wife had run away from him. He'd rather keep it to himself. But overcame his reluctance. With Maggie sitting on the wooden stool behind the cash register, a husband and wife browsing upstairs, and Penny Holt on her day off from the grout factory looking through the Ladybirds for her granddaughter, Tom spoke in a low voice of Auschwitz; of Hannah's first husband, Leon, dead in a week; of her son, Michael, that was his name, who'd vanished forever. And Hannah's vow, that she would never again be a mother, feed and dress a child, read a child stories, sit at a bedside for hours and days depressing the boy's tongue with a spoon to open a channel for breathing,

whooping cough, murmur the prayers of her faith over his head, bless
God with shouts of joy when he recovered.

"And now Peter will be coming here to live, I think. I told you
about Peter one time."

"How?"

"How what?"

"How is he coming to live here?"

"His mum stabbed a pastor."

"What?"

"Have to go, Mag. Talk again later. You're a marvel."

. . .

HANNAH'S VOW. WHAT Tom didn't say, didn't think of saying, but
believed, was that all vows could go to the devil. That's what could be
teased out, picked out from the pain in his heart. All vows could go to
the devil, these stones set up as boundaries that endured the weather
and the change of seasons and would not alter when all around them
was altering each day; everything in the thriving world changing, but
the stones unaltered.

. . .

DAVID MAINE SENT a telegram: Call me, urgent. And a bit more.
Tom, who made sure he caught the mail each day, waiting on Hannah
as he'd waited on Trudy, read the message as soon as Johnny Shields
delivered it. Guesswork told anyone with an interest in the matter that
Tom had experienced the misfortune of a second wife running away,
and Johnny Shields waited on what he might be able to add to the
public's knowledge of the disaster.

"From Dave Maine up in Shep," said Johnny. "What's it say? Haven't read it, cross my heart."

Tom, frowning over the yellow slip, said, "Wants me to call him."

"Yeah? You gonna?"

"Yes I am, Johnny."

"About the boy? The little bloke you used to have running around here?" Johnny had developed, over thirty years as the Rural Mail Delivery postie, a psychic something or other that told him things he couldn't possibly know. It was accepted in Hometown, Johnny's knack, not as anything like nosiness but as a purely supernatural matter. He could also predict the weather, months off. He'd foretold the big flood, if only people had listened. His advice, in its brevity, was always sound.

"Get that little bugger back if you can, Tom. You were a happier bloke when he was here. Get him back." And he added, with less emphasis: "And the missus, too. Good sort."

After Johnny drove off, Tom went to a corner of the farm where neither sheep nor humans would find him. He sat on the trunk of a big ironbark that had fallen decades ago, the boughs sawn off to stop them from blocking the ute track, crusty bark falling away in clumps. The pasture hills where Matty Pearce's cattle roamed on agistment rose to the west, tinged green with the rains of autumn. The bracken had turned brown on the mid-slopes below the tea tree that crowned the hills, meaning that the foxes would come down in their autumn hunger and do crazy things to taste warm chicken. A stone's throw from where Tom sat, the wood ducks had gathered to eat the flesh out of the acorns fallen from trees planted by the Lutherans fifty years past. The ducks couldn't break the outer shells and had to rely on Tom driving over the acorns and crushing them. If he had the time, Tom liked to take the ute down and go forward and back over the acorns while the ducks watched on in approval. Hannah had come with him a couple of times.

"You are a good neighbor for the ducks," she'd said. It was something she liked, that he was too sentimental for farming, and yet made up for it with stamina. "We help the ducks, we sell the books. How did I come here? I don't know. But I love you, Tom. Forever. I love you forever." What an unreliable word that was, *forever*. It shouldn't be spoken. A word like *forever* could kill people.

He still held the telegram in his hand. He'd call Dave Maine; he'd hear that the boy was free to come to him. Peter. And that would bring down the curtain on his life with Hannah. Hector had said, "Three thousand years of history. We know. She'll come back." But she wouldn't. She would keep her precious vow.

Tired of it—that was Tom's mood. The way his legs obeyed the orders of his brain to move him from one place to another—annoying and stupid. Everything about him that cooperated in plodding forward—stupid. Looking at things now—the hills, the red gums at the fringe of the billabong, Beau with his graying muzzle nibbling fleas from his coat—sick of it. The strenuous enterprise of being alive and drawing breath. He was worn out by the circulation of his memories. Images of Hannah in green searching in exasperation for the second of the shoes that matched the dress, and naked, her superb waist that took the circling of his arm; and reading to him in high delight from *The Age* as he painstakingly sawed out the tongue of a dovetail joint. "Tom, your country, it's wonderful. They're saying that Harold Holt was kidnapped by a Chinese submarine. New evidence. Let it be true! The most nonsense I have ever heard. Gorgeous." He had never thought about Australia before Hannah, and then she showed it to him. And now he was supposed to do without her? Just in the way of things, he was supposed to do without her?

He took off his hat and slapped it hard against his thigh. The wood ducks took fright and ran left and right, the females braying like calves.

Then they saw it was nothing and returned happily to the acorns. Too much for him, all of it. And now Peter was coming back. Best plod. Best think. Best use the stupid arms that hung from his shoulders. The heart's bias is always the other one. The heart says: *You, I know. Show me the other one.* The other one was no longer Hannah, but Peter. Tom sighed and stared down at the grass between his spread knees. The boy had suffered. Look out for him. Love him.

.   .   .

He went to the house and called Dave Maine. Dave said, "Yep, he's yours. Paperwork's at the regional office in Benalla." Tom drove there the next morning up through Rushworth and Murchison, across the plain to Miepoll and onto the Hume. He spoke to a shy, dowdy woman in child welfare with the unsuitable name of Desiree. He signed documents. A week later, he drove to Jesus Camp and took Peter from Tilly, with a half-empty suitcase. The place was still in mourning, as hushed as a cemetery. Only two people were left about with any madness left to them, and one was Judy Susan. Her red hair hacked off, she burst into tears when she saw Tom and struck herself on the head with her fist. As he walked with Peter along the path of white pebbles to the front gate, the little girl June came running—the other mad one. She stopped on the path and screamed. And, in her delight, hopped on one foot, then the other, cackling.

CHAPTER 34

Peter's bedroom was as he'd left it. He crossed the threshold with a sigh of relief. Mim Coot's quilt from the CWA fair, magpies and kookas stitched in needlepoint. Peter fell face forward and ground his face into the quilt, kicked his legs. When he turned onto his back, his eyes were wet. Children don't weep for happiness, so it wasn't pure joy he was experiencing. He sat on the side of the bed and told Tom earnestly that he could never go back to Jesus Camp, never.

"Never," said Tom. "I promise you, old chap."

"But, Tom, I mean it. I can never go back."

"You won't be going back, Peter."

"Truly, Tom. I can never go back."

"Never."

He'd seen a knife plunged into Pastor Bligh's guts, and might still harbor mixed feelings about what he'd witnessed. That was his mum with the butcher's knife. That was his mum the Newhaven police took away. Pastor Bligh out of his life, good. By means of murder, maybe not so good. The tears in his eyes—regret, sorrow, complicated feelings about a mum who'd saved him from a forty-stroke thrashing that could've been the end of him, yes. He might (as Tom said) visit his mum if she went to jail, but it would be Tom he wanted in charge. Altered feelings about his mother, but not so altered that Peter would surrender this destination, so desired. Tom in charge.

.　.　.

SCRAMBLED EGGS FOR lunch and six fried cherry tomatoes, cut in half. Two slices of toast from a loaf of white high-tin delivered by Willy McNiff that morning and left on a ledge on the porch out of reach of Beau. A glass of milk from the Ayrshires. Tom sat at the table with the boy, leaning forward on his folded arms, no appetite for a lunch of his own. Beau at the back door moaned for entry and was finally permitted to rush in and dribble over Peter's bare knees. No appetite for lunch, Tom—and no appetite for what he was about to reveal to the boy.

A mongrel's shot dead and it brings a man to your door with a rifle and a conviction that murder will assuage his grief. A woman full of tender love turns away from a child because her own child was murdered. All of this on top of a man mad with pride who died on the floor of a kindergarten with a knife upright in his abdomen. The murders belonged to a realm of experience that Tom recoiled from—as from a powerful stink. To dwell on murder was to foul your nest. He wanted to be the person who took Bernie Shaw's rifle from him before it had been fired; the person who said, "Pastor, let them go," and was heard; the man standing beside Hannah in Auschwitz, holding the child when she lost consciousness. What he needed from the world was a flock of sheep to feed from good pasture; fruit that ripened in response to intelligent care; a dozen dozy Ayrshires; cherry tomatoes thriving on forty-inch stakes; a beloved wife to tend a bookshop in a barn with waxed oak floorboards.

"Peter, we own Henty's spread over the road now. I bought it."

Peter looked up from his plate, inviting Tom to continue, then went back to his scrambled eggs. We can't always discern happiness, strong happiness, without the evidence of laughter, whooping, the dancing of a jig. It's possible to experience the most intense happiness of your life behind a grave, withholding expression. As an adult, at least. Not usually at the age of eight.

Peter was blindingly happy, without wishing to show it. It had grown in him as he'd watched Tom preparing the scrambled eggs. As we usually are not, he was at the place in the world he most wished to inhabit. The fact that he would no longer be thrashed had nothing to do with his mood. It was just Tom. Hannah had often watched her husband for the pleasure of it, her heart and soul a single current that flowed to him. What was most active in Peter's love was admiration, even at the strength suggested by Tom's forearm stirring the eggs and milk in the saucepan.

"Henty, you met him a few times. More than a few. And you met Juliet, of course. She liked you. You remember?"

Peter said, "Mmm." He didn't remember Henty or Juliet.

"Well, they were shot. Shot dead. By Bernie Shaw. You remember Bernie who used to pick for us?"

Peter nodded. The story was about something bad. He didn't care.

"The thing was, Henty shot Bernie's dog. And Bernie was upset."

"Mr. Shaw shot them?"

"He did. He went crazy. With a twenty-two. So Henty's daughters, it was their farm once their mum and dad were dead. They sold it to me."

"Okay," said Peter. He had finished the scrambled eggs and was now picking up the cherry tomato halves with his fork, one at a time.

"So there's that," said Tom. "Bit of a tragedy."

Peter lifted his fork and waggled it in the air.

"Tom, we need more men. With two farms, we need more men."

"We do. Certainly. Then there's the bookshop."

Peter showed a puzzled expression, head on the side.

"Hannah's bookshop," said Tom. "You remember Hannah, don't you?"

Peter was noncommittal.

"My wife. She was here when you turned up last time. Hannah."

Tom was waiting for some acknowledgment, but it didn't come.

"Had a bookshop in town, but moved it into the barn when we took over Henty's spread. Maggie's in there. She's running it. You don't know Maggie."

Peter popped the last half of cherry tomato into his mouth, then picked up the remaining piece of toast and crunched into it. He had nothing to say on the subject of Maggie.

"Here's the thing about Hannah, old chap. She had a boy, a bit younger than you. He was killed in the war. The big war we had before you were born. A long way off. Hannah, she comes from Hungary. Have you ever heard of Hungary?"

Peter shook his head economically—a half turn to the left, half turn to the right. He gulped his milk and left a mustache. Reached for it with his tongue.

"And she misses him. Very badly. Michael."

Without realizing it Tom had leaned further and a bit further across the table. Now, he pulled back. Not to alarm the boy. He pushed his fair hair off his brow, sighed, looked away for a few seconds.

"She's gone away for a bit, Peter. A short time, a long time, I don't know. Maybe for good. I can't say. But if she comes back, be kind to her, old chap."

Peter had developed a guarded way of listening at Jesus Camp. He said nothing in response to Tom's plea. His happiness wasn't eroded.

The little boy, the killed boy, he had no thoughts about him one way or another. The war? He'd attended an Anzac Day ceremony, in honor of the Australian and New Zealand Army Corps, with Tom, and two more at Jesus Camp. He'd seen men, not young, with medals on their chests; medals and colored ribbons. Pastor Bligh had worn medals and ribbons on his blue suit. He'd led the men of Jesus Camp on a march around the dwellings, then back to the church.

Tom gazed at the boy with gladness, not powerful enough to prevail over his heartache.

"You know what, old chap? You're going to be looked after. Right?"

These words—it could have been others with the same message—fed into Peter's happiness and produced the first smile he'd managed in two years. He squirmed in his seat.

. . .

PETER WAS BOOKED into the Hometown primary school, but Tom gave him a week to look around. He introduced him to Hector and his family. Hector blubbered. Here was a boy with black hair and the eyes of Ezekiel, and he would never have such a boy, only girls who mocked him sweetly and sang songs from the radio with synchronized hand movements, swoony expressions. Sharon blubbered. Here was a boy, as beautiful as Jesus, and she would never have such a boy, only the two girls who teased her without mercy and barely listened to a thing she said. Peter whooped when he saw the size of the Henty flocks and the number of lambs, now seven months old. He and Tom walked the rusty red earth of the orchard rows under a blue autumn sky, then took a look at the four Henty dams halfway up the valley slopes. Men would have to be hired, three men, two of them at work all day with the woollies, one in the Henty orchard. It was almost too big, Tom said.

He'd need a second tractor with a slasher, a flatbed truck of their own for the baling season instead of hiring Bon Treadrow's old bomb—it'd be secondhand, not new, said Tom. A three-ton GM could be; Peter would come with him when he took a look at what was on offer at the truck yard in Bendigo.

Strolling along, Peter said, "I've got an idea, Tom."

"Have you, old chap? Let's have it, then."

Making one huge flock of all the sheep and keeping them on the Henty spread, where there was surplus pasture around the billabongs. Tom had to point out that it would take a year for the flocks on Uncle Frank's farm to give up trying to get back across the highway, sheep being set in their ways. But clever thinking.

Then the bookshop. Maggie, growing more officious by the day in her struggle, relented long enough to hug Peter and welcome him and show him all over the two floors of the shop. At the age of eighteen, Maggie had somehow adopted the mentality of someone closer to old maid, burying herself in responsibility and snorting in derision at suggestions (from Tom) that she might like to get about more.

Tom in the ute the next day drove Peter up a track to the top of the highest of the pasture hills on the Henty spread. He wanted the boy to enjoy a view of everything from the eastern rises on Uncle Frank's spread down to the Henty billabongs by the red gums. He wanted to watch the boy marveling, and whisper in his ear, "All this will be yours."

But then . . . maybe not. He didn't want the boy to think he was bound to the farm. He wanted Peter to go to university in the big city and perhaps become—whatever he chose. Anything. Tom himself had come to farming in an indirect way; he wasn't married to the loam. He thought mostly of liberty—north, south, east, west. Let the boy enjoy liberty. Let the liberty sustain him for years and years. Grow straight, and know what was best, what he wanted, instead of growing crookedly along fissures and cracks and giving his heart to a woman mad with grief, too broken to recover.

He watched Peter drawing in his breath at the beauty of it: the slow green river; the big turn at the granite bridge; up the hill to the orchards on Uncle Frank's farm, the pears and apples and nectarines golden in leaf; the big ramshackle cypresses against the fence on the highway. And nearby, the agisted cattle lifting their wet noses to sniff the magical humans who sometimes threw hay about on the banks of the billabongs.

Peter spent three hours on each of five consecutive days in the bookshop with Maggie. He'd never before been in a bookshop and it seemed to dazzle him, so many volumes, spines turned outward. He walked up and down the rows of shelves, reading the names of the books and their authors aloud, as if there were a type of satisfaction for him—poetic, perhaps—in this harvest of plenty. Maggie trailed him, helping with pronunciation, and was soberly thanked for her help at each hurdle. She steered him to the titles he might enjoy reading, urging on him her favorites. He took a chair to the back of the shop and read himself into a Famous Five stupor. Then on the third day, *Swallows and Amazons*. The benefit to Maggie of Peter and his addiction and his earnest endorsement of her being was that he rescued her from her isolation. She might one day—it was possible—be the mother of a child like this. If she found another Tom. If there was another Tom. Or this Tom, if Hannah didn't come back. Well, it could happen. Why say it could never be?

. . .

ANOTHER LETTER CAME from Dave Maine. More paperwork before the Department of Child Welfare could formalize Tom's custody of

Peter. And information: It appeared that Trudy would be tried for murder. The coroner and the Director of Public Prosecutions were inclined to think that the boy's life had not been in danger. A pity, because there was a good record in the Supreme Court of lenient sentences for manslaughter. The boy would very likely be called as a witness. Nonetheless, if somebody wanted to run up the expense of a good legal team—you, Tom?—the lesser charge was still a possibility. Tom wrote back that evening to say that he'd find the money. And because he thought he must, he told Peter, gently, that his mother was to be tried for murder. It was an hour later, at bedtime, before Peter commented. "I wish she didn't." A minute after that: "It was for me."

CHAPTER 35

He loved the boy; the boy adored him. But the love of a child rolls on without any special effort. Six weeks without Hannah and Tom still paused in his tasks each day to shake his head and wipe his eyes because of all that he couldn't share. Husbands are one thing and another, but Tom was made for it: a wife, fond banter, loyalty. Only, he had chosen badly.

These shows of distress disappointed him. Tears and sighs give you a name. Even joy, which ran clear in his blood (not lately), was best kept private. He was, by temperament, a man who might be the winner of the Melbourne Cup or draw a fabled sword from a stone without betraying for a moment the tumult in his heart. But Hannah had driven him to melodrama. In the past week he'd struck out, hit his head with his fist. It could come over him any time of the day. Freeing a burr from the throat of a sheep; trimming the dung from the tails of the Guernseys; replacing the manifold gasket on the ute while considering, like a lunatic, whacking his finger with the spanner; the ring finger.

None of this when the boy was near. Tom kept it jolly. He met Peter at the bus stop on the highway each day and walked with him up to the house, full of tales of the farm, how he'd bathed Stubby's blind eyes in a solution prepared by Don Ford, the vet; had taken a shot at a fox the size of a collie. Really, that big? That big. Almost.

But Peter could see that Tom was not the man he'd been. From the window of his bedroom one afternoon after school, he'd seen Tom standing still in the backyard, his head bowed, raising his hands and letting them flop back to his side. It worried him, but didn't puzzle him. He'd left Jesus Camp with a more detailed map of the passions than most children of eight years ever possessed, or required. It was to do with the lady, Peter deduced. With Tom's wife, who was gone. He didn't think that Tom needed the lady, but he grasped that strange forces were at work in the world around him. In his mother, when she'd stabbed Pastor. And Judy Susan, who'd chopped off all her hair. Mr. Bosk, plunging his hands into boiling water to show he was sorry for the thrashings. The old lady, Pastor's first wife, standing at the door of the kitchen when Pastor's body was carried from the church on a stretcher, calling: "Fare thee well! Fare thee well!" The fixed purpose of his life had been to get back to Tom. It had come about. And now, the flopping hands, the bowed head—he hoped it would pass.

.   .   .

A MORNING IN May. George Cantor, with his eighty-two years, silver hair, and tweed jacket, stood in the doorway of Tom's workshop casting a shadow over the oil-stained floor. Tom, finding solace in the painstaking, looked up from his workbench, stared at George, not seen since the day of his wedding to Hannah, and felt moved to smile by a premonition of welcome news.

"George."

"Mr. Tom Hope. May I enter?"

"Of course. Of course."

George wore his kippah further back on his scalp than was usual among Jews, as he had at the wedding; an affectation of his synagogue in Budapest, according to Hannah. Also, he liked people to notice his silky locks. Such was his vanity.

"You're looking well, George, I must say."

George had approached the workbench, curious about the task he'd interrupted. He shrugged at the compliment, leaned over the latches that Tom was cleaning with Penetrene and an emery cloth.

"I'd shake hands," said Tom, "but mine are dirty."

George snorted, lifted a hand, and shook. "I'm an engineer. Dirty hands, who cares?" Then: "These latches, Tom. Antiques."

"From the barn. The bookshop. I thought I'd give them a bit of a birthday."

George nodded his head in approval at the care Tom was taking. He'd brought the latches back to shiny steel, scraped out every pinpoint of rust.

"The shop," said George. "I'd like to see it."

Tom gave George a more probing look. He was no longer sure he was about to hear good news. "You came all this way to see the bookshop?"

"Maybe. Can I?"

Tom cleaned his hands on the old blue towel kept on a nail above the workbench.

"You won't want to walk," said Tom. "It's on the other property. A good half mile."

George smiled ruefully and gestured at his legs with both hands. "At my most optimistic, I'd say I could manage it. You know what? I'm optimistic today, Mr. Tom. Let's walk. My car is parked outside. Leave it there."

. . .

ON THE RIGHT, the highway paddock, where Stubby and Jo lived in what amounted to a boutique hospice, since both were dying at a lazy pace from being too old to go on living. To the left, the rehab paddock for sheep that had torn themselves on barbed wire, the wounds becoming infected, and others who'd been bruised all over by attacks from hoodlum sheep—mysterious motives, these sheep who battered their brethren. For the torn sheep, antibiotics, and for the battered sheep, verbal consolation from Tom, a scratch between the ears.

The sky was vastly extended in its autumn stillness; the oaks along the driveway turning gold, but gradually. Tom couldn't match himself to the serenity of the season. George would not have come all this way from the city without news of Hannah. Why would it be wrong to stop and say: "George, for the love of God!" But, what—appear avid? No. Happiness, for Tom, was a fugitive. When it appeared, it had to be roused to confidence, encouraged. Anything too gaudy and it might slip back into the shadows, perhaps forever.

Tom said, "I wrote to you. I found your address in the telephone book."

"You did," said George.

"I called your number. Three times. You kept hanging up on me."

George nodded, slowly, to emphasize that he accepted the blame. He shuffled along in his two-toned shoes, cream and brown, for another ten minutes, pausing every so often to admire something close by (the sheep in the sanctuary) or far off (the stands of myrtle beech up on the pasture hills, more vivid than the surrounding eucalyptus), before finally speaking of his mission. He did not look at Tom, but kept his smiling gaze on the myrtle beech.

"Hannah," he said.

"Yes?"

"What is she doing?"

"Doing?"

"What is she doing, Tom?"

"I don't know."

"She is taking her revenge on God."

"What?"

George had stopped in his shuffle and was now facing Tom, looking up from his—well, what was it? Five and a half feet?

"You understand?"

"No, George, I don't. Where is she?"

George resumed his shuffle. "Her boy is taken from her in Auschwitz. You know this?"

"I do."

"She says, 'Never again.' To God, she says this. 'Never again.' So."

They reached the front gate. George had closed it on his way in. He wanted Tom to appreciate this. "Farmers, they like you to close the gate."

"Thank you, George. Where's Hannah?"

"God lets her love. Then he takes the boy. Never again."

Tom ushered George across the highway with caution. The accepted, as opposed to the legal, speed limit on this stretch was whatever you liked. George stopped in the middle of the highway to make a further point, but was not indulged. He spoke up once they were over the highway and through the gate of the Henty farm.

"You hear what I said, Tom? God lets us love. This is all we can ask. If it becomes a catastrophe, that's a horrible thing. But God lets us love."

"Where is Hannah, George? Can you tell me?"

"The boy, you have him? Where is he?"

"He's at school. Peter. Where's Hannah?"

George lifted his shoulders and let them fall. "Everyone wanted her, Tom. You know? She was very fussy. No to this one, no to that one. Then yes to Stefan. Yes to Tom. All of her family died. All of my family, Tom. I shouldn't speak of happiness. But I will. No to everyone. No to me. Yes to Tom."

.   .   .

A GREEN VALLEY Tours bus stood in the parking area beside the barn, passengers boarding with their bookshop carry bags. This was one of Maggie's innovations. She'd petitioned the company that ran twice-weekly tours up the valley to make the bookshop one of the agreed stops. The tourists ventured into a couple of old gold mines led by Teddy Rich, a local history fanatic; studied the river at the cataracts and the marvel of the Mississippi Hole; purchased conscientiously pre-pared meat pies and Cornish pasties from Stella at the Hometown Bakery; gazed in fascination at the granite bridge upstream from Uncle Frank's farm; alighted one final time at the bookshop before returning to the city. THE FINEST REMAINING GERMAN LUTHERAN BARN IN AUSTRALIA, NOW AUSTRALIA'S MOST BEAUTIFUL BOOKSHOP. AN EXTENSIVE RANGE OF NEW AND SECONDHAND TITLES. Maggie's copy.

Tom saw Hannah through the window before she saw him. She was farewelling the last of the customers from the bus. George put a hand on the small of Tom's back. "She told me to drop her off at the bookshop. She said, 'Find him, George. If he is bitter, don't say any-thing.' So I found you. In my judgment, you are not bitter. Forgive her, Tom. She has been six weeks at my apartment. Not a word. A zombie."

Tom stood stock-still. It was as if she'd never been away. Smiling, saying something pleasant to a woman with a haystack of yellow hair and a big woolen scarf, unnecessary on a warm day. What came back to Tom first was an intense, painful, splintery pang of love. Then anger. George must have felt it in Tom's body, his hand pressed where it was. He stepped in front of Tom and seized his hand, squeezed it tightly in both of his. Tom's gaze was fixed beyond George to Hannah, who had yet to notice him.

"Tom, hear these words. Please. This folly of hers—forgive her. You turn your back on her, she is finished."

Hannah had seen him now. She held her chin high, her gaze fixed on her husband. Then she faltered, dropped her head. When she lifted her face to Tom again, the despair was plain. She made a beckoning gesture to him with one hand. Tom remained rooted to the spot for a minute, more, then stepped into the shop. Maggie hurried out to allow them privacy.

The bus, departing, tooted twice. Hannah raised her hand and waved. The hand descended slowly.

"Tom."

David the canary, on top of the cash register, had recovered from his torpor and was twittering away in what must have been gibberish even in birdsong. Gibberish or happy talk. It had been weeks since he'd seen Hannah.

"What the hell, Hannah?"

In a summer dress of pale gold that Tom hadn't seen before, Hannah nodded slowly. "I should go?"

The past exerts itself to influence the future—a bid for immortality. In that room of books, of glowing timber polished with beeswax, Auschwitz loomed, the dead child, a dead husband, the shorn, the doomed, shoes piled outside the door of an underground chamber. But with equal insistence, miraculously, happiness also persists, patches of it, some quite expansive. Creases in a white dress smoothed out with a flat iron, slipped over the head, the smell of the starch, the warmth of the fabric. In the cheval mirror, turning this way and that, a promise of what might follow. Hannah still owned that dress when she met Tom many years later, wore it for him, lifted it above her head while he lay waiting in bed one Sunday afternoon. He'd tried to say something, but it had caught in his throat. She'd said, "We love each other," and ten seconds later was in his arms.

Now, on this day of her return, he took three steps and drew her to him, held her with a fierceness that might have hurt her. With his mouth against her ear, he said, softly at first, "Never again, never, never." Then his anger had to have its way. He stepped back and with his hands on her shoulders, glared at her in warning. "Do you think everyone feels this? Do you think it's just ordinary? Hannah, it's not. And you can't go running off like that."

Hannah looked away, on her face an expression that hadn't quite settled into penitence. She shook her head, tears gathering. It was only at this moment that Tom realized she'd had her curls cut shorter. He wanted to say, "Let them grow back," but couldn't, in the situation.

She managed to speak at last: "Tom, I had to go. And I had to come back."

This is what Tom had feared, if she returned, when she returned. Words that leaked from the muddle within her when all she had to say was what George had said: She'd made a mistake.

"Hannah, you make your mind up now if you're staying. 'I had to go and I had to come back.' What next? 'And then I had to go again.' Enough, Hannah. You stay. You care for Peter. And if you can't, we have to go our separate ways. Hannah, I can't go through this again, waking sick with worry every morning. One thing I learned from Trudy, if your wife doesn't want you there's no hope. It's just pretend."

Hannah let out a wail, brief, truncated. Maggie and George, watching through the pane of the front door, shared a murmur of alarm.

"You think I wanted to go? Are you mad? Tom, he sat at my feet. He thought I would protect him, his mother. In seconds he was gone. And where? Into a nightmare."

"And this is the answer? Another nightmare?"

Hannah paused. Her gaze settled on David. She smiled at him, exciting the bird into an even more extravagant outburst of song. This temporizing might have been designed to keep Hannah from saying something about equivalence. The nightmare that Tom was speaking of could not be compared to a child carried away to be murdered. For her to say so could lead to nothing good.

"Tom, I want to come back."

Nothing was said for a short time.

"I want to come back. I want to stay. Peter, I will care for him. He doesn't like me, but no matter. I will care for him."

Tom looked away. His arms were crossed, giving the impression of a more obdurate state of mind than was actually the case. He uncrossed them.

"Yes, come back, Hannah."

She smiled. "That's what you want?"

"Yes."

Hannah took Tom's face in her two hands. "This is what I have wanted to do every day," she said. "Every day. Your beautiful face."

The grief of Poland coiled itself in corners, banished for the moment by books and beeswax. And by this homecoming. A woman in rags who watched the camp diminish in the distance as she walked away, a woman who lived long enough to love, to marry, to recall the warmth of an ironed white dress, had enjoyed a type of victory. Not to waste it, surely.

On the counter lay the green, cloth-covered ledger in which was recorded the tally of books sold over a period of three years. Sales had not yet reached the magical figure of twenty-five thousand. But it could easily be imagined.

CHAPTER 36

The charge was murder, not manslaughter. The best efforts of Bunny Gorman, Trudy's barrister, to persuade the DPP to see reason had failed. But the judge told Gorman, in private: "Harp away at mitigation."

Peter was not required to give evidence, and needn't have attended the trial at the Supreme Court at all. But Tom said he must, and Hannah agreed. The three of them were permitted to take seats in the courtroom, given precedence over mere stickybeaks. Trudy sat calmly through the preliminaries, nicely dressed, her hair at its most attractive length. She glanced at Peter every few minutes, smiled, lifted her hand once to offer a little wave.

Trudy's mother and sister were also in attendance, distressed, sobbing. And Judy Susan, now as thin as a matchstick, her hair slow to grow back. The voices in the courtroom were subdued. Gorman and the judge appeared to enjoy a genial relationship, and the barrister was once addressed by the judge as "Bunny." It was as if everything that would transpire had already been adjudicated and all that remained to do was follow a script: Bunny murmuring his lines, the judge accepting his cue, the Crown happy to accommodate the mellow flow. Trudy plead not guilty and the judge murmured, "Of course, of course."

Peter listened to everything. He smiled at his mother when she smiled at him. He knew that she cared for him; he knew that she had stabbed Pastor to stop the thrashing. But he didn't love her, and when he smiled, it was only to be kind. He remembered Trudy in the first few months of Jesus Camp screaming at him about obedience, saying he was stupid, calling him a country bumpkin. She had changed over time, and instead of country bumpkin called him "poor child," but the harm was done. She had taken him away from Tom, and kindness was as far as he could go. Or a bit further. Perhaps pity. He knew his mother was mad.

Hannah was mad, too, in a different way. In the four months since she'd returned, Peter had sensed her drawing close, only to back away. Then she didn't back away. Often she couldn't keep herself from putting a hand on his shoulder and letting it run down his back. He saw her catching her lower lip between her teeth. At dinnertime, she would sometimes sit with a fork raised a few inches from her plate to watch him as he ate.

Peter had changed over the two and a half years of Jesus Camp. Many of the people he'd known at the camp were out of their minds. In the midst of the madness, he became calm. Pastor had to be fought, yes, and he would never give up returning to where he belonged with Tom, but otherwise he kept calm. It was like a pool of clear water within. He could go to the pool, drop to his knees, and drink. Trudy said, "Country bumpkin," and he shrugged. Judy Susan said, "You'll cook in Hell in a big pot!" and he smiled. He was not the mad one. He was sure of that.

He could see what was happening to Hannah. Her boy had died, and now she loved him. He was glad Tom had told him about Hannah's boy, otherwise he might have backed away. It did no harm to let Hannah love him. Whenever her eyes filled with tears, he said quietly,

"Don't worry." His boy's soul was filling out, so it seemed. It did no harm. He had Tom.

. . .

PETER RAISED NO objection when Hannah said she wanted him to take the Tuesday off school so that she could drive him to the city and have him fitted for a suit. Just the two of them.

Hannah said, "Will you?"

Peter said, "If you like."

"I want you to look nice for court."

She was talking about the sentencing, expected a week after the verdict. Bunny Gorman had told Tom, who was paying him, that the verdict would be guilty and that the sentence could be as little as eight and a half years, with a non-parole period of four. "Jenny wants to steer her back to the streets and byways, but he has to give her a smack on the hand, alas. Good result." "Jenny" was Judge Jacob Jennifer.

Tom was made uncomfortable by the suit expedition.

"Australians don't dress their kids in suits, Han."

"No? They should. Does every Australian have to look like the Salvation Army is in charge of fashion?"

"We're easygoing, sweetheart. He can wear his school uniform."

Peter said, "It's okay, Tom." Tom shrugged and gave it away.

The tailor was to be Isaac Glick, on Collins Street, next to Job's Warehouse. The dingy entrance and unlit stone stairs let into three bright, spacious rooms paneled in shining teak. Hannah had no acquaintance with Glick, but George Cantor knew him well and had recommended him. Glick was used to dealing with men who put themselves entirely in his hands to be bossed, pushed, and prodded, insulted in their suggestions, and told to be quiet whenever they spoke.

But with Peter, he was gentle. Something of the spell Peter cast over Hannah exercised itself on Glick.

"This is a handsome boy," he said as he measured Peter up, lifting an arm to take the circumference of the chest. "This is a specimen." He showed Hannah and Peter catalogs of cloth samples, broad squares of fabric pinked at the bottom. The two of them stood side by side at the long, varnished counter while Glick turned the samples. Glick was impressed anew with Peter's comments. "Too much green." "No, that's for an old man." "No, the pattern is too big." What Peter did like was a herringbone worsted from the English midlands. One of the delights of the boy was his surprises. Hannah hadn't expected him to take the least interest in cloth samples, imitating Tom, who would rather drink hemlock than take himself off to a tailor's. Glick asked her quietly if the boy was her son, thinking it tactful to substitute "son" for "grandson." Hannah murmured, "Yes, my son," not intending that her reply should carry to Peter. But it did.

. . .

LATER THAT DAY, they visited Trudy at Fairlea. The main business of the trial would conclude on the Wednesday after this one-day break and the verdict was expected the same day. Sentencing would follow a week later. Trudy, who had the sympathy of the prison officers, was permitted to sit with her son and Hannah on a bench in the Fairlea grounds pretty much unsupervised. Trudy was still in civilian dress. She said she knew she would be found guilty and go to prison. She said she didn't care. Peter bore up stoically under his mother's affectionate petting. Trudy said, "I'm glad you're with Hannah. I wasn't a good mum. But I love you." When they strolled back to the administration building, Trudy held Peter's hand. She wept as they parted. She said,

"You stay with Tom and Hannah. That's best. But come and see me." Her self-control gave way at the end. She fell to her knees and hugged her son, and remained on her knees as Hannah guided Peter out the door. A corpulent prison officer, a woman with horn-rim spectacles and a built-up orthopedic shoe, said, "There, there, girlie."

. . .

THEY DROVE TO Hometown over the Black Spur, Peter quiet, Hannah jittery. She feared he'd heard her. "My son," she'd said.

Every time she glanced at Peter she thought she saw a satirical smile on his lips. By the time they reached Dom Dom Saddle at the top of the spur, she could stand it no longer. She veered into the picnic area under the oaks and brought the car to an abrupt halt. With her hands still on the wheel, she turned to Peter and said, "You heard me?" Her expression retained the tenderness that was always there when she spoke to Peter, but made more complicated by remorse. "You heard me call you my son?" Peter, alarmed, but well in control, nodded his head. Hannah looked away, far more badly upset than Peter thought she needed to be.

"Well, that was bad. That was bad of me."

She turned back to Peter.

"I am not your mother," she said. "Trudy is your mother. I am sorry, Peter. Very, very sorry."

She opened the door and slid out of the car, walked a few steps, and stood with her arms folded, her weight more on one leg than the other. She put a hand to her face but then snatched it away, perhaps to avoid giving Peter in the car the impression that she was about to cry.

A month past midwinter and the days were stretching out. At four in the afternoon the sky was still full of light. Rosellas on winter rations gathered in the oaks, ready to hustle for sandwiches and chips. A half dozen gathered at Hannah's feet. Ignored, they gave themselves to a pessimistic picking-over of broken acorn shells. Down on the meadow rabbits stood on their back legs to assess the likelihood of carrots and lettuce being tossed from bread rolls.

A mountain, conical in shape, rose above the picnic area, the slopes densely treed with mountain ash and red box, myrtle beech, black wattle. But the green of the packed foliage gave way in a thousand places to the bone-white of dead trunks, the standing corpses of trees burned in the Black Friday fires of 1939. Enough time had passed since the eruption of the mountain into flame for an intricate pattern of living color and dead color to have emerged. It was as if the thriving foliage of the living trees had undertaken a vast campaign of support for the dead trunks, hemming them in, holding them erect in many places.

Hannah hadn't left the car to look at the mountain but to grimace and hiss and call herself a fool without frightening Peter. It distressed her to see Michael when she looked at Peter. The black hair, the grave expression, the ripple of worry that played around the eyes—the same, even though Michael had been younger than Peter when he'd disappeared. The same, but not the same. It was as if she'd been reading a book and had by mistake turned two pages at once, so that when she resumed reading, there was a jolt of discontinuity. A question at the end of the last page, an episode that was not taken up at the head of the new page.

If she came to love Peter, her grieving might end. If her grieving stopped, the SS had won. Could she not grow close to this child and still be with Michael when they undressed him, handled him, killed him? She saw no path, only tears. A wringing of hands; episodes of anger if she felt the boy was forcing disloyalty on her. At the same time—why not confess it?—she loved Peter. When the tenderness leaped from her heart into her throat, she yearned to hold his face in her hands. Why not confess everything—that she feared she would walk away again, leave Tom with Peter.

Would she? She might. Probably not. No.

The car door opened and closed. Hannah glanced over her shoulder to see Peter approaching shyly. He stood beside her, studying the rabbits. Hannah wished to reach for his hand, but the risk.

"I like the suit," he said.

"Do you? Tom will laugh."

The rabbits, six of them, the boss bunny in the lead, an impressive brute with tufts of black fur in his ears, improved their position once more, not by much.

Hannah said under her breath, "Enough." This was not even the same continent on which Michael had lived. Only she feared the wayward nonsense that surged into her heart. The horrible sense that she had brought the SS to Australia. The smile of that officer, his singsong voice, his unsoiled white gloves, his assurance.

She thought, *You could have died if this is what you feel. A hundred opportunities. Say what you like, you chose to live.*

Hannah could see that Peter was waiting for some sign of recovery. His intelligence showed him distinctly that he must get along with Tom's wife; she was an auxiliary project of his devotion to Tom. This Hannah understood.

But best if she kept it clear in her head that she would come to love him like a crazy person, and he would never love her. Too bad about that. Let him, for the love of God, be the child he was. She had seen him at work on a picture of a steam train in a coloring book, his tongue sticking out in concentration. And the friend he'd made at school—Kerry, Moira Nash's youngest daughter—she'd watched the two of them at play, splashing and shrieking in the Henty dam. He permitted

Sue and Sylvie to fuss over him, combing his hair and leaving lipstick shapes all over his face.

She felt for his hand, and held it. Peter didn't look up at her, but he acquiesced.

Hannah thought, *God knows where this will end.* She wanted Tom in her arms. God bless him that he knew nothing about the camps. May he remain in ignorance forever. She heaved a deep sigh, and Peter glanced up quickly. "It's okay," she said. "I was thinking of Tom. Will he remember the list? Do you think?"

Peter screwed up his face, considering. "He's very . . ." He searched for the word, then looked up at Hannah again. "When you do things like you should?"

"Reliable?" Hannah offered.

"Yes. He's very reliable."

. . .

CARS RUSHED BY on the highway past St. Ronan's Well and down through Narbethong, Buxton, Taggerty, Rubicon. The destination of two or three of the cars would be Hometown Shire, where Tom Hope was locking the bookshop on David and fifteen thousand volumes. It was early to lock up, but Maggie had suffered a blinding bout of conjunctivitis and had to be ferried home by her mother. Tom, unassisted, coped with a busload of tourists and now had to get to the Cash 'n Carry and Juicy's butchery before closing time. If possible. Vern Caldicott and his girl Mandy on the cash register abandoned the grocery section at four-thirty and served exclusively in the liquor department until five-thirty. Closing times in pubs had been extended a couple of years earlier, but Cash 'n Carry liquor was cheaper than pub liquor.

The list, Hannah's list. Where the hell?

On the way to the ute, Tom felt in his pockets, side and back—at the same time cursing Beau, who had taken all this hurry as high jinks and was leaping and yelping. Tom said aloud, "Can I remember everything?" No. But here it was, the list, in the breast pocket of his shirt and thank God for that. He let Beau into the cabin of the ute, climbed in behind the wheel, and roared down the driveway. Maybe ten minutes to reach the shops. He glanced at the list, then dropped it on the seat between himself and Beau:

lb and a half of eye filet steak, trimmed make sure

lb of little potatoes

silver beet, big bunch not wilted

half cabbage

four carrots big, not too big

paprika in packet

self-rising flour packet, small one

butter—lb

three apples, green

ice cream—Neapolitan in plastic tub

Thank you, my darling

ACKNOWLEDGMENTS

My special thanks to Sonia Lovemore,
for sharing her experience of raising sheep with me.

McKenzie Co. Public Library
112 2nd Ave. NE
Watford City, ND 58854
701-444-3785
librarian@co.mckenzie.nd.us